Carol Townend was born in England and went to a convent school in the wilds of Yorkshire. Captivated by the medieval period, Carol read History at London University. She loves to travel, drawing inspiration for her novels from places as diverse as Winchester in England, Istanbul in Turkey and Troyes in France. A writer of both fiction and non-fiction, Carol lives in London with her husband and daughter. Visit her website at caroltownend.co.uk.

Also by Carol Townend

Knights of Champagne miniseries

Lady Isobel's Champion
Unveiling Lady Clare
Lord Gawain's Forbidden Mistress
Lady Rowena's Ruin
Mistaken for a Lady

Princesses of the Alhambra miniseries

The Knight's Forbidden Princess
The Princess's Secret Longing

And look out for the next book coming soon

Discover more at millsandboon.co.uk.

THE PRINCESS'S SECRET LONGING

Carol Townend

MILLS & BOON

First published in Great Britain 2019
by Mills & Boon, an imprint of HarperCollins*Publishers*
1 London Bridge Street, London, SE1 9GF

Large Print edition 2020

© 2019 Carol Townend

ISBN: 978-0-263-08618-8

MIX
Paper from
responsible sources
FSC® C007454

This book is produced from independently certified
FSC™ paper to ensure responsible forest management. For
more information visit www.harpercollins.co.uk/green.

Printed and bound in Great Britain
by CPI Group (UK) Ltd, Croydon, CR0 4YY

To the RNA London Chapter.
Thank you for the many wonderful talks
and much writerly chat.

Chapter One

1396—the Alhambra Palace in the Emirate of Granada

Princess Alba lay in the dark, an unfamiliar noise had dragged her from her dreams. She turned restlessly, unable to work out what had woken her. All she could hear was a trill of birdsong. In her mind's eye, she saw birds flying over lawns and terraces and flitting in and out of shrubs in the wilderness beyond the palace wall. They sounded happy. Free!

A lantern glowed softly in a niche, casting a gentle light on the sleeping forms of Alba's sisters, Princess Leonor and Princess Constanza. Their black hair was loosely tied back for sleep, just like hers, and their eyelashes lay like dark crescents against their cheeks. Princess Alba and her sisters were triplets, identical triplets.

Alba yawned and, as she looked at her sisters, she was gripped by an odd fancy. It was as though she was looking at other versions of herself, versions which had yet to waken. Irritated, she brushed the thought aside. Her sisters' features might mirror hers, but their characters—oh, so very different.

The bedchamber shutters were closed, and it was so early that nothing was visible through the star-shaped patterns cut into the wood. The Princesses hadn't been long in their father's favourite palace—only a few days—but already Alba knew that in daytime the piercings in the shutters turned bright sunlight into starry splashes on the floor tiles.

There it was again! That mysterious noise. Alba sat up. What could it be? The cry of a hawk? No, that was no hawk. That was surely—a baby.

Her breath stopped. Could it really be a baby? Whose could it be? It couldn't belong to her father the Sultan, may God exalt him. The Sultan had only sired three children, Alba and her sisters. Sultan Tariq's unfulfilled wish for other children—more precisely, for a son—was well known.

Alba scrambled to the window. Kneeling on a cushion, for the window was low and the floor hard, she shoved at the shutter and strained to hear more. She'd spent most of her life far away in Salobreña Castle and not once had she held a baby. A pang shot through her, violent and intense. If there was a baby in the palace, she must see it. Hold it.

Loath to wake her sisters, Alba snatched up a robe and veil and was dressed in no time. She took the lantern to light her way, crept softly downstairs and slipped out of the tower.

The stars were fading, the sky was turning pearly grey and the air was pleasantly cool.

Ahead of her, paths ran this way and that. Buildings were visible as black shapes at the end of the paths. So many walls and towers. Alba had yet to learn the layout of the grounds, but in this instance, it didn't matter. That sound, the faintest of whimpers, was her guide. There was a baby in the palace!

Stepping on to the lawn, Alba sped past a hissing fountain. She entered a small grove of trees and was greeted by the heady scent of oranges. A section of the palace wall lay on her left hand and light glowed briefly from a guardhouse at the top. Her father the Sultan had many guards.

Mindful of the need for discretion, Alba tugged her veil tightly about her face. Sultan Tariq insisted that the Princesses wore veils, even when walking here in the palace grounds. Any man who caught a glimpse of her face would be severely disciplined. Alba wasn't sure what form the punishment would take, it was enough to know that her father ruled with an iron hand. She wouldn't be able to live with herself if a guard suffered on her account.

God was with her, she saw no guards.

Several buildings were clustered behind a screen of myrtle bushes, the thread of sound came from the nearest. The strengthening light revealed a line of windows with arches shaped like horseshoes and a large door heavily decorated with ironwork. The door opened smoothly, and Alba entered a shadowy antechamber. An indignant wail echoed across the marble floor.

Excitement fizzing through her veins, Alba hurried towards a curtained door arch.

Since her father the Sultan only had three children, this building had to be part of Prince Ghalib's harem. Prince Ghalib was Alba's uncle. He was much younger than the Sultan and to say that he must find life difficult was an understatement.

Prince Ghalib was her father's designated successor, he was an heir locked in a gilded cage. Like Alba and her sisters, her uncle wasn't allowed his freedom. Alba understood why. Insurrections were commonplace in the long and bloody history of the Nasrid dynasty. Brother would kill brother and seize power. Doubtless, Sultan Tariq feared Prince Ghalib might stage a coup and overthrow him.

Determined to escape such a fate, Sultan Tariq

had kept his brother out of the way at Salobreña Castle for years. The three Princesses had lived there too.

During that time, Alba had seen her uncle happy and she'd seen him angry. Prince Ghalib had many faces. Underneath them all lay a dark and bitter frustration. Alba sympathised, for she'd heard that the Sultan had made his brother promise after promise.

'I'll give you a castle, dear brother, never fear,' the Sultan had vowed. Or, 'I'll put you at the head of an army.'

Her father had broken every promise. While the Sultan lived, Prince Ghalib would never be free, he was too much of a threat. It didn't help that, unlike the Sultan, Prince Ghalib had fathered many children.

Prince Ghalib had been brought from Salobreña Castle to the Alhambra Palace at the same time as his nieces and, like the Princesses, he continued to be granted every luxury. Except his freedom.

Alba reached the curtained archway as the baby paused to draw breath. A woman was crooning softly, and her soft murmurings dragged Alba back to when she herself was little more than an infant. A sharp pain pierced her, like a lance to her heart. Mamá! Her mother, the Queen, had spoken to her in just such a voice. That was the voice of love, it was the most beautiful sound in creation and she'd not heard it in an age.

Curtain rings clinked as Alba pushed inside. If the baby was Prince Ghalib's, it would be her cousin.

A young woman about the same age as Alba was lying on a couch with the baby. She looked across and gave a rueful smile. 'My daughter is keeping you awake? A thousand apologies.'

My cousin. The baby's cheeks were red with anger and she was waving chubby fists in the air. As Alba drew closer, she looked Alba's way and the wailing cut off abruptly.

Alba's heart squeezed. 'What an adorable child.' She tossed her veil over her head. Sultan Tariq's strictures about the Princesses wearing their veils didn't apply when the Princesses were in their private apartments because no man set foot in them. The same rule must apply in her uncle's harem. No guard or manservant would dare enter the women's quarters.

The woman on the couch studied Alba's face, eyes wary. 'I've not seen you before.'

'No.'

Gathering the baby to her breast, the woman sat up. 'May I ask who you are?'

Alba smiled and, since she only used her Spanish name when she was in the company of her sisters or her duenna, she gave her Moorish one. 'I am Princess Zoraida.'

Her uncle's concubine jumped up as though scalded and made a hurried obeisance. 'Princess Zoraida!' The baby in her arms wriggled.

'Please,' Alba said. 'There's no need for that.'

The young woman swallowed. 'There is every need.' Her expression was haunted as she looked Alba up and down. 'You are the middle Princess, I believe?'

'Aye.'

Dawn was breaking, and light was filtering into the chamber. The young mother looked past Alba towards the door arch, her expression pinched. 'Where are the other Princesses, my lady?'

'They are asleep. Please, do not concern yourself.'

The concubine bit her lip. 'My lady, I doubt the Sultan, may he live for ever, would sanction your visiting Prince Ghalib's harem.'

Alba held the girl's gaze. 'I shall say nothing of coming here.'

Her uncle's concubine let out a trembling sigh. 'Thank you, my lady.'

The baby had stopped crying, her eyes were fastened on Alba's lantern. Gently setting it on a ledge, Alba held out her hands.

'May I hold her?'

The girl hesitated and smiled. 'Of course. Here, my lady. Yamina is usually very good, I don't know what has got into her this morning.'

A warm bundle was thrust into Alba's arms and she was transfixed by a painful emotion she could not name. Holding her cousin gave her a sense of belonging. Of completion.

'Yamina is a lovely name.'

Alba could feel Yamina's warmth creeping into her heart. Indeed, it seemed to fill every part of her, warming her in ways that the summer sun could never warm. She'd never felt like this before, such pain—yearning, she supposed. Such joy. Yamina was a sweetheart. Alba's unconfessed miseries coalesced into a piercing spear of longing. A baby. This was what was missing from her life. A baby. For months Alba had felt restless and ill at ease, now she knew why. Deprived of love herself, she yearned for someone to love. She yearned for a baby.

Eyes misting, Alba cradled Yamina. She stroked her face, marvelling at the softness of her skin. Yamina was so trusting. So dear. Aching inside, Alba swallowed down a lump in her throat. 'My cousin,' she murmured.

Dark eyes watched her. 'My lady, her life will be very different to yours. You are a princess.

My daughter will be fortunate if she can remain in the palace. It is lucky she is a girl.'

'Oh?'

The concubine shrugged. 'Who can say what the fate of a male child of Prince Ghalib's might be? However, since I have a daughter, I am hopeful she will be permitted to stay. Perhaps she will attend you, my lady, when she is grown.'

Alba stared. This child was her cousin and she might well become a lady-in-waiting. On the other hand, life was precarious and if something untoward happened to Prince Ghalib—what then? Yamina could be forced into servitude, she could be ill treated. Alba had never seen a servant beaten, but such things were commonplace, her father the Sultan was a hard taskmaster. As for his temper, it was as black as sin. Alba had witnessed his temper first-hand...

When she and the other Princesses had been riding from their old home in Salobreña Castle to their newly built tower in the Alhambra Palace, their father had almost killed three prisoners they had come across on the road. Spanish knights, they were being held for ransom. The knights didn't speak Arabic and were ignorant of local custom, so they hadn't understood they weren't permitted to look at the Princesses.

Sultan Tariq had been so enraged by what he

saw as the knights' insolence, that he'd been prepared to execute them on the spot. If Alba and her
sisters hadn't begged for clemency, those Spanish noblemen would surely be dead.

There was no question but that the Sultan was
inflexible and capricious. However, surely even
he wouldn't allow his niece to be beaten? Whatever happened to Prince Ghalib, she prayed her
father wouldn't force Yamina into servitude.

'Will your daughter have a say in how she lives
her life?'

'No, my lady. Prince Ghalib, long may he pros-
per, will decide.'

Alba held the concubine's gaze. 'Then her life
is little different to mine. I, too, must obey my
father.'

When her uncle's concubine looked at her, face
suddenly blank, Alba knew a moment of shame.
It was true that the three Princesses lived accord-
ing to their father's dictates, but their mother had
been the Queen. The women living here were
simply Prince Ghalib's concubines. The life of
such a woman, even one who had borne a child,
was infinitely more precarious than that of a princess.

'Men can be callous.' Alba shook her head. 'All
they care about is their own pleasure. And war
and conquest, of course.'

The concubine threw a nervous glance over her shoulder. 'My lady, you must not speak in this manner.' Her fingers crept to a silver bangle. 'Prince Ghalib, may blessings rain upon him, is generous. He gives me gifts. He allows me to dress my daughter in the finest linens.'

Alba didn't reply. The Sultan showered the Princesses with gifts too, although Alba had long suspected that the gifts were a means of their father displaying his range of influence. Frankincense and myrrh from the east, silk from Byzantium, silver from Arabia—all these and more had been given to his daughters. Not for a moment did Alba think the gifts were given out of love, Sultan Tariq didn't know the meaning of the word. No, Alba was coming to suspect that the Sultan used gifts as a means of ensuring his daughters' obedience. He wanted to keep them sweet. He wanted them to know how powerful he was. The question was why?

Alba pursed her lips and wondered if she would still be living in the palace when Yamina became an adult. The thought was unpleasant on several levels. The Sultan appeared to be in no hurry to arrange marriages for his daughters. Alba had had her fill of palace life—of the endless intrigues, of the constant tiptoeing around her father's anger. If her father wasn't going to arrange a marriage for her, she would have to find a way to escape.

Pressing her lips firmly together, Alba hugged her cousin. A sturdy leg had escaped its wrappings. Heart hurting, she stroked it gently.

'Your daughter is beautiful,' she said. 'You are very blessed.'

'Thank you.'

Soft voices reached them. A woman laughed. Her uncle's harem was coming to life.

'I ought to leave.'

'That would be wise, my lady.'

Alba handed Yamina back and the young mother's face softened into an expression of love and acceptance. It was then that the realisation hit home. Men didn't understand love, they didn't need it. Alba couldn't be more different, she needed love as she needed air. She craved it. Love was what was missing from her life. This tiny child had shown her as much. If she had a baby...

Her days had felt empty because she had no one to love and care for. Naturally, Alba had her sisters, but she had come to fear that the love she felt for her sisters was all that she would ever have. She was a woman grown and sisterly affection was no longer enough.

Her mind raced. Given the number of concubines that must live in this harem, the bond between men and women must be weak indeed.

How many women lived in her father's harem? She'd heard he kept a harem and had often wondered if that had been true in her mother's time. How long had Father spent mourning Mamá? A month? A week? A day?

The murmur of voices drifted through the arched doorway. Water was being poured. There was much splashing. A loud yawn. It was odd to think that here in Prince Ghalib's harem, Alba had been given a glimpse of real love. The bond between a mother and her child was surely stronger than steel.

Conscious that they might be interrupted, Alba drew her veil over her face. She hesitated. Before she left, there was something she must ask. 'Is my father's harem close by?'

The young woman's eyebrows lifted. 'Why, yes, my lady, if you continue down the path, it's the next building.'

Alba's hands fisted in her robes. 'Was it here when my mother was alive?'

Her uncle's concubine blinked. 'I was not brought to the palace until after the Queen's death, but I believe so. Generations of sultans have kept harems here.'

'So, it's true,' Alba murmured.

'My lady?'

'Never mind. Thank you for allowing me to hold Yamina. Farewell.'

'Farewell, my lady. Blessings upon you.'

'And upon you.'

Curtain rings were clattering, trailing silks were whispering over the marble floor. Another few moments and the women and children of the harem would be fully awake. If anyone saw Alba, she would face a barrage of questions, she had lingered too long. Giving the young mother a parting smile, she slipped out of the chamber.

Swiftly, she retraced her path through the orange grove. The sky was tinged with pink and the tower Sultan Tariq had built for the three Princesses loomed up in front of her. It was an imposing building, so much so, that when Alba had first seen it, she hadn't noticed how far it was from the rest of the palace. That had not been an accident, she realised. Sultan Tariq didn't want his daughters near the rest of the harem.

From this angle the Princesses' tower, though glowing warmly in the rays of the rising sun, looked as forbidding as a prison. Goosebumps ran down her back.

What if the Sultan decided to keep his daughters in the tower until they were wrinkled and grey? He was so controlling, it was entirely possible. Look at what had happened to Mamá. The Queen had been born in the neighbouring Kingdom of Castile and she'd had the misfortune to be captured by the Sultan's troops. The story went that as soon as the Sultan set eyes on his Spanish captive, he'd wanted her.

It hadn't been love. It couldn't have been love, as far as Sultan Tariq was concerned love was all about possession. He'd made Mamá his Queen and she'd never returned to Spain.

Had Mamá been given the chance to refuse him? Alba doubted it.

Had she missed her homeland? Most likely.

Was that why Mamá had died when she and her sisters were small? Was her father's iron will to blame?

Briefly, Alba wondered if she was misjudging him. She burned to know whether he had plans for her and her sisters. They had reached marriageable age, and not once had he mentioned marriage. If she never married, she'd never have a child.

Unfortunately, even if the Sultan were to arrange a marriage for her, Alba didn't trust him to find a good husband. Men were cold and, in her experience, heartless. Her father certainly was, though she ought, in justice, to accept that other men might be different.

Concubinage was another possibility. That girl in the harem had told Alba that Prince Ghalib was good to her.

Unfortunately, Alba didn't think the Sultan would permit his daughters to become concubines. He was too proud.

Alba had done her best to learn about the world outside the palace, and what she'd discovered had made her extremely wary. Men were belligerent. Her father's borders were never safe, there was always a new conflict to worry about. Men cared about power, they craved money, possessions and land, which was why all the great marriage alliances were made with political aims in mind. If men thought about love at all, it must come very low on their list of priorities.

She almost tripped over a paving stone as the realisation hit her. She had no need to marry to have a baby. If she could get away from her father, she could surely find someone to give her a child.

Why tie herself to a man? She would be content on her own. She had caskets overflowing with jewels. She had the means to bring up a child *without* a husband. Her baby would want for nothing. Most importantly, her child would know what it was to have a mother's love. Her child would live free.

Alba's heart ached as she stared at the top of the tower where her sisters were sleeping. That tower was a gilded cage. And there was no way she was going to waste her life in a cage. If her child was to enjoy true freedom, it must be born well away from Sultan Tariq. She must, must, must get away.

Would her sisters come with her? Alba's pulse quickened as she thought it through. That would be wonderful, the three of them would set up home together, they would support each other as they had always done. And she could have a child. Her sisters would love it almost as much as her.

Where? Where might they go?

The Kingdom of Castile—her mother's homeland—seemed as good a place as any. In Spain, Alba could look for her perfect man. A handsome man who would give her a beautiful child and then leave her in peace. An honourable man who would not lord over her in any way. A man who...

A memory stirred in Alba's mind. She was looking into the grey eyes of one of the Spanish knights her father had almost cut down on the road to Granada. She'd only seen him a handful of times, and always from a distance. The first time had been when he'd limped off the prison galley at the port in Salobreña. Captured in a border skirmish, he'd barely been conscious, because of a leg wound courtesy of her father's troops.

Alba reached the tower door, puzzled as to why the memory of that knight kept coming back to her.

The second time she'd seen him had been on the road to Granada. She'd been thankful he'd survived the privations of her father's prison. His green tunic had been somewhat the worse for wear, but he'd been allowed to keep his gold ring—proof of his high status, no doubt.

There'd been something about the way he'd looked at her, and Alba didn't think it was simply that she was unused to a man's regard. He'd made no attempt to hide his curiosity. His gaze had been frank. Admiring. The knight had liked what he'd seen, and he'd made no attempt to hide it. Best of all, she'd seen not the slightest trace of the tyrant in him.

He was brave too. Her father had been bearing down on him, scimitar in hand like a vengeful demon, and that knight had stood firm. For a moment, he'd even looked amused. Amused? Sultan Tariq's fury was never amusing.

Alba could be reading too much into a look. She was, after all, unused to men. She must take care. However, the appreciative glint in those grey eyes gave her hope. That man didn't look like a bully. He liked women and he liked them to like him back.

If life didn't improve here, Alba could think of no better place to settle than in her mother's homeland, preferably with her sisters. All she had to do was to work out how to get there.

Chapter Two

A street in the city of Granada, Al-Andalus

The evening was warm. Moths were fluttering around three lanterns hanging over one of the doorways.

'Three lanterns,' Inigo Sánchez, Count of Seville, murmured. His saddle creaked as he turned to his squire, Guillen. 'This is the place?'

'It must be, my lord.'

The Three Lanterns was a bathhouse. Its popularity with merchants from outside the Emirate gave Count Inigo hope that the presence of a Spanish knight and his squire wouldn't raise too many eyebrows. He was finally on the point of returning home and the last thing he wanted was trouble.

Earlier that day Inigo had been freed from Sultan Tariq's prison in the Vermillion Towers. As Count of Seville, and lord over sizeable holdings in the Spanish kingdom of Castile, a hefty ransom had been paid for Inigo's release. He remained uneasy. Until he left the Sultan's territory, he wasn't going to let his guard down. His incarceration had given him a grave mistrust of Sultan Tariq, and while there was no question that Inigo was free, he wouldn't truly relax until he was back in Castile. One more night and they'd be on their way.

'You have our safe conduct, lad?' Inigo asked.

Guillen patted his saddlebag. 'In here, my lord.'

'Good. And you were given assurances that we may explore Granada unmolested?'

They were still within a stone's throw of the Sultan's palace. If they encountered prejudice, Inigo needed to know he and Guillen had protection. Having won his release, Inigo had no wish to fall foul of city authorities.

'Indeed, my lord. Provided we leave by noon tomorrow, Granada is ours to explore.'

Slivers of light were seeping out between cracks in the bathhouse shutters. Inside, Inigo could hear water being poured. There was a faint tang in the air. Almond oil. It was beyond tempting. After months in captivity, his skin itched. With a grimace, he tugged at what was left of his green tunic. Head to toe, he was filthy. 'I stink to high heaven.'

Guillen grinned and said not a word.

Inigo lifted an eyebrow and prepared to dismount. 'That bad, huh?'

'Yes, my lord.'

'Wretch. Here, hand me that safe conduct, I'm not about to let it out of my sight.'

Guillen unbuckled his saddlebag, drew out a scroll and passed it to Inigo.

'My thanks. See to the horses before you come to attend me.'

Inigo rapped on the door, which opened at his touch. A tiled entrance led to a small courtyard that was starred with lamps. The bathhouse was larger than it appeared from the street, arched doorways led off in all directions. The scent of almond oil mingled with other scents—bay, sage, rose...

Inigo heard the hum of conversation and then a soft footfall. A young boy was bowing at him.

'My apologies, I don't speak Arabic,' Inigo said. Conscious that his unkempt appearance might lead the boy to peg him for a beggar or a thief rather than a customer, he opened his money pouch and took out a handful of silver. 'I am Inigo Sánchez, Count of Seville, and I am hoping you speak my tongue.'

'I do indeed, great lord.'

'That is a relief. I would like a bath and a barber. Your name, lad?'

'I am Mo,' the boy said, smiling. 'Welcome to The Three Lanterns.'

Across the courtyard a door swung wide, and

Sir Enrique de Murcia stepped into the lamplight. Inigo held down a groan. Sir Enrique had been a fellow captive in the Vermillion Towers. Unfortunately, he was the last man Inigo wanted to see.

Desperate though he was for a bath and clean clothes, Inigo found himself wrestling with the urge to turn on his heel and go elsewhere. It was an awkward situation. Sir Enrique was cousin to Inigo's close friend, Count Rodrigo Álvarez. That should have stood in Enrique's favour, but Enrique's foolhardiness had sparked off the border skirmish that had cost Rodrigo's younger brother his life. If Enrique hadn't rushed into battle, young Diego would still be alive, and Inigo and Rodrigo would never have dived into the fray in an attempt to save him. Inigo's capture and subsequent imprisonment lay firmly at Enrique's door.

'Enrique,' Inigo said. 'Didn't think to find you here.'

Enrique stood under an arch, swaying slightly. He was holding a wineskin and he looked drunk, which was quick work, even for him. They'd not been free for long. He lifted the wineskin to his mouth, throat working as he swallowed.

'This wine's not bad,' Enrique said, tossing the empty skin aside and scowling at Mo. 'You, fetch me another.'

'Yes, great lord.' Mo clapped his hands and

another boy appeared and was sent in search of more wine. Mo looked at Inigo. 'You require a private bath, great lord?'

Inigo nodded. 'If you please. My squire Guillen is stabling our horses. He will join me shortly.'

Inigo was shown into a lamplit chamber. After the rigours of his imprisonment, it was like walking into heaven. The floor was white marble and he found himself gazing longingly at a low marble washbowl. Further in, beyond a row of horseshoe arches with red marble columns, steps led into a deep pool fed by a water spout. The water gleamed blue in the lamplight. The wall tiles were earth-coloured, and the ceiling domed. A handful of six-pointed stars were spaced about the dome. Air vents. In the day they would, presumably, admit light. A wooden couch was set against a wall.

This was his bathing chamber? It was fit for a prince.

As Inigo peeled off his clothes, filthy rags he never wanted to see again, he prayed Enrique would have the sense to realise his company wasn't wanted.

He splashed off the worst of the filth in the washbowl before lowering himself into the pool. The water was warm and scented with sage, it felt like heaven. He closed his eyes and was easing his injured leg when a shift in the air told him someone had joined him. Hoping it was Guillen, he opened his eyes.

Enrique stood at the edge of the pool. 'Is Rodrigo joining us?' he asked.

'I couldn't say,' Inigo said, 'I am not privy to your cousin's plans.'

That was a bald lie. In truth, Rodrigo was due later. However, during their captivity, Rodrigo had been unable to escape Enrique's company and Inigo was only too conscious of how difficult he must have found it. To have been compelled, day after day, to keep the company of a man whose recklessness had led directly to the death of his beloved brother must have tested Rodrigo's patience to the limit.

In the interest of harmony, it would be best to get rid of Enrique before Rodrigo arrived.

Enrique grunted, weaved his way to the couch and sat down heavily. He was holding more wine—a bottle this time—and was toying with the cork.

Leaning against the side of the pool, Inigo probed his leg. In the battle to save Diego, one of the Sultan's men had sliced it open. Thankfully, the wound had healed cleanly, though it still ached from time to time.

'They have women here,' Enrique said conversationally. 'Girls seem to like you, I'm sure they will be delighted to accommodate you.'

Inigo cleared his throat. 'Not interested. Enrique, you must be forgetting, I am to be married soon.'

Enrique's lip curled. 'You've been betrothed for years, that's never stopped you before.'

Inigo shrugged. 'Lady Margarita and I have an understanding.'

'She knows about your…flirtations?' Enrique asked.

'Aye, but we will be married shortly and all that will change.'

'You'll be faithful after you're wed?' Enrique sounded incredulous.

'Of course.'

'Good God, man, why? You don't give a fig for Margarita, you never have.'

Inigo was all too aware that his relationship with his betrothed was cool. Lady Margarita Marchena de Carmona was a cool woman, which was exactly why he was marrying her. He wanted a cool wife. An emotional woman wouldn't suit him, such a woman would disrupt his household and destroy his peace of mind. When they were married, he would reward Lady Margarita for her calm by being a loyal husband.

'I won't shame my wife. I shall be faithful.'

Enrique's lip curled. 'It's amazing you can say that with a straight face. You're the biggest flirt alive.'

Inigo couldn't deny that he liked women. It was the emotional baggage they brought with them that made him wary. He liked his relationships simple.

'There will be no flirting when I am wed. It's too much trouble otherwise.'

Idly, Enrique watched him, and a twisted smile formed. 'Crook your finger and those girls will come. They can dry you off. Seriously, Inigo, make the most of them while you can.'

'Guillen will be back from the stables shortly, he can assist me.' Wishing Enrique in Hades, Inigo slid deep into the water.

Back in Castile, Enrique's reputation with women was ugly, Inigo had heard that he had a cruel streak. Inigo had never seen Enrique with a woman, and rumours were only rumours, but having witnessed Enrique's vicious impetuosity in battle, he feared they might be true.

Enrique lifted the bottle and drank. Wiping his mouth with his sleeve, he gave Inigo an unpleasant smile. 'I've been married for years and I've never let it interfere with the real pleasures of life.'

'The real pleasures?' Inigo smothered a yawn.

'I have plans, let me tell you. I'm saving myself for later tonight.' Enrique jerked his head towards the door. 'Otherwise I'd avail myself of the delights here.'

Despite the warmth of the water, Inigo felt a chill of foreboding. 'Plans?'

'I intend to avenge myself on Sultan Tariq.'

Inigo relaxed, it was hard not to laugh. Enrique was ridiculous. Sultan Tariq was safe behind the impenetrable walls of the Alhambra Palace with innumerable soldiers answering to his command. It would take more than a lone Castilian knight with vengeance on his mind to put a dent in the Sultan's armour. 'Oh? How so?' This would be interesting.

'The Sultan will regret the day he made me do forced labour.' Enrique's eyes glittered, and a bitter torrent of words spilled out. 'Damn it, Inigo. I am a nobleman, we are noblemen. It's one thing for Sultan Tariq to demand a ransom for our capture, that I did expect, it's common in war. But when he put us to breaking rocks in that gully outside the palace, he broke every rule of chivalry. The man's a barbarian.'

Inigo decided that an interruption might have a calming effect. 'I don't know, it wasn't all bad. We saw the three Princesses up in their tower, not many can claim that. We even got to serenade them.'

Enrique took another swig from the bottle. 'The devil was tempting us, tempting us with his daughters.'

'I don't believe the Sultan was aware that his daughters saw us.'

'That wretch knows everything, he ordered his daughters to tempt us.'

'For heaven's sake, Enrique, it was a pleasant diversion. The Princesses noticed us, pitied us and gave us food. I truly believe Sultan Tariq had no idea what was going on.'

'Delude yourself all you like, the devil must have known. Nothing happens in that place without his say so. He was trying to drive us mad. Inigo, I will avenge myself for the indignities I suffered, and the Nasrid Princesses will help me.'

'How so?'

'I'm going back to the Alhambra Palace. I'm going to abduct them.'

Inigo stared. Truly, Enrique was a madman. 'Impossible.'

Enrique gave a triumphant grin. 'Not so, it's all arranged. I've been in touch with the Princesses' duenna. She seems to be disloyal to the Sultan.'

'Seems to be?'

'I admit it could be a mistake to rely on the

word of a palace servant, but my honour is at stake, so I'm prepared to risk it. Inigo, this duenna claims credit for arranging for us to serenade the Princesses.'

'Hang on, Enrique, you're contradicting yourself. I thought you said that the Sultan knew what was happening?'

Enrique waved his bottle and the couch creaked. 'Details, details. The point is that I have it on good authority that the Princesses hate their father almost as much as we do. They *want* to run away and they're going to run straight into my arms.'

'When will this happen?'

'This very night, in the gully near their tower.' Enrique studied the wine bottle. 'You might like to know, they're expecting you and Rodrigo to join us.'

'What!'

'Aye, they're expecting the three of us. The Princesses' mother was Spanish, they want us to escort them to Castile to find some lost relatives.' Enrique's mouth tightened. 'Fools. We'll show them, eh?'

'You're insane.' Inigo tried to hide the extent of his dismay. Inwardly, he was appalled. Surely, even Enrique wouldn't be so reckless? 'Have you no sense, why stir up a hornet's nest? We need peace between the kingdoms. We need to get home. Enrique, your plan is foolhardy in the extreme. Suicidal.'

'Rot.'

'The wine has addled your wits, it's suicide. Besides, where's your gratitude? The Princesses saved our lives.'

When Enrique gave him a blank look, Inigo enlarged. 'You can't have forgotten the day the Sultan made us march from Salobreña to Granada.'

'The convoy of prisoners? Walking through dust for days? Throat so parched I couldn't swallow?' Enrique's jaw set. 'I'll never forget it.'

'Well then, you must also remember that the Princesses rushed to our aid. The Sultan had drawn his scimitar and if it weren't for their intervention, he would have killed us.'

'I don't care. I want a princess.'

'Why?'

'There's only one use for a Nasrid princess that I can think of.' Enrique made a crude and very explicit gesture.

Inigo went still. 'Pray tell me you're not serious.'

A flicker of uncertainty crossed Enrique's face. 'You are with me, aren't you?'

'Certainly not. Enrique, this is madness. You're drunk. Deluded. You can't take your anger out on the Princesses. They are innocents.'

'Innocents? Inigo, if anyone is deluded, it's you.

There's an entirely different view of what happened on the road from Salobreña.'

'Go on,' Inigo said. With every moment that went by, Enrique's voice was becoming more slurred. If he drank himself into a stupor, it might be best for all concerned.

'When the Sultan threatened us,' Enrique went on, 'the Princesses raced up to get a better view. They wanted to watch as we were carved into a thousand pieces.'

Inigo blinked, Enrique's version of events was so warped, it was hard to believe he was describing what they had both witnessed. 'You honestly believe that?'

'How was I to know what they were up to? Couldn't understand a word they were saying. They're all heathens.'

Inigo hadn't been able to understand what was said either, but a blind man could tell that the Princesses were in awe of their father.

'The Princesses were pleading for the Sultan to spare us. Enrique, they put themselves at risk for us. It was obvious.'

'Not to me, it wasn't.' Enrique staggered to his feet. 'Tonight promises to give good sport. For the last time, will you come with me?'

'No.' Inigo looked critically at Enrique. Experience had taught him that Rodrigo's cousin could drink most men under the table. The man did have limits—regrettably, he didn't appear to have reached them.

Inigo's squire clattered in. He threw a wary glance at Enrique, propped against the wall with his wine bottle. 'Fresh clothes, my lord.'

'*Gracias*. My thanks. Set them down on that couch, would you?' Inigo said.

Enrique weaved his way to the door. 'I'll be off then. If you're not joining me, doubtless I'll see you back in Córdoba.'

Appalled though he was, Inigo kept his voice cool. 'Enrique, don't do this.' Somehow, he must get Enrique to listen to reason.

'I will have my revenge.' Enrique's voice was slurred and his eyes unfocused. 'I admit I can't take all three of them, but at least one Princess will be coming with me.'

'You would despoil an innocent girl? You talk of honour—what of your chivalric vows? You make me ashamed to be a knight.'

Enrique's laugh echoed around the chamber, harsh and ugly. 'A Nasrid princess has no innocence. And she certainly won't when I've finished with her.'

'No woman should be forced, innocent or otherwise,' Inigo said tightly. He felt like throttling the man. 'Enrique, have you forgotten you are married?'

'Your point being?'

'How would Lady Berengaria feel?'

'She'll never find out.'

'And that makes it right?'

Enrique gave an incoherent reply and fell clumsily against the door frame.

Inigo's squire had listened to their exchange with wide, shocked eyes. Inigo exchanged looks with him, gestured for a drying cloth and climbed out of the pool.

When sober, Enrique was a foolhardy bully. Half soused, he wasn't likely to be very effective. His plans would surely come to nothing. Notwithstanding, Inigo wasn't prepared to take any risks. Peace between the Emirate of Granada and the Kingdom of Castile was shaky at best. If, by some miracle, Enrique managed to spirit away even one of the Nasrid Princesses, there'd be hell to pay.

Enrique straightened as though struck by a sudden thought. 'Inigo, about my lady wife, there's something in what you say, she mustn't hear of this. Give me your word you'll say nothing.'

Half an eye on Enrique, Inigo tossed the drying cloth at Guillen and dragged on fresh clothes. 'It's simple, forget the entire idea.'

'Never. I will have vengeance.'

Realising outright confrontation with Enrique would achieve little, Inigo reached for his sword belt. Apart from the Princesses' largesse, Inigo and his companions had been surviving on siege rations. If he could get decent food into Rodrigo's cousin, perhaps he'd see sense. 'Well, I don't know about you, but I'm starving. We could have supper before you set out.'

Enrique looked blearily at him. 'You're offering to pay?'

'Certainly.' The price of a meal in a tavern was as nothing compared to the havoc that would ensue if a Castilian knight abducted a Nasrid princess. 'If you wait a moment, we can go together.'

'Where are you headed?'

'I am reliably informed that the best local tavern lies about a mile outside the town,' Inigo said. 'The Black Sheep.'

'The Black Sheep.' Enrique laughed and fumbled for the door latch. 'How appropriate. Very well, I accept. See you later.'

'What's the hurry?' Inigo frowned, he didn't want to let Enrique out of his sight, he didn't trust him an inch. 'Allow me to settle up here, we can go together.'

He also needed a moment to leave a message

for Rodrigo. Rodrigo would want to know about his cousin's latest folly, he would object to this plan as much as Inigo. Sir Enrique de Murcia couldn't be allowed anywhere near the three Princesses.

Enrique shook his head. 'I've had my fill of this place, I'll see you at the inn.'

'Good grief, Enrique, you can surely wait until I'm dressed!'

He spoke to an empty doorway.

Tension balling in his gut, Inigo asked Mo to look out for Rodrigo and his squire, making sure Mo understood to give them clear directions to The Black Sheep.

'Mo, his name is Rodrigo Álvarez, Count of Córdoba. Please be sure he understands it's the best inn hereabouts and that I shall meet him there.'

Mo smiled. 'Certainly, my lord.'

'My thanks.' Inigo strode into the lamplit street praying that Enrique would wait for his supper. The sooner Inigo got to that inn, the better he would feel.

Guillen cleared his throat. 'You wish to leave straight away, my lord?' His eyes were shadowed and his voice anxious. 'Didn't you mention a barber?'

Inigo ran his hand ruefully through his hair and beard. 'That will have to wait, we need to find that inn with all speed. I feel uneasy leaving Sir Enrique on his own.'

A line formed on his squire's brow. 'We—that is I—may have to delay. I'm sorry, my lord, one of Raven's shoes was loose. I asked a groom to take him to a blacksmith to shoe him.'

'A smith is working at this hour?' Inigo asked, coming to an abrupt halt outside the stable. They ought to hurry. Left on his own, Enrique was a liability. However, Guillen looked so woebegone, Inigo didn't have the heart to chastise him. 'Hell burn it, Guillen, you're not to blame, horses often cast shoes, but the timing couldn't be worse. With Enrique set on revenge, anything might happen. I wanted to sober him up with food.'

'I know, my lord, and I'm sorry.' Guillen brightened. 'If you go ahead, I can meet you later.'

Inigo shook his head, the idea of leaving his squire alone in Granada while he went tearing after Enrique didn't sit well with him. 'No, lad, we only have one letter of safe conduct. We'd best stick together.'

Inigo collected his horse, Soldier, and he and Guillen were soon at the smithy. Irritatingly, the blacksmith was deep in conversation with a neighbour and Guillen's horse wasn't ready. It was necessary for Inigo to impress upon the man that speed was of the essence. A gold dinar did the trick, and while they were waiting for Raven to be shod, they called for more lamps and Guillen was able to act as Inigo's barber.

At length, Inigo and Guillen hauled themselves on to their horses and took to the road. The whole operation had taken far longer than Inigo had anticipated. He could only pray that Enrique had fallen into a stupor at the inn.

The lights of the town faded, and moonlight became their guide. The road was a silver thread winding through groves of orange and olive. The air hummed with cicadas.

Eventually, stronger lights gleamed, they had reached The Black Sheep. A small area of scrub had been roped off and was serving as a paddock for the tavern's customers. A couple of old men—grooms presumably—sat beneath a tree, guarding a handful of horses. Enrique's wasn't among them.

Inigo held in a groan. 'Guillen, this doesn't look good.'

'No, my lord.'

Leaving their mounts with the grooms, Inigo and Guillen went into the inn. It was crammed to the rafters with big-bellied, prosperous-looking men in fine brocades. Merchants. A couple of shepherds huddled in a corner. The noise was deafening.

No Enrique. And no sign of his squire, either. The innkeeper, a cloth about his waist, approached and greeted them in Arabic.

'My apologies, I don't understand,' Inigo said, over the din. The smell of roasted chicken filled the air and his stomach growled. 'Do you speak Spanish?'

The innkeeper shook his head and gestured towards the serving hatch where a boy was filling bowls from a blackened cauldron.

The boy joined them. 'Sir?'

'I am looking for a friend, a knight. He would have had his squire with him.'

'They are Castilian?' The boy hesitated. 'And the knight had been drinking?'

Inigo grimaced. 'You could say that.'

'They have gone, sir.'

'When?'

'Not long.'

'Which direction did they take?'

'I heard them mention the Alhambra Palace.'

Dear Lord, Enrique had a death wish. Inigo snatched a hunk of bread from a tray and tossed it at his squire.

'Guillen?'

'My lord?'

'Get back outside. Stop them unsaddling the horses and keep an eye out for Rodrigo. If he arrives, don't let him dismount. I'll grab provisions and follow you.'

His squire dashed off and Inigo secured a couple of bundles of food—chicken, bread and cheese. Lord, this was supposed to be his first night of freedom and it looked as though he was going to have to spend it preventing Rodrigo's wretched cousin from despoiling an innocent girl.

Guillen reappeared. 'My lord, Count Rodrigo has arrived.'

Inigo left the inn. Seeing Rodrigo and his squire were still mounted, he let out a breath of relief. Thank God for reliable friends.

'Take this.' He thrust a food bundle at Rodrigo. 'Save it for later.'

'Later?' Rodrigo frowned. 'Inigo, what in hell's going on?'

'Enrique's in trouble again.' Inigo said, hauling himself into the saddle.

'*Madre mía*, this must stop. Last time we rushed to Enrique's rescue, Diego died. Cousin or no, I've no wish to see him again.'

Inigo nodded. Diego's death had upset him, and he could only begin to imagine the depth of Rodrigo's grief. What must it be like to lose a beloved younger brother? His jaw tightened. 'We have no choice.'

Rodrigo's expression was bleak. 'Don't we? Enrique never learns, as far as I'm concerned, he can stew in his own juice.'

'Not this time.'

'What's he done?'

'He's drunk.'

Rodrigo looked at him. 'Is that all? Good grief, given the conditions we've endured, you can hardly blame him for that.' He glanced meaningfully at the tavern. 'I wouldn't mind a drink myself.'

'If only it were as simple as that,' Inigo said. Trusting Rodrigo and the squires to follow, he dug in his spurs and cantered on to the road that led back to the Alhambra Palace. The lights of the inn fell back, they would have to rely on the moon.

Rodrigo soon caught up. 'Slow down, man. What's going on?'

'Enrique's been muttering about revenge all day. Wants to make the Sultan pay for treating us like slaves.'

Rodrigo swore. 'There's no way he can get to Sultan Tariq, the palace is a fortress and he rarely leaves it. Not to mention that entire battalions answer to the Sultan's command and we are in his heartlands. Leave it, Inigo. My cousin can get himself out of the mire this time.'

Inigo grimaced. 'You wouldn't be so sanguine if you knew what he was planning.'

'Surprise me.'

'He's going to abduct the Sultan's daughters.'

'What? That's insane.'

'I assure you, it's true. Enrique's going to lure them out of that tower.'

'They'd never leave the palace.'

Inigo raised his eyebrows and, voice filled with doubt, Rodrigo repeated himself. 'No, they'd surely never leave the palace.'

'Rodrigo, hear me out. Enrique has made contact with someone inside the palace, a maidservant or duenna of some kind, I believe. It's already arranged. The Princesses want to run away. They're to meet your cousin tonight.'

'What? We've only been released a day, how on earth has Enrique managed to organise it in that time?'

'He didn't give me any more details.'

'You're certain it's tonight?'

'That's what he said. Rodrigo, your cousin's a madman when the drink is in him.'

Rodrigo grunted in acknowledgement. 'Unfortunately, he's a madman with a will of iron.'

'Well, he's after vengeance tonight, and he's decided the Sultan's daughters will give it to him. I've never seen him quite so set on anything.'

'I'll thrash him when I see him,' Rodrigo said curtly. 'Those Princesses are very young. Sheltered. What do you reckon he's after, ransom? You don't think he'd harm them?'

Inigo gave a harsh laugh. 'His reputation with women is not good.'

'He's a married man.'

'Don't make the mistake of judging your cousin by your standards. Enrique is roaring drunk and he wants revenge.'

A muscle flickered in Rodrigo's jaw. 'If my cousin carries off just one of the Sultan's daughters, he could set off a minor war. And I'm not just referring to here in Al-Andalus. If Enrique's father-in-law believes my cousin has slighted his daughter by carrying off a Nasrid princess, he will never forgive him. Enrique must be stopped. When did he set out?'

'He'd gone when I got here. The innkeeper says he left about an hour ago.'

'I take it he took his squire with him?'

'Aye.'

Inigo and Rodrigo gave their horses the spur and they and their squires flew into the night.

Chapter Three

In the grounds of the Alhambra Palace

The night of the Princesses' escape had arrived. Leonor and Alba were leading the way even though they had never been in this part of the grounds. The iron gate that marked the entrance to the disused sally port had been almost impossible to find in the dark, and the gardens were so quiet all Alba could hear was her own breathing, fast and flurried. Despite the warmth of the night, she shivered as she peered into the secret tunnel to the outside.

A few yards in, a torch flickered and hissed. Beyond the torch, a gloomy corridor ran deep into the earth. Alba had heard mutterings about this tunnel. Some said it was a secret passageway into the palace, others that it was an escape route for previous sultans fleeing murderous relatives. This last might well be true, many of her father's predecessors had had their lives cut short by ambitious brothers. Her nails dug into her palms. Whatever its use, the passage smelt dank and looked terrifying. Shadowed and seemingly without end, it couldn't have been used for centuries.

This was their route to freedom? Was it safe?

It was certainly narrow. Alba hated confined spaces, normally nothing would persuade her to set foot in a tunnel like this. Unfortunately, life in the palace had become intolerable. The sally port was her only way out. God was good though, and the rusting iron gate on the palace side was open, as her duenna, Inés, had promised.

There would be no turning back.

Alba had no regrets. No, that wasn't entirely true. She deeply regretted having to leave Hunter, her pet monkey, behind. She'd had to do it though, Hunter was exuberant and far too noisy to come with them. He would have given them away in a heartbeat. Alba had wept when she left him in the care of a maidservant.

Another regret was the songbirds. The Sultan had given each of the Princesses a pair of songbirds in a gilded cage. Earlier that evening, Alba had released hers into the wild. Like her, they must take their chances away from the palace. Leonor, too, had freed her songbirds, Constanza had not. A maidservant would care for Constanza's birds.

In the flare of the flickering torch, Alba noticed the tremble of Leonor's veil. Perversely, it gave her heart to see that her brave older sister was unnerved.

'Where's Constanza?' Leonor whispered. 'We can't leave without her.'

'She's just behind, stop fretting. She'll follow us, she always does,' Alba said.

Alba had often wondered if she and her sisters were close because they were triplets or because they had been brought up together. Had the Sultan's policy of isolating them from the rest of the world, indeed, of isolating them from almost everyone except for a handful of servants and their beloved Spanish duenna strengthened the bond between them? The three Princesses ate together, they laughed together, they cried together. They would escape together too. Once in Spain, they would start anew. Together.

Alba gave Leonor a gentle push. 'Hurry, for pity's sake, Father's guards are everywhere.'

Leonor went into the tunnel. A huge key hung on a hook below the torch, it was as rusty and ancient as the gate. Leonor grabbed it and thrust it at Alba.

'Take this, I'll take the torch.' Leonor started down the corridor.

The key was cold and heavy, Alba gripped it as though her life depended on it. As she followed

Leonor, she prayed that the lock in the door at the other end hadn't rusted solid. They *must* escape.

Their father the Sultan was becoming more tyrannical by the day. When Alba and her sisters had asked permission to explore Granada on horseback, he had responded by locking the three of them in their tower. Later, the Princesses had been informed their ponies were no longer in the palace stables. They had been sold.

The sale of their beloved ponies had been the final straw, the moment when the Princesses understood that not only was Sultan Tariq a tyrant, but also that there was no hope for him. He was never going to change. Grimly, Alba set her jaw. She had hopes. Dreams. Her father wasn't going to crush them.

The tunnel twisted this way and that, a dark serpent winding beneath the palace grounds. The air was stale and smelled of earth and rust, and with every step the walls closed in. It was hard to breathe. Alba's skin prickled with sweat and she had the strangest urge to pant.

Torchlight wavered over the tunnel walls. Alba tried to imagine which part of the palace lay above. The orange grove? The lawn beloved of the palace peacocks? The Court of the Lions?

There were footsteps at her back, Constanza

must be close on her heels. Gradually, her breathing eased. *The three of us are in this together.*

The key bit into Alba's palm. Her veil was a nuisance, filmy though it was, it was suffocating. Alba didn't stop to remove it though, the habit of obedience held her, even here in the tunnel.

Alba and her sisters had broken the Sultan's rules once or twice. But tonight, even though they were, she prayed, escaping the life of restriction their father had planned for them, the veil that symbolised their oppression was peculiarly comforting—a shield as it were. There was no saying what was in store for them outside the sally port, she might want to hide.

Leonor forged on without as much as a backward look, clearly, she had no doubts. Suddenly, she stopped. 'I can't see the end,' she said. 'Is Constanza behind us?'

'I think I can hear her. Keep going.'

Alba had strapped a money pouch beneath her clothing; it felt heavy, like a dead thing. Her chest ached for lack of air—she was all too conscious of the weight of earth and rock above them. Her palms were clammy and cold sweat trickled down her spine.

Then the air shifted, it seemed cleaner. Sweeter. Leonor halted, she was frowning at a door so ancient it looked to have grown into the walls. 'We've reached the end.'

Panting only a little, Alba reached past her, fitted the key into the lock and twisted. The handle was rusty and when Leonor wrenched at the door, the hinges moaned in protest.

'Here, let me help,' Alba murmured.

They pushed and shoved, and between them made a narrow crack. As it widened, fresh air wafted in. Leonor squeezed through the gap.

A soft footfall in the tunnel told Alba that Constanza was a few paces behind. Swallowing hard, she gathered her cloak about her and slipped out, breathing properly for the first time since entering the tunnel. Like magic, the tight band about her forehead eased.

They were outside the palace! The danger wasn't past, but at least she was free of that ghastly corridor, it had felt like a tomb.

Trees made dark silhouettes against a starry sky. The moon, barely visible through her veil, glistened through a tangle of branches. In a hollow below the sally port, she could see the faint glow of a lantern.

How odd, the only person Alba could see was Leonor. Beneath her veil, she frowned. Three Castilian knights should be waiting for them. It was all arranged. Their duenna Inés had sworn that their ransom money had been paid in full. Those men should be free. Where were they? Had they, alienated by their captivity, changed their minds?

Alba wouldn't be surprised; her father had treated those knights abysmally. They'd spent weeks clearing a rock-choked ravine outside the palace walls, the same ravine that was overlooked by the Princesses' tower. The Princesses, bored and angered by their confinement and the loss of their beloved ponies, had been quick to notice and recognise them as the self-same men they'd seen first at Salobreña, and again in a convoy of prisoners marching from Salobreña to Granada.

Fuelled by anger, the Princesses had begun a forbidden flirtation from the top of the tower. At night, when the palace was lost in sleep, they had listened to the knights singing. Realising the men were half-starved, they'd sent food baskets down on a rope. In short, they'd ignored all protocols and had behaved quite outrageously. Inés, who had come from Spain with their mother the Queen, and was herself Spanish, encouraged them.

No one had dreamed anything would come of it. It had been a rebellion, a way for the Princesses to channel their anger. Sultan Tariq had locked them in the tower; he had sold their ponies; he refused to listen to reason.

Throughout this dalliance the Spanish knights were distant, mysterious figures, prisoners of their father. Other than that, the Princesses knew next to nothing about them. It was a measure of their seclusion and desperation that they only had these men—strangers—to help them escape.

Inés had contacts outside the palace and she wanted the Princesses to be happy. She had laid her plans with care. The three knights were supposed to spirit the Princesses out of the Emirate of Granada and into the Spanish Kingdom of Castile where they would be beyond the reach of their tyrannical father.

Castile. Alba had longed to see it all her life. In the years since the Queen's death, Inés had taught the Princesses Spanish. Sultan Tariq might have isolated his daughters, but that hadn't stopped them from learning that they had relatives in Castile. They were determined to find them and make a new home for themselves. They would be together, and they would be safe.

Alba peered warily about. The terrain around the disused sally port was all in shadow. It was lightly wooded, resembling the scrubland overlooked by the Princesses' tower—namely a gully, clothed with shrubs and trees, and choked with rocks.

Where were the knights? Her breath was flurried. Nerves, she supposed.

And then she saw them. Six men. Three she recognised as the knights, the others must be their squires. The knights were arguing, their words were sharp and angry. Alba's stomach knotted. Angry men wouldn't be much use. The dark wood seemed to tilt, she was dizzy with an overwhelming mix of excitement, exultation and fear. She had escaped the palace. She and her sisters were free. Could they trust these men? Were they dangerous?

The odd phrase reached her.

'For pity's sake, Enrique,' one of the knights ground out. 'Will you see sense?'

A second knight cut in. 'Enrique's my cousin, I'll deal with him. Rest assured, no one will be hurt.'

Alba recognised the second knight as Count Rodrigo. Leonor had managed to speak to him in private once, and she'd told Alba his name some days ago.

In the distance, dogs were barking. Alba's heart jumped. Had her father released his hunting dogs? Filled with fear, she tried to see through the trees. It was impossible.

With a start, she realised that Count Rodrigo was standing next to Leonor and he too must have heard the dogs, for he cocked his head to listen, took command of Leonor's torch and put it out.

The dark intensified. One of the other knights approached and bowed over Alba's hand. He was touching her.

Alba froze. Save for her father, in her whole life no man had presumed to touch her. She willed herself not to react. This knight was her means of escape. He was not a palace guard, he was Spanish like her mother, and Inés had explained that a Spanish knight would not think it odd or shameful in any way to touch a woman. In the Kingdom of Castile, men often greeted women by bowing over their hands in this manner. For a princess who'd been shielded from men, it was disquieting.

'My lady, I believe you can ride?' the knight said.

Please, sir, be kind.

Alba found her voice. 'Certainly, my lord.'

'This way, if you please. You must ride astride, I'm afraid.'

Alba peered through her veil, but with the torch extinguished she could hardly see. Even so, she knew him. It was the knight her father's men had wounded, the one who had hobbled off the captives' galley when it had made port at Salobreña. He had spent weeks as Sultan Tariq's prisoner and she had no idea how he would treat her.

Would he seek revenge for his imprisonment? He was a nobleman, he was bound to have pride, pride her father's treatment must have dented. At best, he was bound to resent the weeks spent away from Castile.

His tall masculine shape made a black silhouette against the night sky. He was waiting for her decision. Realising she must accept his assistance—and swiftly—if she was to win her freedom, Alba allowed him to help her on to his horse.

Her entire body quivered as he mounted behind her and took up the reins. She was sharing a horse with a Spanish nobleman. A nameless foreigner. Her father's enemy. Yesterday, it would have been unthinkable.

'Your name, sir?' she whispered.

'Inigo Sánchez, Count of Seville,' he murmured. Then, as a blood-curdling howl cut through the dark, he urged his horse on.

God be merciful.

They forged on through undergrowth that prickled and scratched. The stars and moon were gone, the darkness thickened. The air was close and muggy. Alba clung to the saddle, praying the horse didn't stumble. The last thing they needed was a poor horse screaming in agony because it had broken its leg. Sounds were harsh—the thud of hoofs, the baying of the hounds, an ominous rumble of thunder.

Water splashed on the back of Alba's hands. A storm. Months of drought was coming to an end.

Count Inigo reined in. Count Rodrigo drew up alongside, Leonor sat before him on the saddle.

Count Rodrigo gestured at the ground. Small rivulets were swirling around the horses' hoofs, rainwater from a storm high in the mountains was rushing down the gully.

Alba swallowed a groan, it had been a hot, dry summer and a flood was inevitable.

'The riverbed is prone to flash floods,' Lord Rodrigo said. 'We'll use that in our favour. Get the river between us and the palace. With luck, it'll confuse the dogs.'

'Good idea,' Count Inigo said. She felt his hand on her hip, settling her more securely before him.

Leonor touched her elbow. 'Alba, is Constanza behind us?'

Alba twisted to look along the way they had come, her rain-sodden veil clinging to her neck. There was no sign of Constanza. Ominously, other than the two knights and their squires, she could see no one else.

'I don't know, I haven't seen her.'

Leonor turned towards the squires. 'And you, sirs, have you seen my other sister?'

'No, my lady.'

Leonor looked at Count Rodrigo. 'My lord?'

Lord Rodrigo held up his hand. 'A moment, if you please. Inigo, our chances of escape will be better if we separate. I'll head south-west. They won't be expecting that.'

Count Inigo shifted. 'Understood.'

'God willing, I'll be in Córdoba in a week.'

'Very well, I'll meet you there.' Lord Inigo gave his horse the spur and they surged up the river-bank.

Drenched with rain, they pelted into the un-known with Lord Inigo's squire keeping close as a shadow. Alba felt the drumming of the horse's hooves in every bone and kept praying that they didn't lose their footing. *May God preserve us.* Most of all, she focused on keeping her seat. Panic was a breath away. She had no wish to end up alone in this storm-soaked wilderness so close to the palace. The Sultan's troops might catch them. This time Father's punishment would be…

Her mind refused to go down that road. They had done the right thing. They would get away. But what had happened to Constanza?

Lord Inigo's chest pressed against her back. His arms were locked firmly around her.

Was he a kind man? Did such a thing as a kind man even exist outside a fairy tale?

Lord Inigo was a warrior. He'd been caught fighting her father in the recent conflict on the border. He'd been wounded and imprisoned, and the Sultan had demanded a ransom payment, doubtless a large one, for his release from captivity. At best, Lord Inigo was bound to be resentful.

And this was the man she was reliant on to make good her escape?

If only she knew more about him.

However, as the sodden landscape wheeled past—stubby trees, dark bushes whose leaves slapped wetly at her—Alba realised that she wasn't entirely ignorant as to Lord Inigo's nature. Lord Inigo was clearly close to Count Rodrigo whom Leonor trusted. Leonor had only met Lord Rodrigo the once, and he'd made a good impression. Why else would she have been so eager to escape?

What do I know about Lord Inigo?

He'd been wounded by her father's men. He'd come to her rescue. Why? Behind her sodden veil, Alba grimaced. Could she trust him?

* * *

Inigo was cursing the day he had set foot in Al-Andalus. The going was appalling, the sudden downpour had turned what had lately been dust into mud, yet he had no choice but to urge his stallion to greater speed. Soldier slipped, found his footing and charged on.

Riding hard at night was a risky business when visibility was good and now, with moon and stars lost behind a curtain of rain and cloud, not to mention the poor terrain, it was downright foolhardy. Inigo prayed his luck was in. Soldier was the best of horses, he had no desire to lose him.

This race to freedom was, Inigo realised, even more dangerous than when he had dashed into battle to save Rodrigo's foolhardy cousin, Enrique.

As for the slight, feminine form Inigo was wrestling to keep safely in front of him—he couldn't in all honour blame her for his predicament. He hadn't been forced to get involved. The trouble was that as soon as Inigo had got wind of Enrique's plans, Inigo's fate had been sealed. He couldn't stand by while Enrique avenged himself on the Princesses. They weren't responsible for Sultan Tariq's misdeeds.

Thunder shook the heavens and the occasional pause was filled with insistent howling. Inigo focused his mind, he would think about the Nasrid Princess later. He had saved her from Enrique, which was the main thing. The rest—what on earth was he to do with her?—must wait. Other problems were more pressing.

Glancing back to ensure that Guillen was keeping pace, Inigo jabbed Soldier's flanks.

Guillen's background was humble, he mustn't fall into the Sultan's hands. The sole reason that Inigo had survived the Sultan's hospitality was because he was a nobleman and could afford the ransom demanded for his release. Should Guillen be captured, Inigo would be more than willing to pay to get his squire home in one piece, but he doubted that the Sultan's officers would pause long enough to find that out. Guillen must not be caught.

They gained higher ground on the other side of the fast-filling river, and Inigo searched the heavens for a guiding star. Unfortunately, the rain was unremitting and there wasn't as much as a glimmer, he would have to rely on instinct. Summer storms were generally brief, the light must improve soon. He blinked water from his eyes and prayed for the skies to clear. If necessary, he would alter course when the stars reappeared.

They forged on. A flurry of wind caught the Princess's veil and Inigo found himself batting yards of wet, jewel-encrusted fabric out of his face. Swearing under his breath, he slowed, one-handedly gathering the exotic fabric into a bundle. The Princess half turned.

'My lord?' A slender hand pulled at the veil. 'You're strangling me.'

'My apologies, Princess, the wretched thing is blinding me.' Ruthlessly, Inigo tugged. 'It must come off.'

There was a brief pause before her head dipped in agreement and that small hand came up, to fumble with ties or pins, he knew not what, but the veil came free.

Ruthlessly, he gathered the soggy mass into a ball and prepared to toss it aside.

She caught his hand. 'No!'

Inigo lifted an eyebrow. 'It's a nuisance.'

Somehow, she wrested it from him. 'It's a valuable nuisance, my lord. I shall have need of it later.'

Nodding brusquely, Inigo relieved her of the veil and bundled it into a saddlebag. 'I dare say you'll find the ride easier without it.'

Wrapping his arms about her again, Inigo gathered the reins. Inevitably, the movement brought them closer and she didn't face forward immediately. He felt her gaze on him and wondered if she could make out as little as he. He'd seen the faces of all three Princesses, while moving from the prison in Salobreña to hard labour in Granada. It had only been a glimpse, enough to confirm that the stories about them were true. The Princesses were triplets, identical triplets. They were also very lovely. Inigo wouldn't mind seeing Princess Alba's face properly, if only to confirm that she couldn't be quite as beautiful as his memory painted her.

The Princesses had intervened to save Inigo and his comrades from a beating—or worse—when they had inadvertently run foul of the Sultan's orders on the march from Salobreña to Granada. For that he would be eternally grateful. He was also grateful for the food they had sent down in baskets during their time clearing the ravine near the Princesses' tower.

None of which meant that Inigo welcomed having been forced to rescue her. He was betrothed, the last thing he needed was to return to Seville with a Nasrid princess. That would make explanations to Margarita interesting, to say the least. He and the Princess would be parting ways at Córdoba.

'My lord…' her whisper reached him through the dark and wet '…my name is Alba.'

'Princess Alba, I am honoured.' Inigo bowed his head. 'Hold tight.'

'Where are we going, my lord?'

'North. The border's closest there. With luck we'll reach Córdoba before very long.' He wondered how stoic she was. 'It's a fair ride, you understand.'

'It will take more than a day?'

'It could take several days, we are largely in God's hands.'

'Several days?' With a sigh, she faced forward. 'I shall not let you down.'

Inigo dug his heels into Soldier's flanks.

They rode in what he trusted was a northerly direction with the Princess's words—*I shall not let you down*—echoing in his mind. Even though he hadn't wanted this, he felt a reluctant admiration for her.

All Inigo had been able to think about since his release was that his days in Sultan Tariq's prison were over. Even though he knew it was common for lords to be held for ransom after capture in battle, there'd been moments when he'd feared he would never see Seville again. His injured leg still throbbed occasionally. The wound had made him delirious for days. If it hadn't been for Rodrigo, Inigo would doubtless have breathed his last. Thanks to Rodrigo securing the services of a doctor, Inigo's leg had slowly healed. And Sultan Tariq had eventually settled on a ransom.

Fortunately, Inigo's coffers were deep. He wouldn't be crippled, physically or financially, by his ill-fated excursion into Al-Andalus.

The storm rolled on. Inigo swiped water from his face and frowned into the night. Rodrigo had far more cause for regret than he did. Rodrigo's graceless cousin, Enrique, had a lot to answer for. Inigo had merely come away with some grim memories, an ache in his leg and the knowledge that his coffers were slightly lighter. Rodrigo, on the other hand, had lost a beloved younger brother. Inigo didn't envy Rodrigo his homecoming. His mother, Lady Isabel, would be beside herself with grief.

They continued steadily uphill, crossing land that was lightly wooded. The baying of the Sultan's hounds faded and other, less hostile, sounds took over—the startled bleat of a sheep, the thud of their horses' hoofs, the cry of an owl.

The Princess—Alba—held fast. Thankfully, the trembling had stopped. She appeared to be sitting easily before him. Occasionally, a light scent flirted with Inigo's senses. It was flowery and exotic. Jasmine? Inigo wasn't sure, though it was pleasant. As was holding her. How long had it been since he had held a woman in his arms? Too long, clearly.

The face of Inigo's betrothed formed in his

mind. Lady Margarita Marchena de Carmona. They had been betrothed for an age. Inigo was uneasily aware that he'd not seen her in years. That must change, and quickly. His brush with death had brought home to him the importance of marriage. Of getting heirs. He had dallied long enough.

He fixed his gaze on where he thought— prayed—north was and grimaced. In Córdoba, he would have to see the Princess safely stowed before he arranged his marriage. He had no clue how to deal with her. She was a Nasrid princess, for pity's sake. He would consult with Rodrigo, between them they would think of something. Then, with the Princess safe, Inigo could seek out his betrothed.

He'd marry before the year was out. He needed sons, someone to steward the family lands. After Margarita had given him a son or two, he could rest easy in the knowledge that her greedy brother, Baron Fernando, would never lay claim to his lands.

Baron Fernando Marchena de Carmona had a reputation for deviousness and double-dealing. Put bluntly, Inigo didn't trust him. He'd never liked him. While Inigo understood his father's wish to forge an alliance with their close neighbours, the idea of Baron Fernando becoming his brother-in-law filled him with misgivings.

If Inigo's marriage to Margarita proved childless and Inigo were to die without an heir, Baron Fernando wouldn't hesitate to stake a claim to Inigo's lands. Neighbour or no, Baron Fernando wasn't fit to rule. Inigo wanted better for his land and his people.

Inigo tightened his hold on the Nasrid Princess, brought his face closer to her damp hair and inhaled gently. Jasmine. Yes, he'd take his oath Princess Alba's hair was fragranced with jasmine.

The rain slackened, the storm was blowing itself out. When the stars reappeared, Inigo was thankful to see they were, as he had hoped, headed in a northerly direction.

The Princess remained quiet, apparently resigned to the length of the ride and her slightly ignominious mode of transport. She had to be finding this an ordeal, when Inigo had seen her on the road to Granada, she'd been riding a delicate grey mare bedecked with silver bells. The attendant entourage had been huge. Knights. Servants carrying sunshades. Sultan Tariq himself...

Inigo glanced over his shoulder, God help him, Guillen was trailing, they might have to slow down. Had Raven's shoe worked loose? It might not be the shoe though; Raven wasn't as fast or robust as Soldier.

He reined in to allow Guillen to catch up and the Princess looked over her shoulder at him. Her eyes glittered, in the dusky light of the stars and moon, they were enormous.

'I haven't heard the hounds for a while, my lord. Do you think we have outrun them?'

Her voice had a soft, husky quality that sent a frisson of awareness down Inigo's spine.

'I believe so, my lady.'

Inigo studied her, or tried to. The light wasn't strong enough for him to make out much more than her face and her eyes, which were framed by dark eyelashes. The glimpse he'd had of her on that pretty mare had revealed her to be extraordinarily lovely. However, it had been but the briefest of glimpses and Inigo was conscious that he'd been starved of feminine company for so long that he might have exaggerated her appeal.

While he waited for Guillen, Inigo smiled down at her. 'You must be missing your grey mare.'

Those long eyelashes swept down, and she stiffened, an almost imperceptible movement but he could hardly miss it, given how close they were.

'Alas, the grey mares are no longer in the palace stables,' she murmured. 'My father sold them.'

'Oh?'

The Princess didn't choose to enlarge and as Guillen drew abreast, Inigo didn't press her.

'Are we going to stop, my lord?' Guillen asked in his hopeful voice.

'Is Raven's shoe giving you trouble?'

'No, my lord. Raven seems fine.' Guillen gave a loud yawn.

'I'm sorry, lad, I know you're exhausted,' Inigo said. Guillen hadn't been prepared for this race through Al-Andalus any more than Inigo had. 'We'll rest soon. Sir Enrique's folly caught us all unawares.'

'Sir Enrique's folly?' The Princess laid a delicate hand on Inigo's forearm and a dark eyebrow lifted. 'Are you saying that you didn't plan to come to the sally port, Lord Inigo?'

Inigo saw no reason to lie. 'My lady, I had no such plans until the last moment. My sole aim was to leave Al-Andalus and get back to Castile as quickly and safely as possible.' Conscious of the Princess's innocence, Inigo picked his words with care. If Princess Alba had spent her days cloistered with her sisters, she would have no experience of life outside the palace. She must be afraid, and he didn't want to add to her fears. 'However, when Sir Enrique, Lord Rodrigo's cousin, you understand, revealed he was planning to…er…to help you and your sisters escape,

I decided that Lord Rodrigo and I should join him. We wanted to ensure all went smoothly.'

At first the Princess didn't respond. In the east, the horizon was shading to dawn. As Inigo looked at it, he could feel those small fingers, clenching and unclenching on his sleeve.

'My lord, I am sorry to have inconvenienced you,' she said coolly. 'Please be assured, you will be rewarded for your assistance.'

Inigo almost choked. She thought he wanted a reward? What kind of man did she think he was? 'I want no reward.' The only reward he craved was to return to Seville in one piece and get on with his life. 'It is my pleasure to take you to Córdoba where you may join the other Princess.'

Her dark eyebrows snapped together. Her fingers dug into his arm. 'My lord, you must remember there are three of us. Leonor went with your friend, Lord Rodrigo. Did you see Constanza?'

Inigo hesitated. 'I am not sure I saw your other sister,' he said carefully. Rodrigo had sworn to deal with Enrique. Inigo hoped nothing had gone amiss. He caught the gleam of white teeth; the Princess was biting her lip.

'Constanza never left the palace? I could have sworn she was following.' Her voice was small. 'It wouldn't surprise me if she'd lost heart though, Constanza is, well, wary of change.'

'It saddens you to think of her living alone in the palace.'

She shot him a startled look and nodded. 'We have always been together.'

Inigo nudged Soldier into a walk. With the dogs no longer hot on their heels, speed was less important. It was just as well, the horses needed a change of pace. Hearing a stifled yawn, he said, 'We shall rest soon, my lady.'

'As you wish.'

Inigo was himself fatigued. His leg gave a twinge, a slight discomfort that was, he realised with a rueful smile, keeping him alert. And thank heaven for it, he must keep his wits about him until he had found somewhere safe for them to recover their strength. A secluded campsite would be better than nothing. It would have to be soon; the light was strengthening.

They set off again and Inigo was eyeing the terrain, peering into a small olive grove at the side of the road, when Princess Alba pointed.

'My lord, look.'

A dilapidated shack took shape, half hidden by the trees. A shepherd's hut, if he wasn't mistaken.

'Could we stop there?'

'I wouldn't risk it. It's too near the road.' He prepared to ride on when a faint, mewling sound caught his attention.

The Princess gripped his arm. 'Did you hear that?'

'Sounds like a cat,' he said.

The Princess gripped his arm. 'That is no cat.' Her voice held a note of urgency. 'It's a baby. My lord, a baby is in distress, we must stop.'

Inigo looked at the Princess and back at the hut. It really was too close to the highway. 'My lady, we can't stop here.'

'Yes, we can.'

Before Inigo realised what she was about, the Princess leaned back full against him, slipped lithely to the ground and hurried into the hut.

Exchanging a disbelieving glance with Guillen, Inigo handed him his reins. 'Wait here, lad.' He dismounted, jarring his injured leg as his boots hit the ground.

What the devil did she think she was doing, walking boldly into a shepherd's hut dressed like a concubine from a harem? If anyone saw her, the entire area would be awash with rumour, and the world would quickly work out that one of Sultan Tariq's runaway Princesses had come this way.

Chapter Four

Inigo ducked into the shack, the roof was so low he couldn't stand upright. Straw was strewn over a beaten earth floor and a box cradle stood by a crude bed. Smoke spiralled from a sullen fire and a blackened cooking pot stood on a nearby stone. It was all very primitive.

Save for the Princess, the hut was deserted. Almost. A baby was indeed crying, Inigo could see a chubby fist waving back and forth inside the cradle. He watched in disbelief as Princess Alba perched on the edge of the bed and reached for the baby.

'Come to me, little one. Don't cry,' she murmured.

The door was ajar, and the first rays of the rising sun fell on the Princess's face. Her long black hair hung about her—it was slightly dishevelled from their ride, yet it in no way detracted from her beauty. Princess Alba was every bit as lovely as Inigo had remembered. Her face was a perfect oval. As she looked down at the baby, her luxuriant eyelashes lay like dark crescents against her cheeks. Her skin looked smooth, there wasn't a blemish in sight. Her mouth softened as she looked at the baby, it made her seem vulnerable in a way that was impossible to define.

Inigo forgot to breathe. Princess Alba was stunning. Gold gleamed at her throat, gemstones sparkled on her clothes and the sight of her cradling a baby in so humble a setting closed his throat. Such tenderness… His guts knotted with an emotion so primal he couldn't name it.

Swallowing hard, he found his voice. 'My lady, we must go on. We're still in your father's territory and we need to be discreet.' He waved at her jewel-spangled clothes. 'You are rather conspicuous. It is not safe for us here.'

Babe in arms, the Princess pushed to her feet. Her dark eyes sparked.

'This child needs its mother, I will not leave until she returns.'

Inigo ran his hand round the back of his neck. The past few months had been hell. He'd done battle with her father's army. He'd been thrown into prison with a leg wound that had festered. He'd survived the weary trudge from Salobreña to Granada, not to mention weeks of forced labour in the bramble-strewn crevasse outside the Alhambra Palace. He was tired and hungry, and his clothes were damp from the storm. Even so, he was not proof, it seemed, to the pleading in the Princess's eyes.

'My lord, we cannot abandon a baby.'

'The mother won't have gone far,' he said firmly.

During his imprisonment, Inigo had only had glimpses of Princess Alba. He didn't have a clear grasp of her character and he was ruefully aware that his imagination had filled in the gaps of his knowledge. His mind had painted her beautiful, and so she was. Now it would seem that, unbeknown to him, it had also painted her gentle, wise and loving.

Well, she was certainly handling that baby carefully. But as to the rest, Inigo had no clue. What was she really like? As he searched her face, all he could see was determination. Her chin was lifted, and her black eyes held fire.

'My lord, you would not be so cruel as to leave a frightened baby alone.'

He held in a sigh. This fierceness was most inconvenient.

And yet, standing in front of that crude bed like the Queen of Heaven with a baby in her arms and her eyes so intense, she was bewitching. So protective. It was obvious that she would guard that infant with all that was in her.

Princess Alba had courage. Life in the palace could not have prepared her for the world at large, but her bravery was unquestionable. She disarmed him utterly.

She searched his face and what she saw must have satisfied her, for her fierceness faded. She bent over the baby, rocking it. Cooing gently. To Inigo's relief the crying stopped. He hated it when children cried, he felt so helpless.

Inigo wasn't good with babies or children. Never had been. He wanted his own, of course, a man must have heirs. Fortunately, Margarita would have charge of their children if they were so blessed. In Inigo's experience, children, especially infants, were best viewed from a distance.

The Princess frowned at the smoking fire. Her foot tapped.

'The mother can't be far away,' she said, expression clearing. 'I shall find her. It's my belief this child is hungry. My lord, if you please, hold the baby.'

To Inigo's dismay, she thrust the child into his arms and squeezed past, leaving him blinking helplessly after her. He juggled inexpertly with a warm, suspiciously damp bundle.

'My lady, no. Take the baby.'

He found himself staring helplessly at the Princess's back. Moving to the door, he glanced warily at the child. Thumb in mouth, its eyes were open and fixed on him.

The Princess was shading her hand against the morning sun, staring through the olive trees. She must have seen something, for she looked back.

'This won't take a moment,' she said, and made to leave the pathway. 'Someone is coming.'

Inigo hurried over, wrestling with the child. 'My lady, for pity's sake, have a care. It's unwise to draw attention to ourselves. Come back inside. And you had best take this baby before I drop it.'

She looked enquiringly at him. 'Babies disturb you?'

Inigo felt a muscle tick in his cheek. 'Not precisely.' He had no wish to delve into his past and finally settled for, 'Children don't take to me. Come inside, please.'

The Princess relieved him of the child and settled it in the crook of her arm. He had no idea what experience she might have of babies, she was obviously a natural.

The light chime of bells announced the arrival of a small flock of sheep and their shepherdess. Inigo and the Princess watched her approach from the doorway.

Princess Alba's face relaxed. 'Here is our baby's mother.'

Our baby. Her choice of words had an unsettling resonance. *Our baby.*

The mother hurried up and Inigo felt a flicker

of unease. How would Princess Alba—a Nas-rid princess—deal with a simple shepherdess? More importantly, how best to get her to hurry? He wasn't entirely sure they had lost the Sultan's men. The sooner they were outside Al-Andalus and back in Castile, the better. Before that though, they had to find somewhere safe to rest, some-where Guillen's mount could be examined.

Conflict between the two women seemed inevi-table. There the Princess stood in her harem fin-ery, holding the shepherdess's baby. What would the shepherdess think? He stood casually by the door, braced to intervene.

The baby started to cry. Princess Alba smiled, spoke softly in Arabic and handed the child back to its mother.

Inigo couldn't be certain what was said, though the shepherdess didn't seem the least bit per-turbed to have a visitor clothed in silks and hung about with a king's ransom in gems. She nodded at the Princess, retreated to the bed with the child and unlaced her gown. His cheeks warmed, and he looked away to preserve the mother's modesty. A brief silence fell as the baby started to suckle. Then the Princess spoke again, and the conver-sation resumed.

From the doorway, Inigo allowed the two women a few moments before interrupting.

'My lady, the sun is up. We need somewhere safe to recuperate. I cannot be sure we have lost your father's men.'

Princess Alba nodded and rose. Slipping a heavy-looking gold bangle from her wrist, she handed it to the woman. The bangle was so large the shepherdess blinked at it, mouth agape, before plunging into a flurry of what could only be thanks. The Princess responded, and when the conversation began all over again, Inigo lost patience.

'Come, my lady.' He took the Princess firmly by the elbow and steered her outside. 'Was it wise giving a shepherdess so magnificent a bauble, my lady? She might use it to betray you.'

'She won't betray me.' Princess Alba walked towards where Guillen was waiting with the horses. 'She has no husband, she needs a little help.'

'I don't doubt it, but that bangle—it's rather noticeable.'

'It's not as valuable as it looks, it's a sheet of beaten gold wrapped around a wooden block.'

Her naivety was oddly touching. 'My lady, it will be worth more than that woman could earn in her lifetime.'

'She will not betray me.'

Inigo wasn't inclined to argue, they had to find a safe haven. He did, however, unbuckle a saddle bag and pull out his spare cloak. 'I'd like to you put this on.'

'What's wrong with my cloak?'

'It is far too showy.'

The Princess shrugged, swapped her cloak for his and allowed him to help her into the saddle. Having checked that Guillen's horse wasn't lame, Inigo mounted behind her and they continued down the track.

Princess Alba turned her head. 'The road divides a little way ahead. If we take the right-hand fork, we'll find a farm.'

'A farm?' Inigo looked thoughtfully at her. 'I doubt a farm is a good resting place if your father's men are behind us.'

'It's quite remote, I believe. And we'll find someone to care for your squire's horse.'

'The shepherdess told you this?'

'Aye, she was extremely helpful.'

'Very well. Thank you.' He had underestimated her, it seemed. 'I only hope that your faith in that woman isn't misplaced.'

'It is not. She understands my dilemma.' Her eyes were wistful. 'Her baby is beautiful, how blessed she is.'

Since one baby looked very much like another to Inigo, he didn't respond.

The Princess yawned and went on talking.

Inigo had the impression she was struggling to keep herself awake. If he weren't so tired, this ride through the cool of the morning would be pleasant. The faint scent of jasmine, the warmth of her body. Aye, it was very pleasant.

'I've never met a shepherdess before,' the Princess was saying. 'She told me she usually takes the baby with her when she goes out. She has a shawl and carries him on her front.'

'The infant is a boy?'

'Aye. My lord?' She craned her neck and met his eyes. 'You said you are Count of Seville. Is that where you are going?'

'Eventually. First, I shall take you to Córdoba to meet up with your sister and Count Rodrigo.'

And then he and Rodrigo would have to work out what the devil they were going to do with two Nasrid princesses. Only when Inigo was certain that Princess Alba was safe would he return home. To Margarita and marriage. He wasn't immortal—his encounter with the Sultan's troops had brought that home to him as never before. He needed heirs.

The farm the shepherdess had recommended wasn't easy to find, though they followed her directions closely. When at last they saw it, Inigo's spirits lifted. It was set in a small dip, some way from the beaten track. The secluded location was a strong point in its favour. If the shepherdess hadn't told the Princess exactly where to go, they would have ridden straight past it.

It had been hours since Inigo had heard the hounds and he was confident they had lost them. However, he wouldn't relax until they reached Córdoba. Princess Alba was in his care, he must keep her safe. He reined in at the top of the rise.

Humble in design, the farmhouse was little more than a labourer's cottage. It looked half derelict, the door sagged and there were gaps in the planking. Smoke drifted through a ragged vent in the roof. The fence around a vegetable plot was down in places and hens were scratching in the dirt. It looked like the last place a Nasrid princess would choose as her refuge.

In short, it was perfect.

'It looks peaceful enough,' Inigo muttered, even as he was wondering how long they could risk stopping for. The Princess wouldn't be used to riding for hours. Stalwart though she was, she must be exhausted. Guillen too. As for the horses…

He frowned. 'My lady, are you certain the shepherdess mentioned horses? I don't see any.'

'She didn't say that we'd find horses here, my lord, only that there would be someone to care for ours.' She smothered another yawn and looked longingly towards the farm. 'A brief halt would be most welcome.'

Inigo dismissed the last of his misgivings. 'Very well. I doubt your father's men will give this place a second glance. Mind, it won't be what you are used to.'

'As far as I am concerned it is paradise. My lord, for the first time in my life, I am free, that counts for much.'

Wondering how soon Princess Alba would regret those words, Inigo spurred Soldier down the slope. 'In any event, we shan't stay long. Just long enough to ensure the horses won't be lamed when we continue.'

To say that the occupants of the farm—two young women and their ageing father—were startled when their unexpected visitors rode up would be an understatement.

Princess Alba did the talking. Again, it was irritating not to be able to understand what was being said, though the farmer and his daughters seemed friendly. Particularly after Inigo opened his pouch and drew out a palm full of silver dirhams.

The Princess dismounted and entered the farmhouse with his cloak wrapped tightly about her. The cool of the night was dissipating, and she was probably hoping to hide her harem finery. In this, she wasn't entirely successful. Inigo caught the telltale flutter of silk. Her boots, he noticed, were dyed blue, they looked extremely costly.

Wreathed in smiles, the farmer took Inigo, Guillen and their horses to a shack behind the main building. It immediately became clear that the man did indeed have a rare talent with horses, for he spotted Raven's weak leg at once. Confident the animals were in the best hands, Inigo left Guillen with the farmer and returned to the farmhouse.

Princess Alba was standing by the cooking fire, watching the younger sister lift flatbread from a griddle with a wooden paddle. The girl tossed the bread on to a platter and set it on the table while her sister poured what looked like ale into pottery cups.

When the elder sister spoke, Princess Alba smiled and went to the bench by the table. 'Here, my lord,' the Princess said. 'This is for us. And your squire when he gets here, of course. There's a bowl of water to wash in on that side table.'

While Inigo rinsed away the worst of the dust, a round of goat's cheese and a bowl of olives joined the pottery cups on the table.

The Princess sat quietly. Her bright gaze roamed the cottage, taking in the onions hanging from the beams, the bunches of herbs, a small barrel of olives. Inigo wondered if the farmer's daughters had noticed the shimmer of silk peeping out from beneath Princess Alba's cloak. At the least, they must have noticed those blue boots. Women noticed such things.

Inigo remembered the food baskets the Princesses had sent down when he and his comrades had been working like slaves at the foot of their tower. Those baskets had been filled with grapes, chicken, wine, dates...

He eyed the cheese doubtfully and remembered the supplies he'd brought from The Black Sheep.

'My lady? If cheese is not to your liking, I have chicken in my saddlebag.'

'This is fine, thank you,' the Princess said.

She picked up an ale cup and drank with every evidence of enjoyment.

Inigo dragged a three-legged stool to the table and sat down. The sisters, clearly deciding they'd done their duty, edged on to the bench either side of Princess Alba. Leaning their elbows on the table, they stared at him. It was rather disconcerting. They stared and stared.

It was even more disconcerting when they started to giggle and mutter to each other.

Inigo shifted and broke off a piece of bread. 'What the devil are they saying?'

The Princess smiled. 'They think you are very handsome. They are wondering what it would be like to...' she hesitated, flushing '...marry such a man.'

'Saints, have they nothing better to do? Please ask if there is a bedchamber where you may rest a while.'

She pointed towards a stepladder, leading up to a gallery. 'I've already asked. The sleeping loft is ours for as long as we need it.'

'You take the loft. My lady, that shepherdess did well directing us here. I don't speak Arabic, but it's plain this farmer has a gift with horses and my squire's horse seems to have a sprain. I'll not relax until I know how bad it is. In the meantime, I advise you to get as much rest as you can.'

The loft was gloomy and smelled of smoke and dust. Clothes hung, formless as djinns, from hooks driven into the beams. Two mattresses lay flat on the floorboards.

Assuming the larger of the mattresses belonged to the girls, Alba went over to it and knelt. A brief scrutiny showed it to be made with coarse sacking and filled with straw. It felt extraordinary, hard and lumpy. Feathers and down must be beyond the reach of simple farmers. Alba doubted she would sleep, though she told herself sternly that she must accustom herself to living more humbly.

It was noisy in the loft, she could hear much that went on in the main chamber below. The sisters hadn't stopped giggling. They were teasing Lord Inigo and, when his squire joined him, presumably to report on his horse's welfare, they included him in their teasing. Interestingly, the presence of their father didn't curb them, the teasing was relentless.

As Alba listened her cheeks burned. Was this flirting? She had never heard women talking so freely with men. Her duenna Inés had said that in the Kingdom of Castile, men and women often flirted with each other. Until now, Alba hadn't understood what that implied because her father and her uncle kept their concubines in harems. Casual interaction between the sexes in the palace was almost non-existent.

Not so here. This wasn't Castile, they were still in the Sultan's territory, yet the farmer's daughters were teasing Lord Inigo. It was most confusing. In her father's palace, that would never happen. Women belonged in the harem and if they weren't concubines they served the women in the harem. Was it not the same elsewhere in her father's kingdom?

She stared up at a cobweb in the rafters, shocked at how deeply flawed her understanding of the world must be and how unprepared she was to face her new life. Not everyone in Al-Andalus could afford a harem. Unless a family was wealthy, its womenfolk would have to work. Perhaps, if she got to know Lord Inigo better, she might ask him about the differences between life in Al-Andalus and life in Castile.

Downstairs, a door banged and a brief silence fell before one of the girls laughed.

What was going on? More flirting?

Lord Inigo didn't understand a word of what was being said, so what was the point? Maybe the girls wanted to charm him into parting with more money. Alba could think of no other motivation. Unless…

Did they truly like the look of him? Did they find him attractive? They must do.

Lord Inigo was undeniably handsome. He had unruly dark hair and Alba found his face, with its straight nose and square jaw, pleasing. She'd found her gaze straying his way more than once. His mouth was well formed and his teeth white. His body was that of a warrior—broad chest and narrow hips. Lord Inigo didn't rush to speech and his grey eyes were alert, which would seem to indicate a keen intelligence. Alba particularly liked the slight lift to his mouth when their eyes met.

It was mysterious and curious. Those girls were obviously enjoying Lord Inigo's company. Did he find them equally attractive? Impatient with herself, Alba frowned. It was none of her business. In any case, Lord Inigo didn't have time for dalliance, he was eager to reach Castile.

But if he hadn't been in a hurry?

Heavens, she must stop thinking about this. How Lord Inigo chose to live was up to him.

What was important was that the girls below, though they knew nothing about Lord Inigo, appeared to have summed him in a glance. They liked him. They weren't the least bit in awe of him. In truth, their judgement of him was similar to hers.

They trusted him.

Earlier, when Lord Inigo had been occupied with the horses, the sisters had asked Alba, with devastating frankness, whether she was his lover. They had laughed when she had denied it. Alba hadn't been certain they'd believed her.

Did they desire him as a lover? Alba shifted on her mattress.

She wasn't certain what to make of him. She'd felt awkward when he'd admitted that he'd only returned to the palace to prevent—how had he put it?—Sir Enrique's folly. She'd also felt disappointed, though she knew she was being unreasonable. It was perfectly understandable that Lord Inigo should think only of going home. Despite this, he had returned to a place he had every reason to loathe. And he'd done so because he believed that Sir Enrique was too drunk to act responsibly.

Already Alba had much to thank him for. A Spanish knight, a stranger, was turning out to be more honourable than she believed possible. Who would have imagined that a man could be so thoughtful? So kind? It was most unexpected.

Another ripple of feminine laughter came up from below. Alba sighed, stretched out her aching limbs and closed her eyes.

Her thoughts drifted this way and that. She heard the thunder as they fled the palace. She saw the dark, and felt the rain pelting against her skin. She remembered the way her heart had missed its beat when she had heard that baby crying, and she saw the expression on Lord Inigo's face when she'd handed him the child.

Her lips curved. Truly, men were hopeless with children. Didn't they understand what treasures they were? The shepherdess's baby was adorable. The voices from below seemed to fade, Alba's mind blurred and she drifted into a doze.

Chapter Five

Lantern in hand, Inigo stood in the loft staring down at Princess Alba. She was lying on her side with her head pillowed on her hand, lost to the world. A twist of dark hair tumbled past her shoulder and on to the bedding, black silk on humble sackcloth. A slight crinkle in her brow told him that if the Princess was dreaming, her dream was not pleasant. The wonder was that she had fallen asleep.

The Princess intrigued him. It couldn't have been easy for her to walk away from everything she knew. Why had she done it? Outside the palace, she was a fish out of water. How on earth would she survive?

Her necklace gleamed softly in the dull light. Inigo's eyebrows bunched together as he recalled the sparkling gems on the veil he'd stuffed into his saddlebag. And that bangle she'd given the shepherdess! The woman was a walking treasury. Yet what good would that do her in Castile? She wouldn't have the faintest idea how to go on. She could be robbed. Or worse. And for what? Surely life as a Nasrid princess wasn't that intolerable?

Inigo yawned. Princess Alba wasn't his responsibility. True, she'd proved to be brave and resilient, and bravery and resilience were admirable and rare qualities. Particularly in a woman who must have been pampered and cossetted all her life.

Quietly, he hung the lantern on a hook and lowered himself on to the other mattress. Lord, he was tired. What was he to do with her?

There was a convent in Córdoba. Princess Alba and her sister—the one who had ridden off with Rodrigo—would be able to stay there in perfect safety until they decided what best to do.

St Clare's Convent was full of noble ladies. The Princesses would be cared for. Even better, they might learn what life was like in Castile. They might conclude that they'd be better off in Al-Andalus, where they belonged.

A gurgle of earthy laughter came from below. With a sigh, the Princess shifted and opened her eyes.

'Lord Inigo!' Flushing, she pushed herself to sitting position. 'What are you doing?'

'Looking at a princess.' Inigo smiled and allowed his gaze to linger on the curve of her cheek. Her lips. 'A beautiful princess.'

'Please don't.'

'You don't care to be admired?' Inigo felt his

smile grow when, charmingly, her flush deepened, washing down her neck. His fatigue was forgotten. 'You *do* like it.'

Her chin inched up. How delightful and how unexpected. The Princess was a joy to tease, she was very responsive. Unfortunately, this realisation made it well nigh impossible to tear his gaze from her mouth. It was such a temptation, that mouth. Staring at it led inevitably—clearly it had been far too long since Inigo had bedded a woman—to more explicit thoughts.

What would it be like to kiss her? How would she respond? With outrage? No, something in her eyes told him that she'd be more likely to be curious than outraged. Was her skin as smooth as it looked? Would she enjoy being caressed? Princess Alba was, he was sure, far more passionate than Marg—

With a groan, Inigo broke off his train of thought. This was wrong. He was soon to be married and he'd promised himself that from now on he'd look at no woman other than his betrothed. It had been easy to ignore the farmer's daughters, pretty though they were. Princess Alba, however…

'My apologies, my lady, if I disturbed you.' He gestured at the lantern. 'I thought it would be dark up here and assumed you'd feel easier with some light.'

'You are very kind. How is your squire's horse? Will we be leaving shortly?'

'I hope so. Guillen—my squire—is still closeted with the farmer in the stables. There was talk of a poultice and I'm hoping it won't take long. I'll check on progress shortly. Before that, my lady, I'd like to know why you were so eager to flee the palace. You must have lived in great luxury.'

'Luxury isn't everything.' The Princess frowned at one of her rings, a pretty gold one set with seed pearls and amethysts. 'As you know, my father can be difficult.'

Difficult? Somehow, Inigo kept a straight face. Sultan Tariq was a tyrant, all of Castile knew that. None the less, Inigo had assumed that he would treat his daughters well. 'True. And…?'

Confident she would say more, he waited. A bee was trapped in the loft, he could hear it buzzing about near the eaves.

She kept her gaze lowered. 'Father enjoys imposing his will on people.'

'But you are his daughter, a princess.'

'That makes no difference. My lord, the three of us have lived in seclusion for years. We hardly ever saw Father. Then, quite suddenly, he brought us to the Alhambra Palace. We assumed that our lives would change after that, and we'd be given more freedom.' Her mouth tightened. 'Unhappily, we were wrong. That tower became our prison. Father locked us up.'

Inigo's mouth slackened, he could hardly believe what he was hearing. 'I assumed you were free to wander about the palace.'

'When we first arrived, we were given some freedom although we were only allowed near the Sultan when we were summoned.'

Inigo listened, moved by the wistfulness in her eyes as she explained about the restricted lives she and her sisters had led. To his shame, when he and his comrades had stood at the foot of the Princesses' tower and sung songs for their supper, he'd seen it as little more than a relatively painless way of getting extra rations. It had never occurred to him that life in the Princesses' tower might not be as he imagined it.

'We were locked in the tower as a punishment, my lord.'

Her voice was so soft, he had to lean closer to hear her. 'For what? What did you do?'

'We asked too many questions. We wished to explore Granada. Father was beside himself with anger and shut us up in our apartments. That was when we decided life must be better in Mamá's homeland.'

Inigo was hazy about the Queen's background, all he knew was that she had died some years ago. In the bathhouse, he vaguely recalled Enrique mentioning that the Queen was Spanish, but Enrique was hardly the most reliable of sources. 'Pray continue.'

She glanced at her ring, a faint frown on her brow. 'Our mother, the Queen, came from Castile.'

Inigo went very still. Dear heaven, Enrique had been telling the truth. 'You and your sisters are half Spanish?'

'Yes, my lord. We are on a quest to find our Spanish relatives.'

'That explains your name, Alba is Spanish.' Inigo rubbed his chin. Was St Clare's the best place to take her? The convent would certainly be safe and, like a harem, it was filled with women. She'd feel at home. Unfortunately, if the Princess was half Spanish, it didn't seem likely that she would choose to return to her father. She had good reasons for wanting to explore Castile.

'To my father I am Princess Zoraida,' she was saying. 'It seemed easier to give you my Spanish name.'

Inigo had a talent for reading faces and he could tell she wasn't being completely frank with him.

There was something else, something dark that concerned her mother.

'My lady, tell me about your mother. Are you saying that she didn't willingly become Queen?'

The Princess drew in a breath. 'No, my lord, she did not. Mamá was captured by Father's troops and when Father saw her he was so struck by her beauty he refused to release her.' She twisted her fingers together. 'Our mother was a noblewoman, Lady Juana. My sisters and I know little more than that, not even her family name. Mamá married Father when she realised she would never have her freedom. She died when my sisters and I were small.'

'Your duenna is Castilian?'

'Aye, she was captured along with Mamá.'

'Surely this duenna could have told you about your mother's family?'

'Inés?' The Princess twisted her fingers together. 'You might think so. My sisters and I certainly wanted her to. We begged her to talk about Mamá, but in the main she talked about Castile, and then in the most general of terms. Inés is afraid of my father, you see.' Her mouth turned down. 'It can't have been easy for her, torn between love and loyalty to us, and fear of the Sultan.'

'Your duenna knew you wanted to escape.'

'We couldn't have done it without her.'

Inigo made a sound of exasperation. 'This Inés was ill advised to keep you so ignorant. You should know about your mother's past.'

'My lord, she would have told us more, I am sure. However, once she and your friend Sir Enrique starting planning, events moved quickly. There was no time for lengthy explanations.'

'Sir Enrique is no friend of mine.' Inigo had to repress an absurd impulse to cover her hand with his. In truth, he wanted to touch her so much he actually ached. 'I am sorry about your mother and I pray that you find your relatives. I will do all I can to assist you.'

Her smile lit up the loft. 'Thank you, my lord.'

Inigo shook his head. What was he doing, offering to aid a Nasrid princess? He should be thinking about Margarita.

Those dark eyes fixed on him, shy and intent. 'My lord, I too have questions, if you would be so good as to answer them?'

'Of course.'

'I need to ask about my sister.'

'The one who rode off with Rodrigo? God willing, you can meet her in Córdoba.'

Princess Alba made a dismissive gesture and her ring flashed in the lamp light like a firefly.

'No, my lord, that was Leonor and I'm not talking about Leonor, I am talking about Constanza.'

'My lady, as I believe I told you, I didn't see your other sister,' Inigo said, hoping to reassure her. Rodrigo had, he was certain, seen that she was safe.

'She was directly behind me in the sally port, my lord. Her footsteps followed me all along that tunnel. Do you think your other friend helped her get away?'

'Enrique? Lord, I hope not.'

Princess Alba stiffened. 'What do you mean?'

Caught by an absurd wish to tell her the truth, Inigo took his time replying. 'Enrique was drunk,' he said, settling on a half-truth.

Her eyes filled with concern. 'He wouldn't have hurt her, would he?'

Inigo couldn't tell the Princess what Enrique had been planning. In any case, Rodrigo had sworn to see to the third Princess's safety.

'My lady, I can only repeat that I didn't see Princess Constanza.'

She studied him, eyes shy and extraordinarily determined, and gave a small nod. 'I pray she got away.'

Inigo smiled. 'I do too.' And that was the truth. As long as it wasn't with Enrique.

'My lord, may we speak of Castile?'

Those determined eyes searched his, wary and oddly penetrating. Briefly, Inigo felt as though she was trying to see into his soul. It was a ridiculous thought, which he dismissed immediately. The Princess was merely out of her depth and until he got her to Córdoba she would remain so. Under the circumstances, it was perfectly natural for her to want to relate to him. She needed reassurance.

'If you wish. We won't be leaving for a couple of hours.'

'I've been wondering what to expect. You have a king, I believe.'

'King Henry.'

'And does King Henry have palaces, like Father?'

'He has several palaces. For example, in Córdoba the palace is attached to the garrison. There is another palace in Seville, which I am more familiar with.'

'Because it is close to your lands?'

'Aye. My castle is only a few miles from Seville.'

She smiled his way, flushed prettily and lowered her gaze. Did she find this conversation awkward? She must do. She was a Moorish princess and she'd spent most of her life in the women's quarters with her sisters. Her father was so overbearing he'd locked her up in a tower. She wouldn't be used to conversing with men. When she reached for that loosely bound skein of hair and drew it over her shoulder, Inigo saw that her fingers were trembling. His heart clenched in sympathy. She was nervous and trying desperately to hide it.

He braced his hands on his knees, preparing to rise. 'My lady, I should leave you to your rest.'

Her hand reached towards him and fluttered away, like a bird.

'Please stay.' That shy, delightful smile appeared. 'I doubt I shall sleep, I need to know what to expect in Castile. Do men live separately from their wives?'

Inigo felt his expression freeze as he thought of his parents. 'It varies.' He forced lightness into his voice and got to his feet. 'Some people get on better than others. I've known good marriages where a man and wife are inseparable and bad marriages where the couple can't stand being in the same county, let alone the same room.'

She looked up at him, all eyes as she fiddled with her hair, pulling a shining strand loose and twining it round her finger. Inigo had the impression she was understanding more than he was prepared to tell her. She had opened her mouth to say more when a series of thumps reached them.

The farmer's younger daughter was climbing the loft ladder.

The girl grinned broadly at Inigo and rushed into speech. When she came to a halt, Inigo looked enquiringly at Princess Alba. 'Do you care to translate?'

'My lord, her father has asked her to let you know that he has reshod your squire's horse and the animal's leg is fine. We should be able to leave in half an hour.'

'Please thank her, will you?' Inigo rested his forearm against a beam. 'My lady, it would be safer if your clothes were less opulent. Be so good as to ask this girl to give you one of her gowns. I have tried asking. I am not confident she understood. I shall pay her, of course.'

Princess Alba looked the girl over and nodded. 'Your suggestion makes sense, my lord, we are similar in build.'

'So I thought. I shall wait downstairs.'

When Alba emerged from the loft, she was wearing an ochre-coloured gown. It was creased, slightly too large and far too long. It was tricky negotiating the ladder, she had to hold the skirts to one side, so she didn't catch a foot in the hem.

The Count of Seville was sitting at the table under the watchful eye of the older girl. Smiling, he rose as Alba approached and, for a moment, she couldn't breathe.

He looked her up and down. 'That's much better, my lady. Most unexceptionable, though you will have to mind you don't trip.'

'Yes, I see that, I will be careful. As the skirts are so long, I've decided to keep my boots.'

'Very well.'

Despite his smile, Alba couldn't help but notice that Lord Inigo looked exhausted. He had dark shadows under his eyes. And no wonder. Alba glanced at his leg, the one that had been injured. 'Is your leg paining you, my lord?'

He shot her a sharp glance and shook his head. 'Come, we must be on our way.'

'Where's your squire?'

'Readying the horses.'

Lord Inigo reached for her hand and Alba felt a slight frisson when their fingers touched. The sensation was new to her and most strange. It was unsettling rather than unpleasant. Putting it down to fatigue, she quickly released him and turned to the doorway.

'We all need sleep,' she muttered.

'Assuredly.'

'Did you get any rest earlier, my lord?'

He laughed. 'Not much.'

She shot the farmer's daughters a swift glance. 'The girls, I suppose. They gave you no peace.'

His lips twitched. 'You could say that.'

'They like you,' Alba said. Clearly, the farmer's daughters had lived far more freely than she. They had experience of judging a man's nature. And from what Alba had seen, they had both been eager to interrupt their work to talk to Lord Inigo. They weren't afraid of him and they seemed to trust him. Could she do the same?

She rather thought she could. Lord Inigo struck her as an open, honest man. Except for one thing—the way his face had closed when she had asked about men and women living together, it had been most odd. Out of character. What a pity the farmer's daughter had chosen that moment to come up to the loft.

'Those girls are a liability,' he was saying. Eyes laughing, he shook his head. 'Their father should lock them up.'

Alba felt her mouth tighten. 'I don't think you mean that, my lord.'

'Forgive me, that was insensitive.' With a grimace, he shoved his hand through his hair. 'I wasn't thinking. I simply meant—never mind. Come, the horses are waiting, and I need you to help me speak to the farmer.'

They went outside to wait for the horses. 'What am I to say to him?' Alba asked.

'I'm pretty certain we've escaped your father's men, but now we know Raven is fit to ride, I'd be happier if we split up. Are you agreeable?'

'Agreeable, my lord?'

'These tracks near the border with Castile are known to twist every which way. If the farmer will direct us, you and I will travel along one track and Guillen will take another. I am asking if you are content to travel with just me for company?'

Alba's mind worked. What option did she have? If she didn't agree, he might leave her behind. Besides, she had already thrown caution to the winds when she had left the palace. She met his gaze straight on. 'If you believe that is best, my lord, I trust your judgement.'

The farmer joined them in the yard and Alba thanked him for his hospitality and enquired about the various byways. Lord Inigo's knowledge proved to be correct, for the farmer told her that the track that meandered past the farm divided a few miles on. Even better, if the farmer was to be believed, they were already close to the border with Castile.

As Guillen appeared with the horses, Alba pointed in the direction the farmer had indicated.

'My lord, the road forks about two miles further on. Both tracks lead to the border, it sounds to be closer than you realised.'

Lord Inigo reached for her hand and squeezed it and his grey eyes smiled. 'We will have you safe very soon.'

He helped Alba into the saddle and mounted behind her and they were soon on their way. The countryside was quiet, which was a blessing, there was no gut-wrenching howling or barking, no sound of pursuit or telltale dust cloud hanging on the horizon.

Disturbingly, Alba found herself noticing the feel of Lord Inigo's body behind her more keenly than before. She told herself this sudden awareness of him physically meant nothing. It was simply that with her father's hounds no longer on their trail, there were fewer distractions. She was no longer terrified out of her wits.

Quite soon, they reached the fork in the track. Lord Inigo halted and indicated the more northerly route. 'You happy to go that way, lad?'

'Yes, my lord.'

'And you are confident Raven is up to this?'

'Perfectly, my lord. I'll see you in Córdoba.' Guillen directed Raven up the track.

Lord Inigo watched him go, eyes clouded.

'You are concerned for your squire,' Alba murmured.

'A little, he is young and impulsive.' Behind her, his chest moved on a sigh. 'But he knows his horse. If Guillen says Raven is up to this, then he will doubtless arrive in Córdoba before we do.'

They proceeded along quiet, out-of-the-way paths, passing flocks of sheep. A few goats. Cicadas hummed. The sky was blue and the sun hot. As the day grew ever warmer, the shade of the olive groves became more and more tempting. Alba was thankful to set aside Lord Inigo's cloak. Wearing it when the sun was at its height was unthinkable.

The miles drifted by and Alba found herself dwelling on the farmer's daughters and their reaction to Lord Inigo. The way the girls had accepted him interested her. Given that the farm was in the Sultan's territory, and Lord Inigo was obviously a foreign knight, an enemy of her father, she'd expected them to view him with fear and suspicion. There'd been no sign of that.

Why? Was her father so hated by his subjects that they were happy to talk and flirt with his enemies?

It was possible. Rumours of the Sultan ordering beatings and summary executions had reached Alba's ears. All three Princesses had witnessed

Sultan Tariq's rage. They'd learned at an early age that it was never wise to cross him.

Lord Inigo appeared to be different. He hadn't wanted to be burdened with a Nasrid princess, yet he'd taken her up on his horse without complaint. He'd not lost his temper once, on the contrary, he'd been most chivalrous, looking after her in the most trying and exhausting of circumstances. It was baffling and intriguing.

How many other ways might Lord Inigo differ from her father?

It was heartening to know the farmer's daughters liked him because Alba had not known him long and her experience with men was negligible. Her judgement of a man's character had yet to be tested. She would remain wary. Lord Inigo might, on closer acquaintance, prove to be as volatile and violent as her father. For the rest of the way, Alba would watch and study him as if her life depended on it.

In a sense, it did, for if Lord Inigo proved to be as even-tempered and chivalrous as he seemed, it gave her hope that there might be other men like him in Castile, men she might learn to respect.

Alba turned her head. When his grey eyes met hers, her heart jumped, and her cheeks burned. It occurred to her that with a man like Lord Inigo, the act of procreation might not be as terrible as she had feared.

'You are well, my lady?'

'Very well, I thank you.'

Alba faced forward and tried not to think about how one went about getting a child.

Before encountering Lord Inigo, she'd been certain that it was likely to be an unpleasant and demeaning business, something that had to be endured to make a baby. Suddenly, she wasn't so sure.

He was more than ordinarily attractive. That much Alba had known from the start. The women had seen it too, one look and they'd been flirting their hearts out. The questions they'd asked Alba! The teasing. They'd been tempting him. The farmer's daughters would have been delighted if Lord Inigo had taken them up on their offer, which would suggest they thought lying with him would be enjoyable.

Mind in turmoil, she frowned at the horse's ears. The Count had contented himself with smiling at the girls. Why hadn't he gone further? Her father would have done. It was all very puzzling.

As the miles went by, it was a relief to discover that Lord Inigo had an innate sense of direction. When he spotted a smudge of smoke darkening the sky towards the uplands in the north, he muttered something about wanting to avoid the villages and veered on to another path. He knew exactly which route to take and how to avoid other traffic.

Alba looked longingly towards the smoke. 'Was that a town?'

'A small one, I believe.'

'Do you think it will have a market?'

'A market, my lady?'

She fiddled with the horse's mane and said wistfully, 'My sisters and I have never been to a market.'

'It would be dangerous to stop. Wait until we reach Córdoba, the market there is one of the best in Spain.'

His voice had an inflexible tone that warned Alba that argument would be fruitless. He was pushing ahead on her account as well as his own. Neither of them wanted to be caught in Al-Andalus.

'Very good, my lord.'

That evening, they came to a heap of ancient masonry that looked as though it had been there since the time of the Romans.

'We'll eat here,' Lord Inigo said, nodding with satisfaction.

As they dismounted and tethered the horse,

Alba could see it was a good place to stop. Hidden from the track by what was left of the building, they wouldn't be visible.

'My lord, what was this place?'

'An olive press. See?' He pointed at a large circular stone, pitted by age and speckled with yellow lichen. 'That's the press.'

They ate as the sun lowered in the west, turning the sky turquoise and gold. The meal was simple: bread, cheese and olives that Lord Inigo had brought with him from the farm. A flask of ale. In the distance, sheep were bleating. Cicadas sang.

When they had finished their meal, Alba watched as Count Inigo drew a bundle from his saddlebag, moved some distance away, and began scraping a hole in the ground.

'My lord, what are you doing?'

He gestured at the bundle. 'Brought some chicken with me when we left Granada. It will be past its best, so I'm burying it.' When she frowned in puzzlement, he added, 'I'd burn it if I didn't fear it might draw attention to our position.'

Alba lifted an eyebrow. 'We're to sleep here, my lord?' She had never spent the night out in the open. Well, apart from the previous night, which she'd spent sitting in Lord Inigo's arms as his horse carried them away from the palace.

'Aye. Do not fear, my lady, I shall guard you well.'

Having covered the bundle with earth and a small pile of stones, Lord Inigo strolled about the ruin. Three walls of the original building were left, along with the olive press. He pushed at the walls as though testing their resilience, hitting them with the hilt of his sword. He kicked aside a few loose stones and smiled through the thickening gloom.

'There's plenty of space behind the press. Come, my lady, see for yourself. These walls will be our shield. You can rest here, and I shall be your guard. You will be quite safe.'

Faint streaks of red were firing in the west, night would fall swiftly. And, rather to Alba's surprise, the idea of spending the night out in the open wasn't as alarming as it should be. This was largely due to Lord Inigo himself. She was beginning to trust him.

One thing, however, did concern her.

'Are there snakes in these parts, my lord?'

'Probably, though I've made a fair bit of noise. If there were any, they will be long gone.'

Alba bit her lip. Snakes were almost as bad as confined spaces. She told herself that Lord Inigo would be within arm's reach, she had nothing to fear. 'Very well, my lord.'

Later, when Alba lay on Lord Inigo's cloak, disjointed sounds and images flashed in and out of her mind: the dark of the tunnel beneath the palace grounds, the flare of Leonor's torch, the baying of her father's dogs, the incessant rain…

The ground felt like rock and sleep was slow in coming. When it came, the song of the cicadas echoed through Alba's dreams.

She awoke with a jerk. Her makeshift bed was as hard as flint, her skin was sticky from too much heat and the cicadas were unbelievably noisy. Her stomach rumbled. Even though she had eaten earlier, she was ravenous. And deeply unsettled.

It was more than concern for Constanza, though she felt that keenly. Something else was troubling her.

Leaving Al-Andalus had been the only thing to do. So why had the quest to find her Spanish kin suddenly lost its allure?

Chapter Six

Several days later—the City of Córdoba in the Kingdom of Castile

The sun was past its zenith when they clattered along the straw-strewn streets and through the gates of Count Inigo's town house.

Inigo had seen nothing untoward on the road, but he'd been carrying tension in his shoulders for days. It wasn't simply that he was taking the Princess back to the house that his mother had fled to when his parents' marriage had begun to disintegrate, it was more than that. His soldier's instincts were telling him that something was amiss. Dismounting in the courtyard in front of the stable, he told himself he could finally relax. They had reached safety, tired, but unscathed. Swifts were screaming in the skies above them as they did every day. There was nothing alarming here.

Unhappily, a heartbeat after Inigo had lifted the Princess from the saddle, his steward Sir Nicolás appeared. Sir Nicolás was undoubtedly thankful to see him, but his eyes were guarded, and he was clutching a scroll as though his life depended on it.

Inigo's spirits sank, as he suspected, something was wrong.

'Count Inigo!' Sir Nicolás gripped his shoulder and looked him over. 'Thank the Lord you are safe. All is well? We received word you were wounded.'

'I'm fine, thank you. Took a cut to my thigh. I was feverish for a while, but it's healed cleanly.'

Conscious that smiling servants and retainers had gathered under an arch to welcome him back, Inigo nodded a few greetings their way. His servants always welcomed him with open arms, it was as though they knew that returning here resurrected old ghosts for him: his mother's grief caused by his faithless father; the hours of hearing her weeping through the night.

That is all in the past, Inigo told himself as he took the Princess gently by the elbow and drew her towards Sir Nicolás.

He was uneasily aware Princess Alba wouldn't be with him for long. She unsettled him, and the sooner she went to that convent, the sooner he could relax. In the meantime, she was his guest. Everyone must understand she was to have every luxury at his disposal.

'My lady, this is my steward, Sir Nicolás.

Should you need anything during your stay here, you may apply to him.' It had occurred to Inigo that there was no sense announcing to the world that he had brought a Nasrid princess back with him from Granada, so he introduced her with little ceremony. 'Nicolás, this is Lady Alba.'

The Princess smiled at Sir Nicolás. 'It is a pleasure to meet you, sir.'

Sir Nicolás bowed politely. 'The pleasure is all mine, my lady. My wife, Lady Raquel, will be pleased to find you a chamber.' Sir Nicolás gestured his wife forward.

Inigo heard Lady Raquel offering the Princess a bath and a change of clothes and he saw Alba—*Princess* Alba—give her a blinding smile.

'A bath would be marvellous. You are very kind.'

Inigo's mother's house was built in the Moorish style, with the upper floor overlooking a fountained courtyard. As was traditional, the upper floor was reserved for the women in his household. The Princess and Lady Raquel swept towards the stairway.

After the ladies had gone, Sir Nicolás seemed to age ten years. Inigo studied his steward's drooping shoulders and held out his hand.

'Hand me that letter. Who's it from?'

'Count Rodrigo,' Nicolás said. 'My lord, I am unaware of the exact contents, but the Count's envoy begged me to hand it to you as soon as you arrived. I was told it is of the first importance.'

Inigo took the scroll. It was weight off his mind to hear that Rodrigo had got safely away. Doubtless, this letter concerned Princess Leonor. Hopefully, Rodrigo had guarded her well. Alba— *Princess* Alba, he reminded himself again— would be devastated to learn otherwise.

Inigo gestured for Nicolás to follow him. 'Come, I'll read this in my bedchamber. I'll need a messenger to take my reply to Castle Álvarez tonight. Have wine brought in and join me.'

'Certainly, my lord.'

In his bedchamber, Inigo sank on to a leather-backed chair, broke the seal and unrolled the scroll. He recognised Rodrigo's sprawling scrawl and smiled, clearly Rodrigo hadn't waited to summon a scribe. As Inigo read, his smile faded.

Inigo, old friend,
I trust you and Lady Alba met with no accident after we parted.

Lady Leonor and I are residing in Castle Álvarez and we hope to see you as soon as may be arranged. As you may imagine, Lady Leonor is anxious to see her sister.

For the moment, it is imperative you know this: when we first arrived at the castle, I wasn't confident that Lady Leonor's best interests would be served by her settling in Castile. Truth be told, I found it hard to believe that her father could treat his daughters as harshly as she claimed. As a result, I wrote to him, hoping to arrange for Lady Leonor to be reunited with her father.

His reply has reached me, and I am shocked beyond words. It has led me to conclude that Lady Leonor's sire is utterly without feeling.

In brief, he has rejected Lady Leonor. Worse, he has made veiled threats against her, threats which lead me to believe that both Lady Leonor and Lady Alba could be in danger. I doubt their father's reach will extend to Córdoba, but it is best to be safe.

The ladies need to be diligently guarded. If Lady Alba goes abroad, she will need an escort—an armed escort.

I trust we shall speak soon, there is much to discuss.

I also need to mention that, as far as we can tell, Lady Constanza remains with her father. The third woman in the sally port turned out to be our ladies' Spanish duenna, Inés. She

left Granada in the company of my cousin,
Enrique. Sadly, we lost track of her.
  We shall speak more of this later.

Inigo lowered the scroll to his lap and stared blindly at the floor. So, Sultan Tariq had made threats against his daughters. The man was a coward as well as a tyrant.

Rodrigo appeared to doubt the threats had teeth, which was some comfort. Even so, Inigo noted that Rodrigo had been careful not to mention the Sultan by name. Inigo turned back to the letter and reread it. Rodrigo hadn't used the word Princess, he'd said nothing about the Nasrid dynasty, nor had he given any specifics that might link the Princesses back to the Alhambra Palace. Rodrigo was being extremely cautious.

Was Alba truly at risk? A ball of anxiety formed in Inigo's stomach. He thought about the convent and swore under his breath.

His steward walked in, took in Inigo's expression and frowned. 'My lord, is all well?'

'Nicolás, are you familiar with the convent near the Cathedral?'

'Saint Clare's?'

'That's the one. It has high walls, does it not?'

'Yes, my lord.'

'Tell me, Nicolás, do the nuns have guards?'

Sir Nicolás blinked. 'Guards? In the convent? It's very small, my lord, I shouldn't think so.'

Inigo tapped Rodrigo's letter against his thigh. He couldn't in all conscience send the Princess to a defenceless convent if Sultan Tariq was serious in his threats against her. 'It won't do,' he muttered.

A servant scratched on the door and came in with wine on a tray which he set on a side table.

Sir Nicolás reached for a goblet. 'Here, my lord, you look as though you need this. Are you hungry?'

'Starving.' Inigo took the cup and drank deep. 'None the less, I'll take a bath before I eat.'

'Very good, my lord.' Sir Nicolás hesitated. 'I believe Count Rodrigo is anxious for a reply.'

Inigo pushed to his feet. 'I'll reply when I'm ready. I think better on a full stomach.'

Dios mío, Princess Alba seemed to have invaded his mind, he could think of little else. As they'd ridden through the city gate, Inigo had found himself leaning into her, in order to catch a last lungful of that elusive fragrance. Jasmine would be linked in his mind for ever with a pair of gold-flecked black eyes and a quiet smile. Princess Alba was an attractive woman, though it was more than that. Inigo knew the signs, he'd been here before.

He was in danger of becoming seriously besotted.

Inigo had never been in love, but he'd become infatuated—in lust—with one or two women. Being obsessed with a female was inconvenient, it made a man vulnerable and he didn't like it. Fortunately, Inigo had discovered that the best way to exorcise such feelings was to ask the woman in question if she was willing to become his mistress. Feelings were ephemeral, they soon faded.

Lady Alba was different. She would never consent to be a man's mistress, she was a princess. She'd been protected her entire life and was utterly unworldly. Inigo avoided innocents like the plague. In any case, at this stage in his life, when he was on the verge of marrying Margarita, he couldn't afford to become besotted with another woman. Normally, it wouldn't have happened, he would have recognised the warning signs and walked in the opposite direction. The trouble was the Princess had needed him. He'd not been able to turn his back on her.

His mouth twisted as he thought about his betrothal. His father had proposed the alliance with the Marchena family years back, and Inigo was duty-bound to fulfil his wishes. Inigo had never had difficulty remembering his obligations before. The overwhelming desire he felt for Lady Alba—so brave, so beautiful—couldn't have come at a worse time.

He must hold in mind that he would soon be washing his hands of her. The thought left him empty. Hell burn it, he'd miss her.

Which was its own sign that he'd spent too long in her company. Sending her to Saint Clare's Convent had seemed a sensible solution. Unfortunately, Rodrigo's missive meant he would have to think again. If there was the slightest possibility of Lady Alba or the nuns being put at risk, the convent was out of the question.

Inigo would have to have her underfoot for a while longer. If he kept her at arm's length, if he remembered his contract with Margarita, there shouldn't be any difficulty.

At supper, he could bring the Princess up to date with Rodrigo's news. She ought to know everything. Almost everything. He wouldn't dream of mentioning Sultan Tariq's threats. There was no sense alarming her, when in all likelihood the man was merely posturing.

It was a shame he hadn't better news. True, the Princess would be delighted that her sister Leonor was safe at Castle Álvarez, but how would she react when he told her that Princess Constanza had stayed with her father? Would there be tears? Lord, he hoped not. And what would she do when she heard that her faithful duenna had escaped the palace and was presently lost? She would be distraught.

'Nicolás?'

'My lord?'

'Put our best men on guard tonight.'

'At once, my lord.' Sir Nicolás glanced at the scroll. 'We're expecting trouble?'

'It's unlikely, but possible. Nicolás, when I have bathed, I shall eat in my office. Be so good as to invite Lady Alba to join me when she is ready.'

The Princess would wish to write to Princess Leonor. Her letter could be sent to Castle Álvarez along with his.

Alba was much restored by her spell in the bathhouse, which proved to be slightly smaller though every bit as luxurious as the one she and her sisters had shared in the Alhambra Palace. Afternoon sunlight warmed the marble floor and turned ripples in the pool to gold. Serving girls were at hand with drying cloths and perfumed oils. Afterwards, she felt reborn.

The gown Lady Raquel lent her was the colour of violets. Made from fine Granada silk, it was cleverly laced with silver ribbons—a few minor adjustments and it fitted like a second skin. Lady

Raquel insisted that Alba wear a veil and when Alba understood that the veil would hang down her back in the Spanish style, she was more than happy to wear it. In her mother's homeland, few women concealed their faces behind veils. This was the Kingdom of Castile.

The violet gown swished as she was led past the central fountain and ushered into Lord Inigo's office. He was seated behind a desk. On the wall behind him, several shelves were overflowing with scrolls.

As she entered, he came to his feet. Alba dropped him a curtsy and peeped up at him through her eyelashes. Lady Raquel had said she was beautiful in the violet gown and Alba wanted to see Lord Inigo's reaction. This wasn't mere vanity, from this moment on Alba needed to look her best. Inexperienced though she was, she knew enough to realise that if she was going to make a life for herself in Castile, she must learn how to handle its menfolk. Lord Inigo was turning out to be infinitely more reasonable and honourable than she had dared hope. She would start by practising on him.

On the ride from Al-Andalus, Alba had caught him gazing at her more than once. Those grey eyes had lingered on her mouth, her hair and, even though that girl's ochre-coloured gown had swamped her, her shape. She hadn't felt the least bit embarrassed. If the Count liked her woman's body, so much the better. It gave her hope that when she was settled, she might find a good man in Castile.

Lord Inigo gave her a brief, irritatingly unreadable glance. 'My lady. Please, take a seat.'

The desk was laid for a meal—serving dishes and spoons, knives, glass goblets, a jug of wine. Alba frowned. 'We are not eating with your retainers, my lord?'

When explaining Spanish customs, Inés had told Alba great lords usually ate in a hall with their servants and vassals. Alba was aware that this town house wasn't the Count's main holding—that was in Seville—but she had imagined he would eat with his household.

'I need to speak to you privately.' He gestured at a scroll behind him. 'Count Rodrigo sends news.'

Alba caught her breath and sank on to a chair. 'He spoke of Leonor?'

'Aye.' Lord Inigo poured her a goblet of wine. 'Lady Leonor is currently residing at Castle Álvarez.'

'God be praised.' Alba let out a relieved breath and took the wine. 'I would dearly like to see her.'

An answering smile flickered briefly across

his face. 'I suspected as much. I shall be replying to Rodrigo after we have eaten. If you wish to write to your sister, your letter can be dispatched with mine.'

'Thank you, my lord. And what of Constanza?'

'Rodrigo tells me Princess Constanza is still in the Alhambra Palace.'

Goosebumps rose on Alba's skin. 'She did not leave?'

'I'm afraid not.'

Alba's eyes prickled. 'This is terrible news, my lord.'

Everything blurred in a haze of tears and she hurriedly dropped her gaze. Constanza was still in the palace, still at the mercy of their tyrant of a father.

'Of the three of us,' she said slowly, 'Constanza is the nervous one. She is shy and timid. I am shocked she didn't come with us, but I can't claim to be surprised. I don't quite understand it though, I could swear she followed me into the sally port, I heard her.'

Lord Inigo sighed. 'I fear you are mistaken, which brings me to the final part of Rodrigo's news. The woman behind you wasn't Princess Constanza, it was your duenna.'

Her eyes went wide. 'It was Inés?'

'Aye. Apparently, your duenna fled with Rodrigo's cousin, Enrique. I don't know the details, and sadly, she has vanished.'

'Vanished? How can that be? What could have happened?'

'My lady, Rodrigo's letter was brief. When you meet with Princess Leonor, she will doubtless tell you more.'

'I must write today.'

'Naturally.'

'Thank you, my lord.' Alba was unused to men and their ways, but she was coming to know Lord Inigo, and she would swear there was more in that letter. She tipped her head to one side. 'My lord, what else did the Count say?'

Lord Inigo turned his attention to a platter piled high with rice. 'My lady, I am starving, and I am sure you must be too.'

Alba looked searchingly at Lord Inigo and while she was certain something else in Count Rodrigo's communication had unsettled him, she could see that he wasn't about to reveal it. Stifling a sigh, she let the matter drop.

She had much to ponder. With Constanza lost, Alba's plans had been knocked off course. There wouldn't be three sisters learning to live in a foreign land, there would only be two. She took a thoughtful sip of wine. Two could set up house together as well as three. She and Leonor had coin and jewels, they would still be able to hire servants. They would oversee their destiny. And, once she and Leonor felt comfortable in Castile, Alba might start searching for a man, someone kind like Lord Inigo, who could give her the child she longed for.

Alba had decided she had no desire to be a concubine. She wasn't interested in marriage either. She hadn't gone to all this trouble to place herself in a position of servitude. If it was humanly possible, both Alba and her child would be free. It wasn't as if she would be on her own, Leonor would help, as she always did.

Alba stared unseeingly at the food Lord Inigo was setting before her, her mind busy with the letter she would shortly be writing. She and Leonor needed to amend their plans.

Lord Inigo slid a platter towards her. 'Please eat, my lady, you must be hungry.'

Leonor's reply came that evening and it was written in Arabic, for while both Princesses spoke Spanish with some fluency, neither of them could read or write it.

Thankful it had come so swiftly, Alba took it to the central courtyard and sat on the lip of the fountain to read it in the last of the light. The sky above was tinged with orange and purple. Hoofs clopped in a nearby street.

Beloved sister, peace be upon you,
I rejoice to hear that Count Inigo has brought you safely to Córdoba. God willing, we shall meet on the morrow.

Alba, you will doubtless be as grieved as I to learn that Constanza's courage failed her. She remains with our father. It was Inés behind us in the sally port. Inés escaped the palace and was taken up by Count Rodrigo's cousin, Sir Enrique.

I have met Sir Enrique and I regret to say that I cannot like him. When we saw him at the entrance to the sally port you may recall he was most grievously drunk. This is, apparently, normal behaviour for him. It is also why Sir Enrique mistook Inés for Constanza and rode away with her. Sad to say, as soon as Sir Enrique discovered his mistake, he abandoned Inés at the wayside and continued without her.

Count Rodrigo—blessings be upon him— was appalled when he learned of this.

My dear sister, Count Rodrigo is proving to be the best of men. He has sent scouts to search for Inés. Thus far they have found nothing, though we are hopeful that she may find her way into Castile.

Count Rodrigo has surprised me in many ways. He has gone to great lengths to aid us in our search for Mamá's family. Already he has discovered they live in a place called Baeza.

Lord Rodrigo, may God protect him, rides to Baeza tomorrow. He intends to meet our relatives personally. It is my belief he wants confirmation that we will be welcome there.

Rest assured, he has promised to enquire about Inés too. Dearest sister, I know you will join me in praying that Inés finds a safe harbour.

May the angels guard your rest tonight. You have arrived in Córdoba! It is the best of news. Lord Rodrigo has promised me an escort so that I may visit you on the morrow. Until then, beloved,
Your loving sister,
Leonor

The following day, Alba waited for Leonor in an alcove overlooking the sparkling fountain. She was wearing another gown from Lady Raquel's wardrobe, a green damask with a grey trim at the sleeve and hem.

There was no sign of Lord Inigo, though he must have instructed his steward's wife to ensure that she felt at home, because every now and then Lady Raquel would appear. She was warm and friendly, Alba liked her already.

'These slippers look at though they might fit, my lady, would you care to try them?'

Alba glanced at them. Grey kidskin, they were a perfect match for the trimming on her gown. '*Gracias*, they are lovely.'

'And what about these?' More slippers were held out for inspection. 'A perfect pairing, I think, for the violet gown you wore last evening.'

'Lady Raquel, it is kind of you to offer me your belongings, but I have no wish to deprive you of all your clothes.'

Concern flickered across Lady Raquel's face. 'My lady, I realise your taste may not match mine. Please be assured that you will not have to content yourself with my things for long. Lord Inigo has asked a merchant to bring cloth to the house for your approval. And a shoemaker will be arriving later, to take your measure.'

Alba took Lady Raquel's hand, the last thing she wanted to do was offend her. 'You are very kind, I thank you. My lady, I am hoping to see my sister Leonor today. In truth, that is all I can think of.'

It wasn't the whole truth. As the morning progressed and Leonor didn't appear, Alba found herself observing what went on in Lord Inigo's household with great interest and the alcove near the fountain proved to be an excellent vantage point. The courtyard was obviously the heart of the house and sooner or later, everyone went through it. Servants, guards, knights. Everyone, save the one man she wanted to see. Lord Inigo.

'Where is Lord Inigo?' Alba asked Lady Raquel on one of her visits.

'I am sorry, my lady, the Count has gone out.'

'Oh?'

'I believe he went to the Alcázar, my lady.'

'That is the palace of your King?'

'Aye, the Alcázar is King Henry's residence when he comes to Córdoba. The King is not here at present. The Alcázar is also used by visiting nobles. In the main though, it is a garrison. Count Rodrigo is the garrison commander. Since he and Count Inigo have been out of the Kingdom for some while, they will need to catch up with the news.'

Alba's nails dug into her palms. Of course. Lord Inigo had been fighting her father when he had been captured. He had been held in enemy territory and he would doubtless be expected to make a statement on everything that had happened.

'Lord Inigo will have reports to make,' Alba said slowly.

Would Lord Inigo be obliged to reveal her identity—a Nasrid princess—to fellow officers? Alba doubted that such intelligence would be well received. On the other hand, he might not mention it—after all, his friend Lord Rodrigo already knew the whole and he was the garrison commander.

'Just so, my lady. Earlier, I heard Lord Inigo talking to my husband about strengthening the guard on the city gates.'

Alba forced a smile. While it was disappointing not to be able to speak to Lord Inigo, she understood. She told herself it didn't matter. She would see him later to find out what he had told his peers about her.

She spent the better part of the morning near the fountain quietly observing and it wasn't long before she realised that just as she was watching Lord Inigo's retainers, she too was being watched. Everybody who passed through the courtyard glanced her way.

Were they aware that she was a Nasrid princess? She thought not. Too many people smiled when her gaze caught theirs. They would surely not smile at the daughter of their enemy. She must be careful not to betray herself, not until she knew what Lord Inigo had told them.

When the clatter of hoofs announced Leonor's arrival, Alba was pretty certain she must have seen the entire household. Everyone save Lord Inigo.

Chapter Seven

Alba was waiting on a couch in the fountained courtyard when a door under one of the alcoves opened and her sister stepped through.

Leonor, at last! Like Alba, Leonor had adopted the Castilian style of dress, a lightweight cloak over a simple gown. Her black hair was covered in a veil, apart from a twisting strand that had escaped its pins and curled down her breast.

The sisters flew across the courtyard and into each other's arms, and Alba was so choked with emotion that it was a while before she could speak. At length they drew apart, holding each other at arm's length, laughing and crying.

Alba smiled through her tears at features that were an echo of her own. It was truly wonderful seeing Leonor again. 'Spanish gowns suit you,' she murmured.

'I like them very much.'

Alba nodded. 'I agree, they seem to symbolise our freedom from Father.'

'Exactly. This is one of the less showy gowns. Count Rodrigo suggested I wear it today because he didn't want me to draw attention to myself. He was as determined to visit our cousin Sir Alfredo in Baeza as I was to visit you. He only agreed to my coming here if I swore to dress discreetly.'

'The Count sounds very protective.'

Leonor bit her lip. 'He dashed off to Baeza at such speed, I wonder if it isn't rather that he is anxious to be rid of me.' She swallowed. 'Whichever way you look at it, we must be unwelcome. Nasrid princesses in Córdoba cannot be anything but an embarrassment.'

Alba stared at the ground. 'Aye, you are surely in the right.' She still hadn't worked out how much Lord Inigo had told his retainers. She'd had nothing but courtesy from them since her arrival though, so whatever he'd said to them, they were clearly well trained.

Leonor looked about with interest, her gaze taking in the sparkling fountain and a pair of doves strutting and cooing on the tiles. 'Lord Rodrigo also has a town house in Córdoba, it is very like this. There is a fountained courtyard there too.'

A passing maidservant was staring at them in open-mouthed surprise, doubtless her attention had been caught by the sisters' similarity. In their father's palace, where everyone knew the three Princesses were identical, their resemblance to each other had been accepted without comment. Even then, only a select few had seen them without the protection of their veils—their personal maidservants when they were in the women's quarters, the concubine Alba had spoken to in her uncle's harem, and their father the Sultan.

With a sigh, Alba drew Leonor towards the stairway that led to the suite of chambers Lord Inigo had given her. 'We will be more comfortable in my quarters,' she murmured. 'And we shall be able to exchange our news without interruption.'

'Very well.' Leonor looked searchingly at Alba. 'Lord Inigo hasn't told you what Father has done, has he?'

Alba's skin went cold. 'What has he done? Has he hurt Constanza? Has she been punished?'

'No, no.' Leonor gave her a fierce hug. 'Brace yourself though, this will shock you. Come, take me to your bedchamber.'

Leonor stalked the length of Alba's bedchamber, her face set in hard lines.

'Leonor, for pity's sake, tell me.'

'Our beloved father has banished me from Al-Andalus.'

Alba froze. 'You are banished?'

'When Count Rodrigo brought me here he felt sure I was exaggerating Father's treatment of us. He feared that my presence in Castile might cause further violence between our peoples, so he wrote to Father, offering to send me home.'

Alba felt her mouth drop open.

'Naturally, Lord Rodrigo didn't tell me any of this,' Leonor said. 'He was unfailingly kind. He sent scouts searching for Inés. And all the while he was waiting for Father's reply.'

Leonor's eyes were full of pain and confusion. It was plain to Alba that her sister had grown fond of Count Rodrigo and that in writing to the Sultan, he had hurt her a great deal. It must, she realised, feel as though he had betrayed her.

'Most men cannot be relied upon,' Alba murmured.

It was a timely reminder. Alba had come to admire Lord Inigo very much, she didn't think he would ride roughshod over a woman's wishes. That day at the farm when she had rested in the loft, she and Lord Inigo had been alone for quite a while and not for one instant had she felt fear. And then there had been that night by the olive press. On both occasions she had felt perfectly safe. It made the Sultan's overprotectiveness seem ludicrous.

However, Alba hadn't known Lord Inigo for long. Her assessment of his character could be flawed. As Count of Seville, Lord Inigo's main concerns must surely be political.

'We have our jewels, Leonor, we have no need of men.'

Leonor's mouth twisted. 'Just so. And now you have the worst of my news. Father has disowned me and banished me from all his territories.' Her voice wavered. 'Alba, I must warn you, Lord Rodrigo read Father's letter to me and while you weren't mentioned by name, I fear that you also have been banished.'

'Banished,' Alba repeated quietly. She ought to be deeply upset, yet she felt nothing, she must be in shock. 'I am not sure what to think. We spent most of our lives in the castle apartments or in that tower in the Alhambra Palace. Since we were rarely allowed out, I doubt I shall miss one acre of Father's kingdom.'

'A small ray of light is that Father mentioned Constanza in his letter.' Leonor gave a tight smile. 'He acknowledges her and accepts her as his daughter.'

'That is a relief, for it tells us she is safe.'

'I certainly hope so.'

'Father won't hurt Constanza, Leonor. Not now she has, in his eyes, proved her loyalty by staying with him. I am more concerned for Inés. Where can she be?'

Leonor shared Alba's bed that night and they talked until dawn.

* * *

To Alba's joy, Leonor stayed for three days and the talking went on. Constanza's name came up all the time. Alba and Leonor regretted their sister's timidity and speculated about whether the three of them would ever be together again. They talked about Inés and prayed that she succeeded in reaching Baeza.

Not unnaturally, Leonor asked if she was going to meet Lord Inigo. Alba was forced to temporise, for although the sisters never left the town house, they didn't see him, not so much as a glimpse. Alba feared he was avoiding her, and her heart ached.

On the second day of Leonor's visit, the Princesses were informed that Lord Inigo was attending a council meeting at the Alcázar.

On the third, he had, apparently, gone to a horse fair.

As each day passed, Alba became more and more edgy. Count Inigo had to be avoiding her. Had she done something to offend him? Why had he disappeared? Why?

And why couldn't she stop thinking about him?

Sisters often disagree, and this particular disagreement began on the third day of Leonor's visit. It began innocuously enough. They were walking around the sparkling fountain in the central courtyard, their arms about each other's waists. Leonor was wearing a rose-coloured damask gown that Lady Raquel had lent Alba.

'You look well in that colour,' Alba said.

'Thank you.'

Mindful of listening ears, Alba lowered her voice to a confidential murmur. 'Count Rodrigo is certain that Father banished you for ever?'

When Leonor had first told Alba of their father's callousness, she had thought she was past caring. Life with the Sultan was behind her. None the less, now the initial shock had passed, she realised she did feel wounded.

'Yes. As I said, Father has told his men that they are at liberty to punish me if I am caught in Al-Andalus. The letter didn't mention you by name, though Father did say that he only has one daughter, Zorahaida.'

'So I must accept that I too am banished.' Alba sighed. 'I can't say I'm surprised, but what does surprise me is how upsetting it is.'

Leonor smiled sadly. 'I agree, I feel like an orphan. The only brightness in this is that we are reunited. And of course, there's Lord Rodrigo, I've enjoyed coming to know him.'

Alba gave her a thoughtful look. 'You seem to understand him extraordinarily well.'

Leonor fixed her gaze on the jetting fountain. 'He's kind and unexpectedly patient.' She turned to Alba. 'Promise me you'll never go home.'

'I shan't go back. I'm looking forward to meeting our Spanish family.' As the words left Alba's lips, she realised they were no longer true. Leaving the Princess's tower had changed her. While enclosed in the palace, the idea of escaping to meet their mother's relatives had seemed the greatest of quests. Yet was it? Might she merely be exchanging one set of restrictions for another? Freedom was within her reach and she was no longer confident that going to Baeza was right for her. She felt herself flush. 'Before that, however, there's something I need to do.'

Leonor lifted an eyebrow. 'That sounds intriguing.' When Alba didn't continue, Leonor nudged her. 'Well? You've whetted my curiosity. You can't stop there.'

'Ah, but I can. If I succeed… No, *when* I succeed you'll be the first to know.' Alba lifted her shoulders in a careless shrug. 'Rest assured, if I live to be a hundred I will never set foot in Al-Andalus again.'

'I'm glad.' Leonor took in a breath as though to brace herself. 'I thought the same. At first.'

'What are you saying?'

'I need to return home, and before you object, it will be the briefest of visits.'

Alba gaped at Leonor. 'What? You can't warn me not to go home because Father has banished us only to announce that you're going back yourself. The heat must have addled your brain.' She searched Leonor's face and her expression clouded. 'So help me, you're serious. Why?'

'Constanza. We can't abandon her, and if anyone goes back, it must be me. It's my fault we were separated.'

'Leonor, it's not your fault. Constanza's always been timid, we were deluding ourselves to think that she would come with us.'

'Aye, she hates confrontation. I've been thinking about this a great deal in the last few days and believe I know why she didn't come with us. As much as Father terrifies her, she's more afraid of the unknown.'

'I can't blame her for that,' Alba said. 'I was nervous myself.'

Leonor frowned. 'Constanza needs to know life is waiting for her outside the palace walls. She needs to know Mamá's family has been found. Then, when she's ready, she can follow us. She will be free.' Leonor gripped Alba's hand. 'I have to tell her. Outside Al-Andalus, Constanza will be safe. Father won't follow her beyond the boundaries, so there'll be no more living in fear.'

Alba shook her head, Leonor's proposal—to return home!—was chilling. 'It's far too dangerous. Moreover, it won't work. Constanza had her chance and made her choice, it's too late for her.'

'I can't accept that. What will her life be like? We did everything together. She will surely be miserable on her own. Alba, the three of us belong together.'

'Do we?'

Leonor blinked. 'Until we ran away, we were inseparable. It's not right that we have our freedom while Constanza still moulders in that tower.'

Alba opened her mouth to respond when a disturbance drew her attention to an arched doorway leading off from the courtyard.

The door swung wide and a tall, striking man stalked through it, spurs chinking on the stone flags. It was Count Rodrigo. His dark hair was ruffled, clearly, he'd recently removed his helmet. His tunic was dusty and his face ruddy. He'd been riding hard.

Eyes glittering, he scowled at Leonor. 'Lady Leonor, why are you still here?'

Leonor lifted her chin. 'As you see, my lord, I

am visiting my sister. Lord Rodrigo, may I present Princess Alba?'

Lord Rodrigo gave Alba a cursory glance. Curious, Alba watched him. Clearly the Count had no difficulty distinguishing between Leonor and herself. Given that the sisters were the image of each other, this was most unusual.

The Count bowed briefly in Alba's direction. 'Delighted, Lady Alba, I'm sure.' He immediately transferred his attention back to Leonor. 'Were you planning to ever return to Castle Álvarez?'

'Naturally, my lord, I—' Leonor broke off, blinking. 'You can tell us apart!'

'Don't be ridiculous.' Lord Rodrigo ran his hand through his hair. 'Of course I can.'

Intrigued by this exchange, Alba stepped forward. 'Lord Rodrigo, what my sister is trying to say is that most people cannot.'

Lord Rodrigo snorted. 'Clearly, most people are blind.' Imperiously, he held out his hand. 'Come, Lady Leonor, I have news from your family in Baeza.'

Leonor shot Alba an apologetic look though she permitted the Count to take her hand.

'News of our Spanish family?' Leonor nodded pointedly at Alba. 'Then I am sure my sister would also like to hear what you have to say.'

The instant Lord Rodrigo's fingers closed over

Leonor's, he let out a breath and the belligerence in his eyes faded. 'Very well, my lady.' He gestured towards a cushioned divan positioned in the shade. 'I will share the news from Baeza. But first, where's Inigo?'

'He's not here, my lord,' Alba said. 'He went to the horse fair.'

The next half hour passed with Lord Rodrigo telling the sisters about their cousin. 'Sir Alfredo's looking forward to meeting you. He told me you would be more than welcome to stay at Baeza.'

Leonor looked at him, frowning slightly. 'And Inés? Has he heard from Inés?'

'I'm afraid not. However, Sir Alfredo has strong hopes that your duenna will find her way to Baeza if my men cannot locate her. So, as soon as arrangements can be made, the two of you may visit him.'

Leonor fiddled with the fringe on her veil. 'Thank you, my lord. It was kind of you to go to such trouble.'

'My lord, you have my thanks too,' Alba said, rather baffled by her sudden reluctance. She ought to jump at the chance to meet Sir Alfredo, for the sooner she and Leonor found out whether Baeza was the place to set up their household, the better.

She wasn't ready. For the first time in her life she was finding her feet as an individual. Naturally, she adored her sisters, but as the middle princess she'd often felt lost. Leonor was always so certain, Constanza so loving. And she? Caught in the middle.

Alba was finding her feet and, nerve-racking though it was, she was rather enjoying it. Moreover, before she committed to anything, she wanted to speak to Lord Inigo.

'After I have consulted Lord Inigo, I will let you know my decision.'

Lord Rodrigo blinked at her. 'You're not certain you'll go?' He glanced Leonor's way. 'I thought you were set on meeting your family.'

'We are.' Alba smiled. 'However, I have matters to attend to in Córdoba first.'

Leonor cleared her throat. 'Speaking for myself, I've decided I would prefer to meet our Spanish relatives on neutral ground.'

Alba murmured agreement.

Lord Rodrigo's eyes were puzzled as his gaze returned to Leonor.

'You think your family will take advantage of you?' he asked. 'My lady, I assure you Sir Alfredo is anxious to meet you, both of you. You need have no fear of him.'

Leonor's expression was strained, Alba didn't

need a mirror to know it matched hers. She wasn't ready to talk about settling in Baeza, all she wanted was to speak to Lord Inigo. Had she offended him? As soon as Leonor left she would seek him out.

Alba was smiling absently at Lord Rodrigo when the true reason for her reluctance to discuss Baeza hit her. She had left Al-Andalus, hoping to one day have a child, and she had assumed she had plenty of time. Time to learn about life in Castile. Time to discover if she could find the perfect man to give her that child.

She didn't want to leave Córdoba because she had met that man already. Lord Inigo.

Mind whirling, she sat as though turned to stone.

No, no, she scarcely knew him, although admittedly Lord Inigo seemed well suited to the task. He liked women and women liked him. He was chivalrous. The way he had gone out of his way to consider her well-being led her to believe that he'd never hurt or brutalise her. Furthermore, there was a good chance that Lord Inigo's offspring would inherit his traits. They too would be thoughtful and strong and kind.

She couldn't ask him, they didn't know each other well enough. Besides, how would she approach him? Would she ask him outright? She couldn't do it, she simply couldn't.

Alba forced herself to concentrate on the conversation in hand.

'None the less, my lord,' Leonor was saying, 'we prefer to meet our cousin on neutral ground.'

Rodrigo nodded and sent Leonor a wry smile. 'Have you and your sister talked yourselves to a standstill?'

'My lord?'

'You've had three days together, so are you ready to come home yet?'

Leonor laughed and rose gracefully. 'Yes, I think we've caught up.' Her voice warmed. 'It's a relief to know we can see each other whenever we want.'

Princess Alba was too attractive for Inigo's peace of mind. Hoping to avoid her, he delayed his return for as long as he could and crept in like a thief well after dusk. He had barely sat down in his estate office when Sir Nicolás scratched at the door.

'My lord, I have a message from Count Rodrigo.' Sir Nicolás entered and carefully closed the door behind him.

'Very well. First tell me, is Lady Leonor still with us?'

'No, my lord. Lord Rodrigo came today, he spoke at length with both ladies before returning to Castle Álvarez. Lady Leonor went with him.'

'And his message?'

'He wants you to know that he has found the ladies' Spanish relatives, they live in Baeza.'

'Baeza? Is he sure?'

'I believe so. Lord Rodrigo interviewed Sir Alfredo, who has accepted the ladies as kin. Sir Alfredo assures him that they will be welcome in his household.'

'Sir Alfredo of Baeza,' Inigo muttered. He felt strangely put out. It had occurred to him that the Princess's belief she had relatives in Spain might be little more than a fairy tale, an excuse to run away. He'd never met Sir Alfredo, though he had heard of him. If Rodrigo trusted the man, Inigo could be confident the Princess would be safe. She would be planning to leave. The thought was surprisingly disturbing. He forced a smile. 'So, it's true. There'll be no need of that convent now.'

'My lord?'

'Never mind.' He yawned. 'It's late. Get to bed, Nicolás.'

'*Buenas noches*, my lord.'

Confident that the lateness of the hour meant the Princess would be safely abed, Inigo strode across the shadowy courtyard. Silvered by moonlight, spray from the central fountain arced upwards. Bright ripples danced and quivered across the water. The night was warm.

He had deliberately given Princess Alba a day or so to find her feet. Aware of her sister's visit, he had instructed his household to leave them to themselves as much as possible. He'd been praying that the bond between them remained strong. Clearly, it would be sensible—and safer—for them to seek out their mother's family together. Then he could stop worrying.

Inigo had been fully occupied since he had last seen the Princess, yet not an hour had passed without her intruding into his thoughts. He would miss her, he realised, shaking his head. The way she occupied his mind was confirmation that she should leave his protection as soon as possible. His future lay with Margarita. His days with the Princess would soon be a memory.

The fountain tinkled into the basin.

'My lord?'

That soft voice, an alluring combination of innocence and sensuality, had Inigo's body snap into wakefulness. He focused on the shadows beneath one of the arches.

'Lady Alba?'

The Princess stepped into the moonlight. Had she waited for his return? She must have done.

She stood before him in a Spanish gown, doubtless lent to her by Lady Raquel. She had discarded her veil, and that glossy black hair was swept back to reveal the sweetest of faces. Inigo stared at her hair like a man transfixed and found himself wondering what it would look like when fully unbound. Did she have any idea how alluring she was? She was driving him mad. Was she doing it on purpose?

Saints, what was he thinking? The Princess was an innocent. Tempting though he found her, she wouldn't dream of thinking of him in the same way. She'd lived her life in the company of women. Further, it was clear that Sultan Tariq's harsh treatment had left her with a grave mistrust of men.

Long-lashed dark eyes glowed up at him and she gave him a shy smile which made it hard to remember all that she had been through. Her smile, quiet though it was, warmed him to his heart. It held not the slightest trace of mistrust.

His pulse sped up. Hell burn it, despite distancing himself from her over the past few days, he remained in her thrall. He had grown to like her far too much. *We are soon to go our separate ways.* It was a dispiriting thought.

'Good evening, Lady Alba.'

'My lord.' The Princess dipped into a brief

curtsy, reinforcing the impression that here was a Spanish lady. This evening, no one would imagine that she was a Nasrid princess and that her father was none other than Sultan Tariq, the ruler of Al-Andalus.

What kind of a father locked his daughters up in a tower? Had the Sultan ruined her for all men?

'It's late, I thought you would be abed,' Inigo said.

'I need to speak to you, my lord. My sister Leonor has visited and your friend Lord Rodrigo was also here today.'

'Sir Nicolás mentioned Rodrigo's visit. I hear he brought news of your mother's family?'

'Aye.'

Inigo waited, trying not to stare at her mouth and wishing he could convince himself that it would be a relief to see her on her way. It wasn't true. Even though the responsibility of caring for Princess Alba had turned out to be far more complicated than he could have imagined, he wouldn't have changed it for the world. The feelings she evoked!

They were uncomfortable, he told himself. Unwanted and unacceptable. She was too pretty, too brave, too—everything. The sooner she was united with her Spanish relations, the better. She wrecked his peace of mind.

'When do you leave?' he asked.

An unreadable expression flitted across her face. 'I... I am not decided. Lord Rodrigo has discovered that Sir Alfredo of Baeza is a cousin of sorts. Leonor will contact me when everything is arranged. We shall discuss it then.'

'I understand Sir Alfredo will be happy to welcome you.'

'So we were told. Lord Rodrigo is hopeful that Inés will find her way to Baeza.'

'That is good to hear. I know how worried you've been.'

The Princess tilted her head back, and those shining dark eyes smiled into his. 'Lord Inigo, I must thank you for all you have done. You have been kindness itself. I shall never forget it.'

Inigo bowed his head. 'You are very welcome, my lady.'

Alba—no, he must really remember to think of her as the Princess—opened her mouth to say more when a maidservant entered the courtyard to light the wall lamps. Shooting a wary glance the maidservant's way, Al—*the Princess*—pursed her lips and watched silently as the girl moved from lamp to lamp.

How strange, Princess Alba appeared nervous. Of a maidservant? Inigo couldn't think why. She must have dealt with scores of servants.

'If that is all, my lady, I'm to bed,' he said. *'Buenas noches.'*

A small hand lifted. 'A moment, my lord. I have a…a favour to ask.' Her gaze flickered in the direction of the maidservant, and she lowered her voice. 'It is of a personal nature.'

Lamps glowed all about the courtyard. The maidservant bobbed a curtsy and slipped away.

Inigo stepped closer, caught a hint of jasmine and drew up short.

He and Princess Alba had spent days on the road. They'd been flung together in the most trying of circumstances and as a result the scent of jasmine would be associated for ever with a pair of black eyes so enthralling they stole his breath. Eyes in which he'd glimpsed a constellation of golden stars. A twist of longing squeezed his heart. He wanted this woman. He'd wanted her from the first. With a wrench, he forced his mind away.

He had no business longing for a Nasrid princess. He focused on a wall lamp and tried to conjure Margarita's face. *Dios mío*, why was it so hard? He'd known Margarita all his life. Lady Margarita Marchena de Carmona. His betrothed.

Inigo's leg throbbed. It was a sharp reminder of why he was marrying, he wasn't immortal. His parents, God rest them, had long championed an alliance with the Marchena family and he intended to honour their wishes. Not least because he needed heirs and Margarita would supply them.

Clearing his face of expression, he looked the Princess in the eye. 'A favour, you say?'

'Aye.' Her voice was soft and clear, and it reached further inside him than was comfortable. Her cheeks darkened into a deep blush. 'My lord, our days together are numbered. That is why I must ask you now.'

'Ask what?'

'Lord Inigo, I would like you to give me a child.'

She spoke so quickly that Inigo knew he had misheard. A child? The Princess wanted him to...

'I beg your pardon?'

She moistened her lips. 'Lord Inigo, I would very much like a child. I am hoping that you will agree to father it.'

Chapter Eight

A bat whisked silently past and vanished into the night while Inigo stood staring at the Princess. He was stunned. Already, the Sultan's daughter had proved to be an unusual woman—getting to know her had been both fascinating and tantalising. Yet it seemed he didn't know her at all.

A child? The Princess wanted him to give her a child? Inigo took a firm step backwards.

'No.' It was all he could manage. Unfortunately, he betrayed his innermost desires, for even as the word left his lips, his gaze was devouring her. Taking in those black, gold-flecked eyes, that tempting mouth, that lissom body. *'No.'*

The Princess drew in a deep breath and squared her shoulders. Closing the distance between them, she touched the back of Inigo's hand. There was a new vulnerability in her manner and her fingers were trembling. In truth, she looked as stunned as he and it occurred to him that she had surprised herself. She hadn't set out to make so bold a request. That squaring of her shoulders told him as much.

Despite his attempts at control, Inigo's skin

tingled at her touch. It was as though the years had rolled back and he was a callow youth in the first throes of calf-love. Could it be that, where this woman was concerned, his emotions might not be under his command? It was an unsettling possibility.

'My apologies, my lord.' A soft sigh vanished into the night. 'I don't know how I came to ask such a question. I withdraw my request, please forget it.'

Inigo watched her face intently, slowly shaking his head. 'My lady, you can't unsay something like that, any more that I can forget it. What worries me is why you would make such a proposition in the first place. Are you having second thoughts about meeting your Spanish kin?'

Aye, that might explain it. Alba and her sister had been so eager to escape their father that they'd given little thought to the realities of setting up a household in Castile. They were within sight of their goal and it was dawning on them that making a home for themselves in a new land might not be as easy as they had imagined. Dreams were one thing, reality quite another.

White teeth worried her lower lip. 'Please forgive me, my lord. May I be candid?'

'As you wish.'

'My lord, Inés explained much about Spanish

life, but her information was patchy. Clearly, there is much that I must learn. All I can say, apart from begging your forgiveness if I have offended you, is that I have seen you…looking at me. On the road, you behaved most circumspectly, you were very gallant, but your eyes followed me.'

Conscious of the disturbing warmth of her fingers on the back of his hand, Inigo cleared his throat. 'It was my duty to protect you. I couldn't do that without watching you.'

A small smile curved her lips and with a jolt of surprise, Inigo realised that deep down, he was flattered. Startled, yes, but definitely flattered. He had learned to like this woman and she, it would seem, had learned to like him too. Which was why it was imperative he send her to her Spanish relatives as soon as possible. The longer he spent in her company, the more she would tempt him. He must remember he was soon to be married and, unlike his father, he fully intended to honour his marriage vows.

She tipped her head to one side, looking at him as though he were a riddle that she was intent on solving. Well, he wasn't crass enough to deny that he wanted her. Nor was he about to start lying to her, even if he'd made a botch of hiding his desire.

Princess Alba peeped up at him through her eyelashes. It was a flirtatious trick. Women were probably born knowing it, and over the years Inigo had been at the receiving end of many such looks. This one was devastating. That peculiar combination of innocence and curiosity was all too compelling. It was utterly charming.

'My lord, I see I shouldn't have asked. The words slipped out somehow. I am very sorry.'

A disturbing pulse throbbed in Inigo's loins. Manfully, he ignored it. 'You do me much honour. My lady, I won't deny that I find you attractive. That doesn't mean I could contemplate bedding you.' Clutching at straws, scarcely able to believe he was having this conversation, he added, 'I am betrothed.'

'Betrothed?'

When a crease appeared between the Princess's eyebrows, it occurred to Inigo that one of the things her Spanish duenna hadn't told her about was Spanish marriage customs.

'I plan to marry quite soon, my lady. My father arranged the betrothal years ago. It is a dynastic alliance.'

'And the name of your betrothed?'

'Lady Margarita Marchena de Carmona.'

'I see. I wish you blessings in your life together,' she murmured.

He smiled down at her and never had a smile

felt more forced. 'You will understand then, why I cannot…do what you ask.'

'Not really, no.' She released his hand with a frown. 'Would you grant me my request if you were free?'

'Since I am not free, that question is irrelevant.'

'Is it? Your customs seem most odd.'

Inigo wanted nothing more than to end this tantalising and disturbing conversation, however, the Princess needed to understand, and he felt impelled to help her. 'Do they? How so?'

'When my mother was Queen, my father had many concubines. He was in the habit of visiting his harem long before Mamá's death.'

Inigo wasn't often at a loss for words, but this was one of those times. Clearly, Princess Alba's upbringing had been unlike that of almost every lady of his acquaintance. The women in Sultan Tariq's harem were held exclusively for his pleasure. Further, it seemed that the Sultan ruled his daughters with an iron hand. Why else would he have shut them—his only offspring— in that tower?

A few moments in Princess Alba's company and Inigo had seen that she was as innocent as a newborn lamb. She was unaccustomed to the company of men, no, it was worse than that, life had taught her to mistrust them. Fiercely.

All of which made her impulsive and scandalous proposition even more mysterious. She wanted him to father her child? It was preposterous. Inigo wasn't inexperienced where women were concerned, yet this entire conversation had him way out of his depth.

'Why me?'

She shrugged. 'I know no other men whom I...'

He smothered a sigh. 'My lady, you have my deep apologies. As I have explained, I am betrothed. I could never marry you.'

Dark eyes, lustrous in the lamplight, held his. Her lips twitched. 'Since I don't want marriage, I consider your betrothal irrelevant. I merely hoped that you would give me a child. Please, my lord, forget I ever asked.'

She went on watching him, her puzzlement almost tangible. She really didn't understand.

'My lady, you need to know that in Spain, children born out of wedlock are frowned upon. Your duenna might have taught you to speak our tongue, she should have done more to explain our traditions.'

A dark eyebrow arched. 'My father had concubines although he was married. I imagine that Spanish lords have mistresses?'

He nodded.

'Isn't a mistress the same thing as a concubine?'

'Aye, but…'

Her eyebrows bunched together. 'My lord, Spanish mistresses cannot be so different from concubines. They must surely have babies?'

Dios mío, what next? Inigo shoved his thumbs into his belt and struggled for a suitable answer. She didn't have a clue. Princess Alba was dangerously innocent. She knew barely a soul in Castile, so it was up to him to explain. The question was how to manage it without destroying the very innocence that was so charming.

Her foot tapped. 'My lord, do Spanish lords give their mistresses babies?'

She wasn't used to being kept waiting. Innocent she might be, patient she was not.

'Some of them do. I am not one of those men.'

'Oh?'

'My lady, you would do well to remember that in Castile, children born to mistresses rather than wives have a lower status. We call it illegitimacy. Illegitimate children, or bastards as they are sometimes called, can be mocked, even reviled. The word bastard is a derogatory term. Life can be especially hard for them.'

'That is sad, indeed.' The Princess lifted her wrist, toying pointedly with a jewel-encrusted bangle. 'However, if you had agreed to my proposition, you need not have feared for that. I have the means to ensure that our child would have been well cared for. It would not have been reviled. It would not have had a hard life.'

Our child. Briefly, Inigo closed his eyes. Lord, how she tempted him.

'Tell me, my lady, if I had agreed how did you intend to live? Without the protection of a husband or lover life wouldn't be easy.'

'Protection is a double-edged sword, my lord.' Her mouth firmed. 'And as you have pointed out, I am not bound by your conventions. I intended to establish a household with my sister. We thought to live alone.'

'In that case, my lady, the pair of you may as well have stayed in the Alhambra.'

'My lord?'

'It strikes me you have yet to leave the harem. My lady, I meant no insult when I told you I could not oblige. I will not sire an illegitimate child.'

'Because you are betrothed to this Lady Margarita Marchena de Carmona.'

'That is so. And since I believe that fidelity is vital to a lasting and happy marriage, that is an end to it.'

There she stood, calm and beautiful. Was she confused? Troubled by his rejection? It wasn't easy to judge. Inigo certainly was, desire was an ache in every bone. Turning down her outrageous, seductive request was one of the hardest things he had ever done.

He had to send her away. In her company, he turned into a needy stranger who ached to wrap his arms about her and carry her to his bed. He no longer knew himself. No longer knew what he might do.

'Very well.' Princess Alba gathered up her skirts as if preparing to retire. She looked up at him, apparently studying his features in much the same way that he had studied hers. 'I am curious, my lord. How long have you been betrothed?'

'Ten years.'

Her sigh melted into the night. 'So long? Are you saying that in all that time you have not had a mistress? You have been faithful to your Lady Margarita for ten years?'

Heat scorched Inigo's cheeks and it was hard to maintain eye contact. Of course he'd had mistresses, he and Lady Margarita had an understanding.

'My lady, you are too forthright. This conversation is unseemly.'

She bit her lip. 'I embarrass you, my lord, and am sorry for it. My world and yours cannot be so very different, I am trying to understand. Do you have a mistress?'

'Not at present.' He made his voice dry. 'If you

recall, I have been enjoying the comforts of your father's prison.'

'I meant before the fighting, before you were taken captive.' A smile trembled into being. It was charming as usual—shy and incredibly alluring. 'A man like you would be bound to have mistresses.'

How she did it, Inigo had no idea. He had no wish to prolong the conversation, yet he found himself returning her smile. 'One or two.'

'And they never had babies?'

'Certainly not.'

The Princess's eyes sparkled with interest and Inigo's heart sank. What would she say next? Any moment, she'd be asking how one went about enjoying a mistress and yet avoided having a child. It was a question he had no intention of answering.

This woman was a princess. She was untouched, pure both in body and mind, and one day a fortunate man would thank him for keeping her that way. The thought left him with a bitter taste in his mouth.

'My lady, it is late.' He faked a yawn. 'If you wish, we can continue this conversation in the morning. Meanwhile, you might like to consider that relationships between men and women are different in the Kingdom of Castile. Marriage matters. Legitimacy matters.'

'Very well.' She inclined her head. 'I shall reflect upon what you have told me. In the meantime, I'd like you to answer one final question. After you are married, will it be hard to remain faithful to your wife?'

Inigo almost choked. 'Really, my lady. Such questions—you must learn to curb your curiosity.'

Her lips curved and her eyes gleamed. He had a strong suspicion she was laughing at him.

'I shall try.' Gripping her skirts, she curtsied. *'Buenas noches,* my lord.'

With a swirl of silk, she was gone.

Inigo sank on to a bench and put his head in his hands. Lord, what a handful. Shaking his head, he smiled ruefully at the floor tiles. Princess Alba was going to lead some poor wretch a merry dance. Thank heaven she was too innocent to have tried a more flirtatious approach, he was all too aware it would probably have worked. She was temptation incarnate. Fortunately, he'd managed to resist her.

Other men, however?

He swore softly. Other men might not recognise that her forthright manner masked genuine innocence. Worse, they might not care. Lady Alba could walk into a lion's den and not know it. So, relieved though he was that she would shortly be joining her relatives, he couldn't help but be concerned.

What would she do next?

Reminding himself that after Princess Alba left his house she would no longer be his concern, Inigo pushed to his feet and headed uneasily for bed.

Alba's breakfast was brought to her bedchamber by a polite maidservant. Alba wasn't fooled. Despite his promise to continue their discussion, Lord Inigo was trying to avoid her. Well, she wouldn't be avoided, she had an apology to make. Last night, she had surprised herself. She should never have asked him to consider entering into a liaison with her. She hadn't meant to, the words had simply slipped out.

It was a pity, because she liked Lord Inigo very much. She felt easy with him and she wanted that sense of ease to continue. She would never forgive himself if he took against her because of her ignorance. And what he clearly saw as her brashness.

As soon as she had eaten, Alba dragged on a blue gown and headed down to the courtyard. Picking a bench under a shady arch, she sank on to it.

While she waited, several people passed by.

The first was a guard in a green tunic with a distinctive black falcon emblazoned on his chest. The green of the guard's tunic matched the colour of the tunic Lord Inigo had been wearing when he'd been imprisoned by her father's soldiers. Alba stared at the falcon, realising it must be his device. Servants crossed this way and that. A couple of knights appeared, spurs chinking as they headed towards the stables.

The sound of water playing in the fountain, so reminiscent of the Alhambra Palace, was bittersweet. Alba's throat tightened. Al-Andalus was no longer her home. She had turned her back on it and had no regrets. So why the prickling at the back of her eyes? It made no sense. The Alhambra Palace, with its marbled courts, honeycomb plasterwork ceilings and carefully tended gardens could have been paradise on earth. But when one's father was a tyrant who terrorised his own children it was far from that.

Father has banished us, I shall never go home.

A tear ran down Alba's cheek, impatiently, she brushed it away. Even though she never intended to return to Granada, she'd been wounded by her father's decree. Worst of all, however, was Leonor's decision to contact Constanza. If Father caught Leonor, what would he do to her? She felt faint thinking about it.

Leonor couldn't be serious about going back after they had risked so much to escape.

Constanza has made her decision, we shall have to accept it.

She focused on the fountain. Sunlight was gilding the arching spray as prettily as any in her father's palace. The leaves of a vine trailing along a sunlit wall trembled in a light breeze. There was beauty here. It was less ostentatious than the opulent grandeur of her father's Granada palace, but Castile was not the wilderness Sultan Tariq had led his daughters to believe.

A white dove fluttered to the edge of the pool and dipped its beak into the water. Almost immediately, brisk footsteps had it whirring away.

Lord Inigo had entered the courtyard. He broke step on seeing her and gave a slight bow.

'My lady.'

'Buenos días.' Alba rose. 'My lord, I have been thinking about our conversation last evening and I should like to apologise.'

His grey eyes were wary. 'There is no need, my lady.'

'I hadn't realised the extent of my ignorance about Spanish customs. I am truly sorry to have caused you embarrassment.' She clasped her hands together. 'I value your friendship. Please say you are not offended.'

He inclined his head. 'Not at all. My lady, it will take a while for you to find your feet. Do you wish to visit your sister? If so, you will need an escort.'

'That won't be necessary, I shan't be seeing Leonor today.' Alba tipped her head back to look at him. It was a relief to see that with her apology his whole demeanour had relaxed. 'I was hoping to see something of Córdoba. I think I mentioned that my sisters and I were forbidden to explore Granada. My lord, bearing in mind the Sultan's letter to Lord Rodrigo, do you think it would be safe for me to see the market?'

Lord Inigo's gaze sharpened. 'Your sister mentioned the Sultan's threats?'

'Yes, my lord. And our banishment.'

He swore under his breath. 'That was badly done, I wasn't going to tell you.'

'Why ever not?'

'I didn't want you worried.' He rubbed his forehead. 'My lady, it's doubtful Sultan Tariq's scouts could penetrate this far into Castile, none the less, it's wise to take precautions. To that end, it might reassure you to know that I've doubled the watch on the city walls. More guards have been assigned to the main gate.'

She looked pensively at him. 'So I can't explore Córdoba? Even with an escort?'

'Provided your escort is reliable, I think something might be arranged.'

'Thank you, my lord.'

Lord Inigo's gaze drifted briefly to her mouth. Then he stepped back. Alba frowned, she'd seen him step away from her like that many times. She'd catch him looking at her in a way that suggested he found her desirable. He'd look at her, realise she'd noticed and look swiftly away.

She'd thought—no, hoped—it meant that he desired her. She truly hoped that her request hadn't pushed him away. She'd spent half the night worrying about that, and the other half trying to understand the reasons for his rejection. He'd admitted to taking mistresses and he'd told her he was marrying Lady Margarita for dynastic reasons. For heirs. How she wished she had a firmer grasp of local culture. All she truly understood was that it didn't seem likely he'd change his mind.

Lady Raquel had told her that Lord Inigo's main holding near Seville was vast. He was a great lord. Doubtless, he had houses like this all over Spain and hordes of knights and servants catering to his every whim. Regret pierced her. It was such a shame he couldn't have a mistress as well as a wife.

'Will you accompany me, my lord?'

'I regret I cannot. I have an engagement later this morning. I'll ask Sir Ruys to attend you.'

Alba felt her face fall and forced a smile. 'Very well. I am sure Sir Ruys will be an admirable escort.' Noticing that Lord Inigo's gaze was fastened on her mouth, a demon in her prompted her to add, 'Sir Ruys is very handsome.'

Lord Inigo's grey eyes sharpened. 'My lady, you will behave.'

She opened her eyes wide. 'Behave, my lord?'

He leaned in, a pleat in his brow. 'There is to be no propositioning Captain Ruys.'

Alba hesitated, he'd spoken softly, yet there was an edge to his voice. It would seem she'd hit a nerve. She couldn't resist probing. 'No?'

'No. You will leave my captain alone.' His grey eyes were hard as flint. 'You will leave all my men alone, is that understood?'

'Perfectly, my lord.'

Strong fingers gripped hers. 'There will be no flirting and absolutely no propositioning. It would be disparagement, you are a princess and you must never forget it.'

'Disparagement? I am not so sure. It seems that being a Nasrid princess is not good currency outside Al-Andalus.'

His face darkened, he looked so angry that she

lost her breath. 'Don't even think that.' That grey gaze held hers. 'Swear you will behave.'

'Very well, my lord. I will behave.'

He released her hand and glowered down at her. 'You're a witch, you're deliberately provoking me.'

She lifted an eyebrow. 'Is it working?'

'Witch.' Lips curving into a smile, the Count crooked his arm at her. 'You will leave Sir Ruys alone because he won't be taking you to the market. I will.'

Joy filled her. 'Thank you! I can't think of a better escort.'

'I do have a meeting though, you mustn't take long.'

'I won't, I swear it.'

Delighted her tactics had worked, Alba tucked her hand into his arm. Lord Inigo had no idea that she wouldn't dream of propositioning Sir Ruys or any of his men. She hadn't even planned to proposition Lord Inigo. The trouble was that now that she had done it, she couldn't stop thinking about it.

It had been a blow to discover that Lord Inigo was soon to be married. And despite knowing it was wrong of her, she regretted he was so principled. Still, he'd proved himself an ally. He'd helped her flee Granada and he appeared to have her interests at heart. God willing, he would remain close.

In the future, would Lady Margarita object to their seeing each other as friends? She hoped not. The idea that she might not see him after she went to Baeza was surprisingly painful.

She shot him a sidelong glance and struggled to keep the smile on her face. It was such a shame Lord Inigo wouldn't give her a child. She'd never dreamed a man could be so fascinating. His brown hair was thick but otherwise unremarkable. He had a straight nose and a strong jaw, but so did many men. And just as Lord Inigo looked at Alba's mouth, so she had looked at his. She wasn't quite sure why she enjoyed looking at it, though she'd come to see she found it attractive. It was pleasingly shaped, particularly when he was smiling.

On their journey to Córdoba, Lord Inigo had smiled a great deal. He'd smiled in reassurance. He'd smiled to amuse her. He'd smiled to let her know that although she was ignorant of the ways of the world, he would protect her and would demand no toll in payment. He even smiled when, after too many hours in the saddle, his injured leg pained him. Above all, his smile told her that he would never treat her as cruelly as her father had done. His smile told her that he was her friend.

A friend who had made it plain she should expect no more from him than friendship. It shouldn't hurt, but it did.

Alba's father had taught her a harsh lesson. Men didn't understand the nature of love. She'd steeled herself to escape and to set her wariness of men aside for one thing and one thing alone. A child. A child she could love and who would love her unreservedly, like the concubine's baby in her uncle's harem.

A child would give her a new role in life, that of a mother. She would no longer simply be the middle of three sisters, she would find herself in motherhood. She had anticipated a brief, possibly painful liaison before she got herself with child and she had deemed the pain a price worth paying.

And then, by that sally port, Lord Inigo had bowed over her hand and offered to help, and her defences had begun to crumble. Doubtless that was why Lord Inigo's rejection last eve hurt more than her father's declaration of banishment.

Mind overflowing with doubts and wishes, Alba glanced at the knight beside her and reminded herself that she hadn't known him long. Back at the palace, she'd been certain that no man was worth fighting for. This one, she suspected, might be different.

Could he be persuaded to change his mind?

Chapter Nine

As Inigo led Princess Alba out of the courtyard, he was wondering what the devil he was doing. Now she was safe, he had no business continuing to act as her escort, even on so innocuous an outing as a visit to the market.

Yesterday, he had received a sharp reminder of his betrothal in the form of a communication from Sir Pero de Carmona, a knight who owed fealty to Margarita's brother, Baron Fernando Marchena. Sir Pero had news concerning Margarita, and Inigo had arranged to meet him later that morning at the garrison.

King Henry's Córdoban military headquarters was more than a fort. Sited a stone's throw from the river, the palace, or Alcázar, adjoining the garrison was a huge, rambling structure. Visiting noblemen from all corners of Castile often stayed there.

When the Princess had ambushed him on the way to bed and had made her astonishing and unsettling request, the meeting with Sir Pero had dropped from Inigo's mind. Truth be told, Inigo would far rather escort the Princess to the market than discuss Margarita with her brother's knight.

Meeting Lady Alba was casting new light on Inigo's relationship with his betrothed. He'd known it was cool, and it had taken the Princess to show that part of him had long been dreading his marriage. Still, duty must be done.

'My lady, I am prepared to escort you, but remember we cannot be long.'

Eyes dancing, she hugged his arm. 'I won't dally, I swear it.'

The market was close, so they went on foot. As they left the house, it was immediately apparent that Inigo's time in the garrison had been well spent. A pair of guards was stationed in the street outside, and as Inigo directed the Princess towards the market, he counted off the patrols on every corner. A small contingent of men were posted by the Cathedral. Mounted knights were keeping an eye on the market. His advice had been taken, thank the Lord. King Henry's Guard was out in force.

And as well they were, because despite her promise to hurry, Princess Alba was soon distracted. She wanted to look at *everything*. Her bright gaze darted this way and that. First she dragged him to a cloth stall. She oohed and aahed over silks from the east, and damasks from

France. Releasing his arm, she slipped into the crowd and forced her way through. When Inigo caught up with her again, she was staring round-eyed at bowls of amber shipped in from the north. She picked up a block of frankincense, closing her eyes as she inhaled. Her pleasure was unfeigned and very refreshing. Inigo enjoyed watching her.

As they neared the goldsmiths' quarter, however, Margarita entered Inigo's thoughts and it was as though a cloud had blocked the sun. He frowned, shook his head and walked on. There was no need for guilt. He wasn't planning on dishonouring the commitment his father had made with the Marchena family.

The Princess was talking to a pedlar with a tray of ribbons. A small purse hung from her belt, she dipped into it, produced a gold coin and pointed at a violet ribbon.

Inigo frowned. 'That's far too much. Allow me, my lady.'

Firmly he closed her fingers over the gold and paid for the ribbon.

Dark eyes flashed. 'I can pay, my lord. I want to pay.'

He shrugged. 'If it pleases you, we can keep a tally.' He lowered his voice to a confidential murmur. 'If you throw gold about in the market, you will cause a brawl.'

'Very well.'

'Take this.' Inigo pressed a handful of silver into her hand, lips twitching as he watched her carefully count the coins. She was a menace. Let loose on her own she would cause a riot, just as she'd cause a riot among his men if she proceeded with her scandalous plan to find a man to father a child.

Dios mío, if his men got wind of that, he'd have the devil's own job with discipline.

The violet ribbon safely stowed in her purse, several other things caught her eye. Simple things that Inigo was surprised she would notice. A length of filmy gauze. A plaited belt with coloured beads threaded on to the leather strips. Her delight was infectious and beguiling. More than once, Inigo found himself smiling as he watched her.

They had worked their way right into the goldsmiths' quarter when someone hailed him.

'Count Inigo!'

Inigo swallowed a curse and forced a smile. It was the knight he'd agreed to meet later, Sir Pero. Inigo wasn't sure how he would react when he realised Inigo was escorting Lady Alba.

'Well met, my lord. I was glad to hear you had

returned.' Sir Pero clapped him on the back and glanced meaningfully at his leg. 'I believe Sultan Tariq's men left you with a little memento. I trust you are fully recovered?'

'Thank you, yes.'

The Princess was occupied with a selection of bangles on one of the stalls and, happily, Sir Pero didn't appear to have noticed her. Inigo gave him a cool smile.

'Lady Margarita is well, sir?'

It was odd, asking about Margarita felt strange, even wrong. Worse, it was impossible not to notice the way his heart sank at the very thought of her. It was also impossible not to notice the tightening in Sir Pero's jaw.

'Lady Margarita is in good health. She and her brother are here in Córdoba.'

Inigo's chest felt cold. He lifted his eyebrows. 'Baron Fernando and Lady Margarita are in Córdoba?'

'Yes, my lord. When news reached Carmona that your ransom had been settled and that you were in the company of Rodrigo Álvarez, the Baron realised you were likely to come to Córdoba before returning to Seville.'

'Certainly Córdoba is closer to Granada than Seville,' Inigo murmured, hoping he didn't look as stunned as he felt.

Margarita was in Córdoba. He managed not to glance towards the Princess. There was no need for guilt. None whatsoever.

'Quite so, my lord. At any rate, when news came of your release, the Baron and his sister set out at once. They are anxious to welcome you home.'

'That's strange, I've spent much of the past few days at the garrison. I didn't see them.'

'The Baron and Lady Margarita are in the palace, not the fort, my lord,' Sir Pero said. 'By the by, Lady Margarita is planning to celebrate your marriage before the year is out.'

Gripped by a sense of impending doom, Inigo kept his expression neutral and nodded. Margarita was in the Alcázar. Unwelcome as this news was, running into Margarita or her brother when he hadn't been braced for it would have been far worse. Indeed, his betrothed could be mere yards away, she too might be visiting the market.

'Is Lady Margarita with you this morning? Are you her escort?'

Sir Pero glanced quizzically in Princess Alba's direction and shook his head. 'You may be at ease, my lord,' he said in a dry voice. 'However, when you are free, I am sure Lady Margarita and Baron Fernando will be glad to see you.'

The surge of anger caught Inigo by surprise.

Not only had Sir Pero noticed the Princess, he had assumed that Inigo and she were lovers. Inigo willed himself not to react. It shouldn't matter, it wasn't the man's business.

Inigo gave a tight smile. 'Please convey my greetings to Lady Margarita and her brother. I shall be glad to attend them at the Alcázar later today.'

The knight smiled. 'Very good, my lord.'

'I take it that now that we have spoken, our meeting at noon is unnecessary?'

'Yes, my lord.'

Inigo inclined his head and turned away.

The Princess had left the stall. His stomach lurched. She wasn't at the next stall either, she seemed to have vanished. Well, she couldn't have got far, not with her poring over every trinket in sight.

Alba had been examining an enamelled bracelet when a man at the edge of her vision caught her attention. Having spent most of her life looking at the world through a veil, she was getting used to walking about without one. There were times she felt shy looking directly at people and this was one of those times.

Broad and darkly handsome, the man was well dressed with a fine sword hanging from his belt.

A nobleman. He was staring at Lord Inigo and his face broke into a smile.

'Count Inigo!' The man clapped the Count on the back.

Wryly, Alba shook her head. She had no wish to embarrass Lord Inigo among his peers. It could be awkward if he was obliged to present her. He could hardly say, 'Here is Princess Alba, a Nasrid princess and daughter of the man who held me captive and set me to hard labour.'

She turned quickly back to the bracelets. A woman brushed past, a willow basket over her arm, and a young girl skipped up to the goldsmith's stall. The girl was so short that she had to go up on tiptoes to look at the silver rings laid out on a tray.

A loud crash, like breaking pottery, came from a gloomy side street. Alba heard a man groan. Replacing the enamelled bracelet on the stall, she went to the head of the alley.

The houses on either side were so close they almost touched and the shadows were thick. A door a little way in hung slightly ajar, presumably it led into a goldsmith's workshop. She heard another muffled moan.

A child was crying. 'Papá! *Papá!*'

Picking up her skirts, Alba flew into the side street.

As she reached the workshop door, the shadows seemed to twist and it took a moment to interpret what she was seeing. A hooded man was crouched over a figure slumped against the wall of one of the houses. He looked up briefly and Alba's skin chilled.

A knife flashed and she heard the hideous and perfectly distinct sound of choking. The hooded man—an assassin, for Alba was certain she was witnessing a murder—glared at her.

It was astonishing how much you could see when gripped with horror. Time was at a standstill, everything was starkly, hideously clear. Beneath the hood, the assassin's face was swarthy. He had dark eyebrows, a nose like a hawk and he was sweating profusely. His legs were bandy and his build bulky. His clothing was nondescript. He was wearing a stained leather gambeson and was wielding a slim, lethal-looking dagger.

His sword stood out, for it was exceptional. The hilt was patterned with complicated swirls of black and gold. Alba had seen one like it in her father's collection. Fiendishly expensive, that sword came from Toledo.

Giving the hooded man a final look, Alba stumbled over the threshold and into the workshop. Trembling from head to foot, she slammed the door and shot the bolt home.

A man was sitting on the floor, rubbing his head. He looked dazed and disorientated. This must be the goldsmith. A small child, a girl, she thought, was clinging to the man's tunic, sobbing.

'You are the goldsmith, sir?'

The goldsmith nodded. With a groan, he clambered to his feet and scooped up the child who clung to him like a barnacle. 'Domingo Romero, at your service.'

'That man…' Alba gestured wildly at the door. 'He's still there?'

'Aye. He… I think he murdered someone.'

The child gave a hiccoughing sob.

Face white, the goldsmith swayed. 'Jesu.' He held out the child. 'I beg you, see to Marta, will you? Take her to the back and keep her quiet.'

Alba smiled at the child and opened her arms. '*Hola*, Marta.' As she prised the child from her father, a violent crash bowed the workshop door. Alba stifled a scream. 'He's out there. Be careful.'

'I'll be fine.' Grim-faced, the goldsmith snatched up a fearsome metal tool. 'Get my daughter out of here.'

Marta hugged to her chest, Alba fled. A narrow corridor led into the living quarters. She hurtled through a neat, flower-filled courtyard and entered a chamber to be faced with two doors. She wrenched a handle at random. A cupboard. What a blessing the child was so small. Built into the wall, the cupboard was large enough to hide in if they squeezed in under the shelf.

Sweat broke out on Alba's brow. It would be incredibly cramped. Thankfully, Marta was no longer sobbing, she was sniffling quietly, sucking her thumb as though her life depended on it.

'Good girl,' Alba murmured, scrambling into the cupboard. She curled up tight, prayed the child didn't mind the dark and closed the door. The latch clicked. It was warm and gloomy in the cupboard. Airless.

'I really hope we are not shut in,' she murmured, panic rising. 'I hate being confined.'

Marta sniffed, caught a strand of Alba's hair and tugged gently.

The shelf pressed down on Alba's head as she wriggled into a more comfortable position, leaning against the relative cool of the cupboard wall. She truly hated being shut in and the dark made it worse. She forced herself to take slow, steadying breaths. As she struggled for calm, she felt another pull on her hair. Marta must have wound it about her fist, it was too dark to see. Another tug. It was strangely calming. She kissed the child's cheek.

'Good girl,' she whispered. 'All will be well.'

The child hiccoughed and fell blessedly quiet.

* * *

The sun beat down as Inigo stalked the street. The crowd was thinning. Shops were starting to put up their shutters, they would remain closed until the worst of the heat was over.

Where the devil was she?

A shutter thudded closed and he heard the clack of a bolt being thrown. He heard laughter from the stall behind him, and the cry of a child. And then—a muffled gasp. A woman. The hairs lifted on the back of his neck.

Princess Alba?

Disquieting noises were coming from a dark alley that cut between the goldsmiths' workshops. Hand on his sword hilt, Inigo hurtled towards it.

A hooded man was crouched over a body, his dagger was gore-stained. Inigo whipped out his sword. What was this? Murder? Where was the Princess?

The door to the goldsmith's workshop was closed. Was she in there? Inigo felt frantic. Desperate. She must be safe, she had to be safe.

The hooded man straightened and loped away. The soldier in Inigo noted the man's legs were bowed and his gait awkward. He gave a last searching glance down the alley for Princess Alba, put his shoulder to the workshop door and burst in.

A man lurched towards him brandishing a tool of some kind. Inigo recognised him as Domingo Romero, the best goldsmith in Córdoba, a man so talented that King Henry regularly gave him work.

'Domingo, hold.' Inigo moved swiftly to disarm him. Domingo had a cut on his head and a line of blood was trickling down his temple. Otherwise, he seemed unharmed. 'You've seen a young lady in a blue gown?'

'Aye.'

'Is she hurt?'

Domingo shook his head and, wincing, rubbed his brow.

'Where is she?' Inigo clenched his jaw. It was plain Domingo was half dazed, but if he didn't answer in a heartbeat, he'd shake the answer out of him.

'Bless her, she…she's in the house. Took my daughter to safety.' Domingo pointed.

Inigo tore through the house like a whirlwind. Banging doors. Calling.

'Lady Alba? *Alba!*'

In the last chamber, a faint cry came from behind a door. He jerked it open and his breath left him in a rush of relief. There she was, sitting on the ground beneath a shelf with her knees drawn up, the child tight in her arms. *She is safe.*

'*Dios mío*, Alba.' Inigo gasped, his lungs ached, he'd run so hard. 'You had me worried.'

She smiled unsteadily and swung her legs out of the cupboard. Inigo helped her to her feet, and she stood there, cradling the goldsmith's daughter. Faint tear tracks stained her cheeks.

Inigo's guts tangled. 'Alba,' he repeated, ignoring the fact that she was a princess and she had not given him permission to address him in so familiar a manner.

Alba drew in a shaky breath and a small sob escaped her. The little girl sucked her thumb, eyes solemn.

Inigo couldn't help himself. Forgetting the deference that was Princess Alba's due, forgetting everything save the need to offer comfort, his arms went around her, child and all. 'You are safe, my lady. Safe.'

He felt her nod. A soft murmur warmed his ear and for the first time that day, all was right in his world. He heard her swallow.

'My lord, it seems I am a coward.'

'Not at all.' Inigo ran his palms up and down her arms. Soothing. Gentling. Domingo's daughter was toying with a glossy strand of her hair. 'You have the heart of a lion. And you kept the child calm.'

'Marta's the brave one, aren't you, sweetheart?'

The Princess kissed the child and her black, gold-flecked eyes found his. She jerked her head in the direction of the courtyard and the workshop beyond. 'It was I who was afraid. Is her father all right?'

'He is fine, though I suspect he will have quite a headache.'

'Lord Inigo.' Her voice wavered before strengthening again. 'A man's been killed in the side street outside. I saw the assassin.'

She'd seen the murderer? No wonder she was so distressed. 'Never fear, he will be streets away by now,' Inigo said. 'Sadly, there are cut-throats everywhere, even in Córdoba.'

'My lord, you are quite certain he has gone?'

'Aye.'

'Thank heaven.'

Alba sagged a little. When she rested her head against his chest, Inigo felt a sharp pain. Longing. And fear. He was still caressing her arms, he couldn't seem to stop. Since she made no objection, he went on doing it. He was uncomfortably aware he was no longer certain whom he was comforting, Alba or himself.

Was she in danger?

'That poor man,' she said, voice shaking.

'King Henry's Guard will investigate.'

Alba didn't move away. Small fingers were

weaving in and out of her hair, the child seemed to have forgotten whatever horrors she'd seen in her father's workshop. Eventually, Alba raised her head and stepped back.

'Thank you, my lord, I feel calmer.'

Inigo's hands dropped to his sides. Only then did he notice that his sword lay on the floor, he must have dropped it when he had helped her out of her hiding place. Saints, what this woman did to him. Hastily, he retrieved it.

She stroked the little girl's cheek and gently extricated her hair from her grasp.

'It's a mercy you came so quickly, my lord. A thousand thanks.'

He bowed. 'You are most welcome.'

She gave him a straight look. 'I apologise for my weakness. I don't care for confined spaces. And I don't like the dark.'

And I don't like not knowing you are safe.

Inigo smiled. 'Think nothing of it, my lady.'

He stood back and allowed the Princess to precede him out of the chamber.

The goldsmith's workshop was in uproar. Half of Córdoba seemed to be crowded round the scarred workbench and everyone was shouting.

'That man out there is dead! Dead, I tell you.'

'He's the King's man.'

The goldsmith groaned. 'There'll be the devil to pay.'

'The King's man?' A woman crossed herself. 'God help us.'

'Enough!' Inigo spoke sharply. Waving the townsfolk to one side, he fixed the goldsmith with a hard stare. 'The King's man, Domingo?'

'Yes, my lord.' The goldsmith looked past Inigo to where Alba was standing, child in arms and his face softened. 'You have her safe. Thank you, my lady. I'll take her.'

Alba handed the girl to her father. Everybody was watching. Inigo scowled, there were far too many people in here. He gestured at the door.

'I need to speak to Domingo, the rest of you— out.'

They filed out, muttering, and Alba gave him a questioning glance. Oddly, it was at that moment that Inigo realised that it was no use constantly reminding himself to use her title whenever he thought of her. Some time that morning Princess Alba had become too dear to him for formality. However, when addressing her, he ought to use the expected mode of address.

'Not you, my lady.'

Inigo didn't want Alba out there with a cut-throat on the loose. She'd witnessed a murder, she could be in danger. Until he was certain that the man had fled the area, he wasn't going to let her out of his sight.

When the workshop door closed, Inigo gave the goldsmith a direct look. 'Domingo, what's this about?'

Domingo hugged his daughter and bit his lip. 'Well, my lord...'

Light from an open shutter slanted across the workbench. The goldsmith gestured at a small pot. A clutch of seed pearls was nestled inside and next to the pot lay a curl of gold leaf.

'I was working on a special commission for King Henry, my lord.'

Inigo stiffened. 'Go on.'

'It was a Book of Hours.'

'Was?'

'It's been stolen. The scribes and bookbinder had done their part, I was embellishing the cover with jewels and my work was almost done when someone burst in. He was quick. Before I could turn, I was hit on the head.' Domingo smiled faintly at Alba. 'The next thing I knew this lady appeared. My lady, my apologies if I made little sense, my head was reeling and all I could think of was that Marta must be safe.'

'There is no need to apologise, I quite understand,' Alba said softly.

Domingo touched a fingertip to his daughter's

small nose. 'Truth be told, I was too dazed even to think of the book. The King's man had been told when to collect it, poor fellow.' His mouth turned down. 'With his death on my doorstep, I don't suppose I shall be given such a commission again.'

'You're the best goldsmith in Córdoba, I am sure you will,' Inigo said.

The latch rattled and a young woman rushed in, her face was the colour of chalk.

'Domingo, your head! Marta, my love, are you all right? Oh, Domingo.'

'This is my wife, my lord.'

While Domingo's wife fussed over the goldsmith and their daughter, Inigo transferred his attention to Alba. He spoke softly, for her ears alone. 'You saw the murderer clearly?'

'Quite clearly, my lord.'

'And he saw you?'

'I am certain of it.'

Madre mía, if the assassin saw Alba again, he would want her silenced. Someone reckless enough to kill the King's man wouldn't hesitate to kill again. Alba needed to be taken to a place of safety. Furthermore, the death of the King's envoy must be reported to the Captain of the Guard at the Alcázar. Rodrigo, in his capacity as Commander of the Córdoban garrison, would also have to be told.

And then there was Princess Leonor.

Dear Lord, complexity was piling up upon complexity. The Nasrid Princesses were triplets, and they were said to be identical. If the assassin mistook Lady Leonor for Alba, she too could be in grave danger. Inigo's mind raced. He had seen Lady Leonor from a distance, and he knew the Princesses were similar in looks, but he couldn't say whether they truly were identical.

'My lady, you and your sisters—how similar are your features?'

'We are identical.'

Inigo grimaced. 'I must contact Rodrigo without delay,' he said. 'It's a mercy Princess Constanza didn't come to Córdoba as well.'

'My lord?'

'My lady, you witnessed the murder of King Henry's man. I have no wish to alarm you, but we need to get you somewhere safe.'

Her cheeks paled. She wasn't stupid, she understood what he wasn't saying.

'I would like to see Leonor,' she said.

'In good time, my lady.'

With a murderer loose in Córdoba, there was no way in hell Inigo was going to allow her to see her sister. It was far too dangerous. He would send a message to Rodrigo, explaining what had happened and alert him to the possibility that Lady Leonor too might be in danger.

In the meantime, Inigo had an urgent report for the Captain at the garrison. And as sole witness to the murder of the King's man, Alba would have to go with him.

'My lady, I shall need your help. Would you accompany me while I report to the Captain at the garrison?'

She glanced fearfully towards the door. 'You want me to describe what happened out there?'

'Please. If it makes you uncomfortable to speak to the Captain, I can do most of the talking.'

'That will not be necessary. My lord, I saw the assassin quite plainly. He had dark eyebrows and a hawklike nose. He was wearing a hood.'

'Aye, I saw he was hooded.' Inigo lowered his voice, though it proved unnecessary as, with a brief 'Excuse us, my lord', the goldsmith and his family drifted into the living quarters. 'My lady, what else did you see?'

'His gait was awkward, he was bow-legged, I think.'

'Anything else?'

'His sword caught my eye, it was most remarkable. I believe it was forged in Toledo.'

Lord Inigo's eyes widened. 'Toledan steel, eh? Now that I didn't see. Are you certain?'

Her chin lifted. 'My father the Sultan has a collection of swords, he is very proud of it. The star in his collection has similar markings. Toledan swords have distinctive hilts.'

'They do indeed. Thank you, my lady, that is most helpful.'

Black eyes held his. 'I wonder you didn't notice that yourself, my lord.'

Inigo felt his cheeks warm. 'I was too busy chasing after you to notice much else.'

She nodded. 'My lord, do you think my father could be involved?'

'I doubt it, this appears to touch on the commission the King gave Domingo. Unfortunately, with the murderer getting a clear sight of you, that doesn't help us.'

'Or Leonor.'

'Exactly. That is why I shall be writing to Rodrigo. He needs to know what has happened, so that he can ensure no harm comes to your sister.' He crooked his arm at Alba. 'Come, my lady. Let us make our report at the garrison.'

And God help me if I run into Margarita with Alba on my arm.

Chapter Ten

Mercifully, presenting Sir Gui García, the Captain of the Guard, with a report proved relatively painless. Alba spoke clearly and concisely about what she had seen. Inigo was relieved when her word was accepted without question.

Afterwards, as Inigo escorted Alba to the antechamber over the garrison gatehouse, he found himself dwelling on the challenges facing him. Returning from Al-Andalus with a Nasrid princess was turning out to be fiendishly complicated. Given the fragile balance of power between Sultan Tariq of Granada and King Henry of Castile, Inigo had known that bringing a Nasrid princess into Spain was going to be a trial. He'd rescued her on impulse, and he ought to be returning to Falcon's Castle and his estates in Seville. Yet he could hardly abandon her in Córdoba. He needed to know she was safe.

Other problems were demanding Inigo's attention. His own estate aside, Sir Nicolás had warned him that Crown Revenues from the city of Seville had fallen short. King Henry would want an explanation, he would be relying on Inigo to investigate.

As for that unfortunate meeting with Sir Pero in the market—Sir Pero's reaction to Alba had made it plain that he believed Inigo and Alba to be lovers.

Had Sir Pero told Margarita that her betrothed had returned from Granada? Had he mentioned Alba? Inigo's nostrils flared. His reunion with Margarita was going to be devilishly tricky and the timing—with Alba in the Alcázar garrison—was impossible.

His mouth twisted. Irony was piling on irony. The safest place for Alba—the Alcázar—was the self-same place that presently housed his betrothed.

He had to tell Margarita about Alba. Not to do so would be to insult his betrothed and jeopardise their future together.

Would Margarita accept his word that nothing untoward had happened between him and the Princess? Save for that weak moment in Domingo's house when Inigo had comforted her, he'd only ever touched her out of necessity. His behaviour had been exemplary.

He gave Alba a sidelong glance and a twist of longing tightened inside. He'd never felt anything like it. Was this the lure of forbidden fruit? It must be.

By the time they had finished with the Captain, Inigo had concluded that frankness was the best policy. With luck, Alba would agree to remain in the antechamber while he spoke to his betrothed.

'My lady, while we were at the market I had news concerning Lady Margarita, my fiancée. She has arrived in Córdoba.'

Dark eyes met his and a shiver of regret went through him. Regret? Inigo had no business feeling regretful—he had been betrothed to Margarita long before he'd met Alba.

'Lady Margarita will need to speak to you,' Alba said calmly. 'Is she residing in the Alcázar?'

'Aye. My lady, would you be so good as to wait for me here? You will be quite safe, I assure you. I will return as soon as I may.'

Her smile was gracious. 'Of course, my lord. I shall await your return.'

Heaving a thankful sigh, Inigo gestured at a side table where a jug of wine and half a dozen cups were laid out ready for guests. A small bell stood next to the jug. 'My lady, Sir Gui is in the chamber below. Should you want for anything, that bell will summon him.'

'Thank you, my lord.'

Inigo bowed and went in search of his betrothed. His belly felt as though it was full of stones. Dread. He didn't want to see her. The very qualities that had once drawn him to Margarita—her coolness, that sense of distance—no longer attracted. Did he truly want to marry her? How could an arrangement that had once seemed logical and inevitable now feel like a death sentence?

He strode through a palace courtyard with the sun warm on his head, wondering at his change of heart. It had something to do with Lady Alba, meeting her had changed him. The idea of a cool and calm marriage had lost its allure.

Inigo's next thought robbed him of breath. Would Margarita release him from his betrothal vows?

She might. It wasn't a love match on either side, Inigo's father had arranged it. Given the proximity of the two estates, it was a sensible alliance. Margarita's brother Fernando was eager for the marriage to go ahead. What did Margarita herself think? Inigo was startled to realise he had no idea.

Dutiful. The woman was dutiful to her marrow. Did she even have feelings?

Upon enquiry, a guard told Inigo that Lady Margarita was in the water garden behind the palace. He went out on to the terrace. Yes, there she was, sitting with a couple of ladies in the shade of a cypress tree. He leaned against a pillar for a moment, silently watching her. Analysing what exactly it was that he felt. About her. About their betrothal.

Margarita looked exactly as she had always done. Calm. Unemotional. She was slightly paler than he remembered. Overall Inigo felt nothing, absolutely nothing. There was no lifting of his spirits. Only a dull feeling of dread and impending doom.

He was to tie himself to her for the rest of his life?

'It would be dishonourable to ask her to set me free,' he muttered as Margarita smiled quietly in response to something one of the ladies said.

What would Margarita say if he asked for their contract to be set aside? He truly did not know. She had lived for years in the knowledge that she was one day to be his bride. And he had no idea how she would react—about anything. It was an appalling indictment of their relationship. He ought to know what she would feel. And he didn't. He didn't want to make her unhappy, but he must know if she was willing to release him.

Inigo pushed away from the pillar, pinned a polite smile on his face and walked slowly towards her.

* * *

Alba didn't want refreshment. She wanted what she couldn't have.

Hollow inside, she glanced at the bell on the side table and then back at the door. By now, Count Inigo would be with his Lady Margarita. How would they greet each other? Would he take her in his arms? Would he kiss her?

Lord Inigo was, she was sure, an ardent, hot-blooded man. Yet he had told Alba that his forthcoming marriage was dynastic. It wasn't a union born of passion and Alba believed him. For a man like Lord Inigo that was very sad.

A reminiscent smile trembled on Alba's lips as she recalled Lord Inigo laughing and flirting with the farmer's daughters. There had been nothing in it and no harm done. In an odd way, it had been perfectly innocent. Lord Inigo had enjoyed those girls' company and they had enjoyed his.

Was his marriage to Lady Margarita to end all that? It didn't seem right. He'd have to kiss the woman. Would he enjoy it?

Her smile faded, and she found herself scowling at the hand bell. Lord Inigo was too honourable for his own good.

It was a shame he was set on marrying so quickly. If he hadn't been, perhaps Alba would have been able to persuade him to father her child. As matters stood, however…

He had refused to bed her, and Lady Margarita was here in Córdoba.

Alba wrapped her arms about her middle. Her mind felt muddled, she was conscious that she hadn't fully understood Spanish marriage customs. Lord Inigo had admitted to having had mistresses in the past. In Alba's view there was little to distinguish a married man with a mistress and one who was merely betrothed.

Lord Inigo seemed to think otherwise. This must touch on his honour. And honour, Alba was learning, meant much to him.

It was so confusing. The relief that had filled her when Lord Inigo had freed her from that cupboard had merely confirmed her feelings for him. When he'd put his arms about her, all fear had melted away. It had felt like stepping into Paradise when all he'd done was hold and comfort her. He'd ran his hands up and down her arms and dozens of pleasurable tingles had weakened her knees. A simple touch, yet it had meant so much.

She hadn't been wrong about Lord Inigo. If he hadn't made his rejection of her plain, she could quite easily have lain with him.

It wasn't to be. Lord Inigo was marrying Lady

Margarita. If Alba wanted a child, she must pursue another course. She must look elsewhere...

The Captain of the Guard, Gui García, was a handsome, well-made man. He'd been polite and reasonable. His smile was attractive.

A twinge of guilt had her biting her lip. Lord Inigo had expressly forbidden her to flirt with his men. Well, Lord Inigo was about to learn that he had no right of command over her. In any case, Captain García answered to Count Rodrigo, not to Lord Inigo.

Was the Captain married? Might he consider a brief affair?

There was only one way to find out. Alba stiffened her shoulders and rang the bell.

Almost immediately, heavy footsteps sounded outside. The door swung wide.

'Lady Alba.' The Captain bowed. 'May I be of assistance?'

'I hope so, Sir Gui.' Alba gestured at a pair of chairs. 'I was hoping we might talk.'

'Talk?'

Captain García's gaze flicked down her, top to toe. Alba was watching him keenly and she noted the heat that flared briefly in the back of his eyes. Confused blue eyes, she noticed, not laughing grey ones. He couldn't decide what to make of her. Alba's heart jumped about in her chest, that sudden heat had unnerved her.

Assuming calm, she drifted to the tray on the table and picked up a cup. 'Wine, sir?'

'Thank you, but no. My lady, I can't stay long, I have duties elsewhere. If you need company, I can ask the wife of one of my men to join you.'

That sounded as though the Captain wasn't married himself. That was good. Wasn't it? Alba was no longer so sure.

'There's no need to look so suspicious, sir. I merely mean to learn a little about you.'

The Captain's eyes narrowed. 'I see no reason for your interest. My lady, may I enquire who you are exactly?'

Alba's mouth dried. She daren't admit to being a Nasrid princess, what could she say? 'As you know, I am a…a friend of Count Inigo.'

His smile became suggestive. 'A friend. A friend who returns with Count Inigo from Al-Andalus. My lady, pray tell me what sort of friend you are. A friend who will be discarded when the Count marries? Perhaps you are in search of a new friend?' Captain García's smile vanished. 'Or is your presence in Córdoba more sinister? Lord Inigo recommended that the City Guard be increased. Are you responsible for that? I repeat, who are you?'

Alba's mouth dried. 'I am no threat, sir, I assure you. I merely want to…to discover if you…' Alba stuttered to a halt as the Captain stood before her. He was doing it again—eyeing her from head to toe.

He grinned. 'Lord Inigo is to marry soon. You are looking for a new protector.'

Large hands gripped her shoulders and without warning, his mouth flattened hers.

Alba stood like a statue as the Captain's mouth worked against hers. It felt brutal. She had hoped for an echo of the pleasurable tingles evoked by Lord Inigo's touch, and all she felt was an overwhelming impulse to tear herself away. It was hard to remain still.

The kiss—her first—was horrible. He was bruising her and what on earth was he doing with his tongue?

The Captain pulled back, frowning. 'Don't pretend innocence with me. Open your mouth.'

'Wh…what?'

Alba blinked up at him and he hauled her close. She was cold to her core. God save her, he was pushing his tongue into her mouth. He was shoving her veil aside, disordering her hair.

She jerked out of his hold and stepped back, panting, noting absently that he was equally breathless. If this was kissing, it was a repellent business. And if kissing was a prelude to…

'No. *No.*' She wiped her mouth with the back of her hand. 'My apologies, sir. I have made a terrible mistake.'

There was a brief silence, a silence in which Alba saw anger flare in the Captain's eyes.

'I am sorry, sir, truly sorry.'

Dreading that Captain García might chase after her, Alba stumbled to the door with one thought in mind. Lord Inigo, she must find Lord Inigo.

Recognising that extricating himself from his betrothal was best done out of earshot of the other ladies, Inigo had secured the use of a private chamber for his meeting with his betrothed. He'd no wish to embarrass her.

Opening the heavy door, he ushered Margarita inside. First, he must discover her true feelings. Did she want to marry him?

Margarita's face looked flat, it was expressionless even for her, and her eyes were dull. All in all, there was little sign of pleasure on her face, no hint that she was eager for their nuptials to take place.

Closing the door, Inigo bowed formally over her hand. 'It is a pleasure to see you, my lady.

I didn't dare hope that you would tear yourself away from Carmona. You look well.'

In truth, Inigo's last comment was a bald lie, Margarita's skin looked sallow. He knew she didn't enjoy travel—had the journey unsettled her?

Margarita drew her hand from his. 'Naturally I needed to see you, my lord.' Her gaze flickered briefly to his leg before fixing on his belt, she seemed to be having trouble meeting his gaze. 'I believe you were injured.'

'The wound festered for a while, but it has healed well.'

'I am glad.'

Inigo frowned. Modest as always, Margarita kept her gaze lowered. Had she always been so reluctant to look at him? He couldn't remember, although it was plain that she'd aged quite a bit. That shouldn't be surprising, it had been five years since they'd last met, he too must have aged.

Inigo frowned at the top of her head and racked his brains to remember the last time they'd spoken. Surely, she'd been livelier? More…forthcoming.

He kept his expression neutral as Alba's face took shape in his mind. Her black, gold-flecked eyes, sparkling with laughter, were all too easily summoned. And Alba's mouth, which was far more tempting than—

He cut off the tail of his thoughts. This was no good, if Margarita hoped to marry him, he must forget Alba. He—as a man of honour—ought not to break his betrothal.

However, it would be an entirely different case if Margarita no longer wanted him…

Alba. That sweet ache rushed back in full force. He needed heirs. Lord, it didn't help that Alba had asked him to give her a child. He mustn't think about that, even if the idea was beyond tempting.

Margarita's gaze lifted briefly before she resumed her contemplation of his belt buckle. 'My brother will be pleased to hear we have met, my lord,' she said in a dull and joyless voice. 'He is anxious for our union to take place as soon as possible.'

Icy fingers danced across Inigo's neck. Margarita looked listless and depressed, and the mismatch between her words and her manner was profoundly worrying. His gut was telling him in no uncertain terms that she wanted this marriage no more than he did.

Gently, he put his finger under her chin and raised her head, the better to read her expression.

'And you, my lady? Are you as eager for us to exchange our vows as Baron Fernando?'

Her mouth worked. Why was it so hard for her to look him straight in the face? She'd never been this shy before.

She gave a bright, brittle smile. 'Of course, my lord. I am looking forward to our wedding with all my heart.'

Margarita shifted to free herself and looked away. And at that moment, the thing that Inigo had been dreading happened.

The door groaned open.

Alba stood on the threshold. Her veil was askew, and her hair disordered. Giving a swift glance over her shoulder, she shut the door smartly behind her and blinked at him. Her breath was coming fast.

'Lord Inigo, a thousand apologies for this intrusion,' she said.

Margarita's eyes widened. For once, she met his gaze directly. 'Who is this lady, my lord?'

Never had Inigo felt so torn. Alba looked so distressed, it took a supreme effort of will not to enfold her in his arms.

'Margarita, this is Lady Alba,' he managed. 'Lady Alba, this is Lady Margarita Marchena de Carmona. My betrothed.'

Even as he introduced them, Inigo was conscious that Alba, as a princess, outranked Margarita. By rights Inigo should have introduced

Margarita to the Princess rather than the other way around. He couldn't do it. Much as he wanted to be open with Margarita, until he knew that Alba was safe in Castile, her identity must remain secret.

Margarita dipped into a curtsy, and Alba returned it. Other than that, the two women's reactions to each other were very different. Alba was quick to recover her poise. Her expression was open and curious. Frankly interested. Margarita, after that first startled moment, pursed her lips. Dear heaven, he'd intended to tell Margarita how Alba came to be with him, and he was grimly aware this wasn't the way to go about it.

'Lady Alba?' Margarita's eyebrows lifted. Unspoken questions hung in the air. Who are you? Margarita's eyes were asking. What are you to Lord Inigo?

He and Alba were walking a tightrope. If word about her parentage got out, she could be in grave danger.

Her father, Sultan Tariq, regularly broke peace accords with the Spanish Crown. The Sultan moved heaven and earth to avoid paying the tribute he owed to Castile. His troops made regular and violent incursions beyond his borders, they captured Spanish noblemen like Inigo and Rodrigo so that their estates could be milked for ransom money. Ransom which the Sultan then deigned to pay back to the Spanish crown as tribute.

Alba could quite easily become an object of loathing. She might be attacked, imprisoned...

Margarita swallowed. 'Where did you meet?'

'Lady Alba and I met on the road.'

Alba nodded agreement. 'I had suffered an... an accident. Count Inigo was kind enough to lend aid.'

Inigo let out a breath he hadn't known he'd been holding. Thank the Lord, Alba had followed his lead. He narrowed his gaze on her. She must know that interrupting his discussion with Margarita would cause untold difficulties.

He'd left her safely in the garrison not half an hour since. What had happened? Her mouth looked bruised. Inigo focused on a tangled skein of black hair. Someone had touched her. Worse, they had frightened her. He gritted his teeth. How dare they?

Alba's voice broke through his anger. 'Lady Margarita, I was indeed fortunate to meet Lord Inigo. He is the most gallant of men. I dread to think what could have happened if he hadn't saved me.'

'Gallant?' Margarita's eyebrow lifted. Her tone was dry. Disbelieving. 'Of course.'

Inigo's jaw tightened and shame washed over him. For the first time it occurred to him that his betrothed knew of his reputation with women and didn't care for it. Margarita had been so aloof he could have sworn that what he did before they were married didn't matter a whit.

Had he misjudged her? Still, she must know that once they were married—if they married—dalliance with other women would stop. Inigo had seen first-hand how faithlessness could wreck a good marriage and he had no intention of repeating his father's mistakes. Margarita must understand that.

His betrothed inclined her head and gave him the thinnest of smiles.

'And so I bid you good day, my lord. It has, as always, been an enlightening meeting. I shall inform my brother you have arrived, he will be arranging our nuptials.'

Margarita swept from the chamber, leaving in her wake a heavy silence.

'Lady Margarita is very angry,' Alba murmured.

Inigo grimaced. 'I think you are in the right. I had no idea she cared.'

Alba frowned thoughtfully at a scroll on the steward's desk. 'She wants to be loved, poor thing. She doesn't realise she's looking in the wrong place.' Her tone lightened. 'I hoped for love once.'

'What are you saying?'

Alba shrugged. 'Men…women—I have seen how love between them is impossible.'

Inigo let out a short laugh. 'It's rare, I'll grant you, but it can happen. When they were young, my parents, God rest them, loved each other with a passion.'

A dark eyebrow lifted. 'I can tell from your tone that their love died.'

'I am not certain.'

'What happened?'

'Pepita happened,' Inigo said.

'Pepita?'

'Pepita is my half-sister.'

Alba's brow wrinkled. 'Explain, if you please. Also, it would help if I knew your parents' names.'

'My father was Count Javier and my mother Countess Elena. In the beginning they were inseparable. They laughed together and cried together. They had no secrets and their marriage appeared perfect. And then came the day when Father brought a small child to Falcon's Castle.'

'That is your castle in Seville?'

'Aye. The child's name was Pepita. Father told my mother everything. He'd had a brief affair with a widowed noblewoman and Pepita was the result.'

'Countess Elena found that hard to forgive.'

'That is an understatement. Pepita's arrival turned the household upside down. Father insisted he had never stopped loving Mamá, but she was never the same after that.'

Alba stepped closer, dark eyes full of concern. 'This upsets you a great deal. It is why you are determined to have only children who are legitimate.'

Throat tight—even though this was ancient history—Inigo nodded. 'My mother became a ghost of her former self. Father was desperate to make it up to her. They decided to go on a voyage to visit a cousin in Mallorca. Father pinned his hopes on the journey, he was determined to win Mother back. I fear that he failed, though I shall never know for sure. All that voyage did was cause yet more misery.' With an effort, he roused himself, he was getting maudlin. 'My apologies, I haven't spoken of this in years.'

'My lord, as a friend, there is no need to apologise. What happened?'

Inigo became conscious that Alba was touching his hand. He wished she wouldn't, it made him want to entwine his fingers with hers. He cleared his throat. 'There was a storm at sea and the ship foundered. All lives were lost.'

Her breath caught. 'Your parents drowned? That is very sad.' Then her voice strengthened and took on a sharp edge. 'Count Javier sounds like my father.'

Inigo went rigid. 'My father was nothing like yours. Nothing.'

'You are mistaken, my lord. My father the Sultan insists he loved my mother—the only woman he chose to make his Queen—yet he has always maintained a large harem. Even while Mamá was alive he visited his concubines.' She shrugged. 'Like it or not, our fathers sound very similar. You are betrothed, yet by your own admission, you have enjoyed other ladies. You do not love Lady Margarita.'

There was no answer to that, Inigo didn't love Margarita, he never had. That didn't mean a union between them couldn't be successful. Love wasn't necessary to produce an heir.

Alba sighed. 'It is the way of men. Men love power and politics and little else. You marry to fall in with your father's plans. Your mother's mistake was to look for love in the wrong place. She should have looked to you.'

Inigo's eyebrows lifted. 'To me?'

'The bond between a mother and child is one

of love. You loved your mother once, I am sure. That is why you mourn her.'

Inigo almost choked. 'I love her still.'

Her eyes widened. 'Do you, my lord?'

She was standing so close, Inigo could see the gold flecks in her eyes. He rubbed his face. He found her responses baffling and not a little confusing. Of course, he loved his mother, how could she think otherwise?

She directed a frown at the door. 'My lord, Lady Margarita is desperately unhappy.'

Here Inigo agreed, though Alba's insight disconcerted him. 'How the devil did you work that out? You've never met her before.'

'I can see she is distressed that you brought me back with you. There is something else though, her eyes were shadowed.'

'I agree her manner was extremely subdued.' Not to mention that Margarita had refused to meet his eye and the very tenor of her voice spoke of a woman who was being browbeaten in some way. It was obvious, now he thought about it.

'I wonder if your lady is being forced into this marriage,' Alba said slowly. 'Is her brother a violent man?'

'He has a temper, though I've never seen signs of violence towards his sister.' Inigo swore under his breath. Coercion, however, was a distinct possibility. Was the Baron forcing Margarita to marry him? If so, would she agree to Inigo reneging on their betrothal agreement? His heart lifted, and it was as though the world was suddenly filled with light.

'My lady, I beg you to excuse me, it seems I must have words with Fernando Marchena.'

A dark tress trembled as she shook her head. 'I wouldn't do that.'

He threw her a puzzled look. 'Alba—my lady—I will not have Margarita coerced into marriage.'

'You mistake me, my lord, of course not. However, it might be best if I spoke to Lady Margarita first. Her brother could be using violence against her. If so, a discussion with you is likely to make matters worse.'

Bemused, Inigo looked down at her. The gentle touch of her fingers on his, subtle though it was, had him almost entirely at her command. Almost.

'Sweet Mary, you cannot be that naive. Margarita already suspects you are my mistress, if she discovers who you really are, it would be disastrous.' When the Princess opened her mouth, he ignored it. 'My lady, if you care not for your own safety, think of your sister. Lady Leonor might come to harm.'

She hesitated, eyes pensive. 'Very well, my

lord. I shall take your advice, though I think it's a pity. Lady Margarita needs a friend.'

'Rest assured, I shall speak to her,' Inigo said. Realising that at some point he had inadvertently laced his fingers with hers, he released her. 'Why did you leave the garrison? I asked you to stay put.'

Her chin lifted. 'I don't take orders well.'

He lifted an eyebrow. 'That is an understatement.' Resisting the urge to touch that wayward curl, he gestured at her veil. 'What happened?'

'I was foolish, that is all.'

'What did you do?'

Fixing her dark gaze on the wall behind him, very much as Margarita had done earlier, she shrugged. 'Nothing much.'

'My lady, I asked you to wait for me and you tear in here as though a troop of demons are at your heels. I repeat, what happened?'

Deep colour washed into her cheeks. 'I did something stupid. It won't happen again.'

She was fiddling with her girdle, she looked nervous and edgy. Guilt? Suddenly, he had it. No. *No.* She could not be that foolish or that innocent. 'You asked someone to give you a child.'

She flushed. 'No! Not exactly. My lord, I... I merely asked for help.'

He pulled her hands from her girdle and enfolded them in his. 'There's more to it than that. Pray continue.'

'I asked a man if I could get to know him.'

'And?'

She looked at him then, eyes troubled. 'He misunderstood. He thought I was asking to become his...his...'

'He kissed you, didn't he?' Inigo was overwhelmed by rage. That would explain her dishevelment and her bruised mouth. Whoever he was, he'd mauled her. Hurt her. 'Who was it?'

'Since I am entirely to blame, I shall not tell you,' she said, voice wavering.

Shaken by the depth of his anger, Inigo turned aside. He felt like punching a hole in the wall. After a few steadying breaths, he turned back to her. 'You are not seriously hurt?'

She shook her head. 'Other than feeling rather stupid, no. My lord, I am sorry to be such a trouble.'

'What were you thinking?' Inigo paced about the chamber. Should he have anticipated this? He'd known the Princess longed for a child. Even so, never in a thousand years would he have anticipated that she would march up to a total stranger in order to discover whether he would fulfil her desires. The combination of boldness and naivety took his breath away. 'You were attempting seduction, weren't you?'

'Lord Inigo!'

'Be honest, my lady.'

She stared at the floor. 'I wanted to see if he might suit.'

Inigo swore. 'You aren't fit to be left on your own. My lady, you must take care.'

'I will.' She swallowed. 'It was a huge mistake. It was horrible.'

'What was?'

'His kiss.' She shuddered. 'I didn't know what to expect. I certainly had no idea his touch would be so repellent.'

A little of Inigo's rage ebbed away. 'You didn't like it.'

'No.'

She shrugged, an attempt at nonchalance that didn't fool him. The man had truly upset her.

'It made my flesh creep. To be honest, my lord, I was surprised at how strongly he repelled me.'

He looked at her through narrowed eyes. 'Oh?'

She bit her lip. 'You see, when you touch me, I quite like it. I… I delight in your touch.'

Inigo felt a sudden flare of heat which, for his sanity, he tried to ignore. 'My lady, you should not speak in this way.'

'My apologies if I have embarrassed you. But

there it is. I enjoy your touch. Unfortunately, I imagined it would be the same with another man. Since love between men and woman is an impossibility, I thought that—how can I put this?—mutual attraction was assured if one wanted to go about getting a child.'

'Lord save us, you can't go around propositioning every man you meet.'

She scuffed the floor with the toe of her shoe. 'I didn't get that far.'

'That is a mercy. My lady, you are a danger to yourself.'

'Never fear, I've learned my lesson. I am thoroughly embarrassed, and I would be grateful if you didn't pursue this.'

'Very well, my lady, on one condition.'

'And that is?

'From now on you will keep your promise to behave. You will leave the King's knights alone. There will be no more propositioning.'

'Very well, my lord, I agree.'

He looked at her downbent head, wishing he could believe her. 'My lady, there are many dangers in Córdoba, and it would seem that you are your own worst enemy.'

'I am very sorry, my lord. I have no wish to repeat the experience, believe me.' She shuddered and lifted her gaze to his. 'I had no idea kissing would be so repugnant.'

A hot surge of want and jealousy ripped through Inigo. He'd wanted to kiss the Princess himself and thus far he'd managed to resist. He knew he ought to change the subject, yet that seemed impossible, he had to know more. He cleared his throat.

'It was your first kiss?'

It was a ridiculous question, given he already knew the answer. Of course it had been her first kiss. The Princess had lived in a gilded cage. There would have been no opportunity for dalliance.

'I thought it would be pleasant.'

Her voice was so soft he barely heard her. Unable to help himself, he moved closer, stopping when he stood mere inches from her. He could feel the warmth of her body, pulling him in.

'Pleasant, my lady?'

Black eyes held his. Inigo was entirely in her thrall.

'How else are babies made? It starts with a kiss, does it not?' She gave a pretty shrug. 'I thought kissing must be pleasant.'

Inigo grimaced. 'Sadly, that is not always the case.'

She sighed. 'To be sure, Inés did mention that

sometimes men force themselves on women. I should have remembered it. You made me forget.'

'I?'

'My lord, when you touch me, I feel warm inside. Nervous, yet content. It is most pleasant.' Her expression was puzzled. 'Since we rode away from Father, you have touched me many times. When we were riding, when we were at the farm. And this morning, when you pulled me out of that horrible cupboard, you held me. I liked it, very much. I assumed that kissing another man would evoke a similar response.'

Inigo's throat dried. All he could see was her sweet face, turned trustingly to his. He could see her confusion. And more than that. Her eyes were huge. So black, with those bright flecks dancing in their depths. He saw hope. And longing. And, though it was possible that all he was seeing was the reflection of his own desire, Inigo could swear she wanted him.

Thought left him, he moved without it. One hand reached up to cup her face, the other rested gently on her hip. He pulled her close. There was no resistance. Only those wonderful gold-flecked eyes, mirroring his every desire. And that body, lissom and lithe, leaning softly against him.

She let out a soft breath. Slowly, giving her

every chance to draw back, Inigo covered her mouth with his.

Warm, welcoming lips softened beneath his. She gave a sensual murmur and her body melted against him. Inigo tightened his hold and deepened the kiss. Her mouth opened. Their tongues met and played, and Inigo's knees weakened, something which had never happened to him before. An alarm rang in the back of his mind. This was dangerous. Wrong. He forced himself to draw back.

Alba whimpered and reached for his head, pulling him to her. When their lips met again, her moan of pleasure drew an answering groan from him.

He drew back, he had to. Her eyes were closed, she opened them and he leaned his forehead against hers.

'This must stop.' His voice was rusty, it sounded as though he hadn't spoken in an age. 'We cannot go on.'

She nodded and stroked his cheek, a wistful smile playing at the edge of her mouth. Her veil was even more disordered than it had been when she had run through that door. Her lips were pink from his kiss, and she was smiling. Lightly, she touched his mouth, it felt like a blessing.

'Thank you, my lord. I knew that kissing you

would transport me. You need not fear I shall approach anyone else.'

Inigo found himself groping for words. He shouldn't have kissed her. All it had done was make him want even more. And to see her gazing up at him, all starry-eyed…

With an effort he released her.

'No, don't say it,' she muttered, on a heavy sigh. 'My lord, I accept that, beautiful though it was, that kiss changes nothing. You are promised to Lady Margarita.'

Inigo felt as though he'd been pierced through the heart. He had never met anyone like her. Nor had he, an insidious voice said quietly, met a woman he wanted more.

Chapter Eleven

Mind in disarray, Inigo gave Alba a tight smile, placed her hand formally on his arm and led her to the door.

'Where are we going, my lord?'

'Back to the town house. I ought to speak to Margarita again, but that will have to wait. I don't want you wandering about on your own.'

She hung her head, apparently chastened. Inigo wasn't fooled, a ghost of a smile trembled at the edge of her lips.

'Irrepressible,' he muttered.

'My lord?'

Inigo didn't trust himself to reply and they passed through the gates of the Alcázar and out into the streets.

He really must order his mind. First, Margarita…

The idea that Baron Fernando might be forcing Margarita into marriage was discomforting and—Inigo glanced at Alba—painfully tantalising. Yet he could hardly seek a second meeting with his betrothed with Alba on his arm. As far as Margarita was concerned, careful reflection was needed. She would, for the time being, come to no harm.

Next, the Princess…

Alba was disconcertingly innocent. She wasn't to blame, but she needed protecting from herself. Who had she propositioned? If it weren't so disturbing, it might be amusing. Inigo found himself suppressing a smile. The poor fellow probably didn't know what had hit him.

His humour faded. If only that were the sum of their problems. A man had been murdered and Alba had witnessed it. Initially, Inigo had assumed the murderer was an opportunist thief. However, the victim had been the King's man and a valuable Book of Hours had been stolen. Everything had to have been carefully planned. Most worryingly, the murderer had seen Alba, which meant that neither she nor Princess Leonor were safe.

Who was behind it? Where were they? Was it possible Sultan Tariq was involved?

Inigo's skin prickled and, without thinking, he covered Alba's hand with his.

Did her father's reach extend to Córdoba? No, no, that was surely not possible.

It was one thing for the Sultan to declare his daughters banished in a letter to Rodrigo Álvarez, quite another for him to steal a book destined for King Henry of Castile.

Lord Inigo drew Alba swiftly through the side streets and no sooner had they reached the fountained courtyard of his town house than Sir Nicolás was hurrying towards them, his brow furrowed.

Alba had been smiling ever since Lord Inigo had kissed her—she had known it would be wonderful. One look at Sir Nicolás, and she felt her smile waver.

'My lord,' Sir Nicolás said, 'when you have concluded your business with Lady Alba, I crave your attention.'

Alba kept her expression steady. She and Lord Inigo would be parting soon and though she regretted it, she must not show it. She dipped into a curtsy.

'Doubtless your estates need much attention. Please excuse me, my lord.' A strong hand caught her elbow. It was the lightest of touches and despite her best efforts it had her heart leaping. 'My lord?'

Grey eyes smiled down at her. 'My lady, be so good as to pack clothes for a stay in the country. Nothing opulent, you understand,' he said, walking with her into the cool of the stairwell. 'We shan't be staying in a palace.'

Over Lord Inigo's shoulder Alba saw Sir Nicolás's frown deepen, disapproval was writ large on his face.

'Where are we going?'

'Count Rodrigo's hunting lodge. He rarely uses it, it's rather out of the way, which is why it's ideal.' Lord Inigo lowered his voice. 'I should warn you, it's very basic. Pack as little as possible, you will have two saddlebags, no more. Oh, and be so good as to change that gown for something to ride in.'

'I am to have my own horse?'

'Of course. Please hurry.'

'I understand. Will we travel alone?'

'Not entirely. I'll be posting a contingent of guards along our route, they will be on the lookout for anything unusual.'

'You are thinking of the assassin?'

'I am taking precautions. There is also your father to consider.'

Alba stared at her feet. 'I am a great nuisance, my lord, I am truly sorry.'

'It is my pleasure to see you safe,' he said.

He sounded sincere and when Alba looked up, his eyes were still smiling.

'My lady, I'll also be sending Guillen to Rodrigo with a message about this morning's events. Guillen will join us at the lodge when he has Rodrigo's reply.'

At the foot of the stairs, Lord Inigo bowed over her hand. 'I'll wait for you in my office.'

Fired up by his sense of urgency, Alba hurried up to her bedchamber. A painted chest at the foot of the bed held the gowns and cloaks Lady Raquel had lent her. She was busily sifting through them when a maidservant appeared with the saddlebags.

Shortly after that, the maidservant carried the saddlebags down the stairs and led Alba to Lord Inigo's office. The maid rapped at the door.

'Enter.'

The maid deposited the saddlebags on the floor and retreated. Lord Inigo was writing at his desk and Guillen stood at his right hand. There was no sign of Sir Nicolás. As Alba entered, Inigo set the quill aside and pushed to his feet.

'You've perfect timing, my lady, I've finished. Here, Guillen.' He sanded the letter, rolled it into a scroll and sealed it. 'There you are, lad, off with you. Take that straight to Rodrigo, he alone must read it.'

'Understood.'

'Be sure to wait for a response. When you have it, you know where to find us.'

'Aye, my lord.' Guillen tucked the letter into his tunic.

Alba watched the squire go. 'My lord, you did warn Count Rodrigo that the assassin may mistake Leonor for me? He will watch out for my sister?'

'I did warn him, and I am sure of it.'

Inigo delayed their departure long enough for them to eat a simple meal and they were on the road soon after, several guards and a sumpter mule in tow.

His mind remained a mess, conflicting urges were fighting each other. He was concerned for Margarita. When he had Alba safely hidden at Rodrigo's lodge, he must return to Córdoba and speak to his betrothed. At the same time, he would reassure himself that Rodrigo had heeded his warning concerning the assassin. Alba would never forgive him if Princess Leonor came to harm.

He glanced across at Alba, guilty tension tightening his shoulders. How was it that she had become a priority? By rights, he should be on his way to Seville, not seeing to the safety of a runaway princess.

Sir Manuel's report from Seville had unsettled Nicolás. The shortfall in revenues was certainly a concern and as tenant-in-chief of the County of Seville, Inigo was honour-bound to head an enquiry. As soon as he could, he would investigate. Inigo's personal estates lay slightly out of town. Thankfully, they were in good order despite his enforced absence.

His gaze flickered to Alba and his troubles seemed to fade. His mind was filled with images of the future that could be theirs: the confidences, the laughter, the lovemaking...

She sat easily on the mare, a sweet grey that had reminded Inigo of the pony he'd glimpsed her riding in Al-Andalus. He'd spotted the mare at the horse fair and had bought her on a whim. When Alba leaned forward to croon in the grey's ear, Inigo knew he'd done the right thing.

Alba appreciated being in the saddle again, particularly since she had a horse to herself. She had learned to enjoy Lord Inigo's arms about her on their flight from the Alhambra, but this was far more comfortable, not to mention that it gave her the sense that she was in command of her life. It was exhilarating.

Because of the mule, which was laden with supplies, they travelled at an easy pace. At intervals, the guards fell back to take up posts along the route. By the time Lord Inigo came to a halt at the top of a small rise, Alba and he were on their own with their horses and the mule.

Alba found herself looking down at an unpretentious wooden building flanked by tall cypresses. A thin stream meandered downhill, appearing and disappearing at random among the stones at the side of the track. Goodness, was this Count Rodrigo's hunting lodge? It was smaller than she had expected. The door was shut, and no smoke was winding out of the roof. In short, there was no sign of life.

She raised an eyebrow. 'That's the Count's hunting lodge?'

Lord Inigo grimaced. 'I did warn you.'

'I think you said it was basic.' She laughed. 'Well, that is certainly true. Where are the caretakers? It seems completely deserted.'

'There are no caretakers.'

'That door looks solid, how will we get in?'

Face lightening into a grin, Lord Inigo patted his scrip. 'Rodrigo gave me a key years ago.'

Alba looked doubtfully back at the lodge. The roof was thatched with reed, although a small hole was visible on one side. 'And if it rains in the night?'

'We shall choose our sleeping space with care.' He sighed. 'My apologies, my lady. I haven't been here in years.'

'Neither has Lord Rodrigo, by the look of it,' Alba said calmly, though his comment—we shall choose our sleeping space with care—held most of her attention. *We? We are to sleep together?* Half of her was thankful—the idea of resting alone in the wilds was alarming. It would be good to have him close. Yet if they slept together…

'My lady? What's the matter?'

Lord Inigo was watching her face and, judging from the amused glint in his eyes, he'd read her thoughts with embarrassing accuracy.

She flushed. 'Nothing, my lord, you did warn me. Lead on.'

Inigo's conscience stirred. It had been impossible to miss the look of surprise that had crossed Alba's face when she had realised they would be staying at the lodge on their own. He could have taken her somewhere more comfortable. Where there were servants. It was, after all, what she was used to. And, bearing in mind that he was a betrothed man with duties waiting for him in Seville, he should be washing his hands of her sooner rather than later. He couldn't do it. With a dangerous murderer on the loose, and Sultan Tariq making threatening noises, St Clare's Convent was out of the question.

There had been other options. Alba would be well guarded if she went to Castle Álvarez. Rodrigo was already caring for her sister, one more lady wouldn't be noticed in that vast keep. Yet the idea held little appeal. For some reason, Inigo was reluctant to allow Alba out of his sight. Besides, he was certain it wouldn't occur to anyone to look for her here. She was out of harm's way at Rodrigo's lodge. His guards would sound the alarm if they spotted any suspicious traffic on the roads. Further, with Alba tucked away in the wilds, the stray knights of the world would be safe from temptation. There would be no danger of Alba propositioning anyone else.

All Inigo had to do was keep her at a respectful distance. It shouldn't be hard.

They rode up to the lodge and her gaze flickered over everything—the stunted oaks, the dry goat tracks leading deep into the scrub, the lichen-covered bench beneath a cypress tree.

After they had dismounted, Inigo unstrapped their saddlebags and set them by the sun-bleached door.

'My lady, please hold the animals while I unburden the mule.'

Alba did as he asked and when the last bag sat

by the doorway, he took the animals' reins. 'I'll join you shortly, my lady.'

A dark eyebrow lifted. 'There's shelter for them here?'

'Aye, around the back.'

He reached into his purse for the key and handed it to her. As he led the animals away, he heard the rasp of the key being fitted to the lock and the click of the door latch. She was already exploring.

A wooden trough stood in the shade of the trees. The stream was little more than a dribble, so Inigo found a bucket and took time to draw water from the well. He left the animals hobbled under the trees and returned to see how Alba was faring in what, to her, must be dismal accommodation.

The lodge had been built in a time-hallowed manner, it was rectangular with a storeroom at one end and a central fire. Alba had dragged the saddlebags inside the door. She hadn't touched the shutters and shadows crowded in. Inigo went to the first shutter, slid it open and moved on to the next. The gloom lightened as he moved around the lodge, opening shutter after shutter.

There was no fireplace as such, merely a simple ring of stones to contain the flames and a spit which had been knocked over. An iron tripod stood to one side, next to a couple of blackened pots that had seen much service.

Alba bent over one of the cooking pots, touched it and frowned when her finger came away blackened with soot.

'We are to cook here, my lord?'

'Certainly.'

'What is this iron thing?' She indicated the tripod.

'It's for hanging pots on.' Coming across, Inigo nudged a cauldron with the toe of his boot. 'We can boil water in this or make soup.'

'And this?' She waved at the spit. 'What is its purpose?'

She was asking questions a child could answer and for the first time, Inigo recognised how at sea she must feel. The poor woman, she had been so cossetted, so hedged about, she didn't even know how to heat water. What had her father been thinking?

Inigo had known she was innocent, he'd known Sultan Tariq had told her nothing of the world outside the palace, even so he'd underestimated the extent of her ignorance. Keeping his face straight, he didn't want her to think he was mocking her, Inigo righted the spit. 'It's a spit, for roasting.

You turn it so. If I catch any game, we'll be sure to use it.'

'We?' She swallowed, and her face fell. 'My lord, you must know I've no knowledge of cooking.'

Her brow had puckered in a most endearing way. Quelling the urge to smooth the lines away, he said, 'I know how to cook.'

Her mouth fell open. 'What, a great lord like you?'

'In the field, a knight learns to fend for himself if he wants to survive. And don't forget, this is a hunting lodge, the area is teeming with game. I've brought cooked meat with us for our first night though. And cheese and olives. We won't starve while we settle in.'

That frown was still puckering her brow. Inigo wasn't certain what was worrying her the most, the fact that she might have to cook, or being alone with him.

'My lady.' He spoke gently. 'I trust you know you are safe with me.'

She glanced at his mouth and nodded. 'Yes, my lord.'

She still looked worried.

'Alb—' Swiftly he corrected himself. 'My lady, something is preying on your mind, what is it?'

A faint smile flickered across her lips. 'Apart from being carried off into the wilderness, you mean?'

He smiled back. 'Aye, apart from that.'

'I should like to see Leonor.'

'My lady, you shall see Leonor as soon as I am confident you are not in danger.'

He stepped closer and found himself wrestling with the ever-present urge to reach for her hands.

She looked about her, smile fading. 'I hope I don't disappoint you, my lord. I fear I am unsuited to this life.'

'Nonsense.' Inigo gave in, enfolded her hands in his, and his whole being was suddenly at ease. 'It's a matter of adapting, you're an intelligent woman, you can learn.'

And he, God save him, would enjoy teaching her. He eyed the bags at the doorway. A wooden bucket stood nearby, Inigo remembered using it on his last visit.

'My lady, we need to unpack our supplies before nightfall, but there's something you must learn first. Come with me. Be so good as to bring that bucket with you.'

Half expecting an explosion, for he doubted she had lifted a bucket in her life, Inigo led the way to the well.

He leaned against the housing and folded his

arms. 'I'd like you to fill that bucket with fresh water.'

'Why can't I fill it from the stream?'

'It's almost dry. In any case, water from the well is cleaner.'

She stared at the well and her foot tapped. Her eyes flashed. 'I don't understand the mechanism. My lord, I would far rather learn to cook.'

Inigo nodded. 'We shall come to that soon enough. I need to know that you can draw fresh water. If for any reason we are separated, you will have to survive on your own. Water comes before all else.'

'I understand,' she murmured, and the belligerence left her eyes. She turned her attention back to the well and bent to remove the cover. Carefully, she set it aside. 'I have seen servants operating a well, I am guessing that if I turn this handle so, another bucket will appear.'

Inigo watched her wind up the bucket.

She made a good job of it until the bucket reached the top, when she almost let it fall back as she slackened her hold on the handle. She was quick to get the knack of it though and was soon pouring water into the spare bucket.

Eyes alight with success, she picked up the full bucket. 'Shall I take this inside?'

'Aye, but there's something you've forgotten,' Inigo said.

She frowned at the well and set the bucket down. 'The well cover,' she murmured. 'I should put it back.'

'Very good, my lady. If an animal fell in, not only would it drown, it would also foul the water.'

He followed her back to the lodge. She only staggered once, although by the time she had set the bucket by the hearth, it was half full, and her gown was dark with spilled water.

'Oh, dear.' She brushed at her skirts. 'Never mind. My lord, that was most interesting. Will you teach me to cook next?'

Slowly Inigo shook his head. 'Not yet. The hearth needs cleaning. Then you will learn to set a fire.'

Inigo was dragging out pallets for them to sleep on when she finally leaned back on her heels.

'My lord, I've done it!'

In the centre of the hearth, a tiny flame flickered into life. She'd taken an age to get a spark from the flint, outside the light was fading. The important thing was that she had, in the end, done it unaided.

'That's it. Take care it doesn't go out. Feed in

the small twigs first, my lady, then gradually larger and larger ones.'

He hid a smile. Alba was so pleased with her efforts she remained on her knees at the hearth, staring proudly at the fire. The bodice of her dress was covered in ash, her hands were filthy and at some point she must have rubbed her cheek, it was streaked with soot. Strangely, she still managed to look beautiful.

Inigo cleared his throat. 'Once a good blaze is going, please fill that cauldron with some of the water. We need to wash before we sup.'

'Then we start cooking?' she asked, eagerly.

'No, my lady. The sun's almost down, what we need tonight is hot water.' He placed a bundle of candles on the table. 'Rodrigo used to keep glass lanterns in the storeroom. See if you can find them and light a few of these, would you? And while you're in there, you might like to consider how the storeroom should be ordered. It will be your responsibility while we are here.' He felt his lips twitch. 'I should warn you, it's probably dusty, it will need cleaning.'

Rising, she filled the cauldron with water and set it on the hook over the fire.

'Cleaning? Marvellous.' Her voice was dry and her face lit with mischief. 'Pray tell me, my lord, what are your duties to be?'

The idea that Alba apparently trusted him enough to tease him was warming, particularly given her sour relationship with her father and her belief that men were incapable of love or true affection. Inigo enjoyed teasing her, testing to see where her limits were. And she, apparently, enjoyed teasing him back. What a rare creature she was.

'I shall be hunting, my lady,' Inigo said blandly.

Her eyes narrowed. Rather to his surprise, she made no comment. She merely stalked to the table for the candles and swept, somewhat sootily, into the storeroom. He heard banging and thumping as she shifted things about.

When she emerged, she had the glass lanterns. She soon had them lit and disposed about the lodge. She spread her skirts in a mock curtsy.

'And now, my lord, what is your will?'

Inigo choked back a remark that would have been extremely inappropriate and nodded his head towards the fire. 'If the water's warm, we can wash. And then we shall eat.' He felt himself smile. He owned a castle and had vast estates; hundreds of soldiers and servants were his to command, and yet here, alone with Alba, just the two of them, he had never been happier.

'Very well. My lord?

'Mmm?'

'I have enjoyed today.'

Inigo felt his eyebrows rise. 'Even the household tasks?'

'Especially the household tasks.' She shrugged. 'It's clear I still have much to learn. My lord, this may sound odd, but I feel so much happier knowing how to draw water and light a fire. Without you, I wouldn't have known where to start. Thank you.'

'You are very welcome.' Inigo's heart warmed as he looked at her.

Alba's gown was sooty, her veil had been shoved into a corner, and her dark hair hung down her back, a tangle of glossy black silk. There was little sign of the Princess, yet she still drew him. The sense of connection he felt with her was extraordinary. She was so open, so honest. It was most engaging. She had been her own sweet self the entire day.

She smothered a yawn and looked ruefully at him. 'I must confess though, today has been a little tiring.'

Sunrise didn't see Inigo in the saddle, hunting for game. On the contrary, he found himself lingering at the lodge. He taught the Princess to tend to the animals, moving them into the shade and ensuring they had enough to eat and drink.

'Won't the horses need exercise?' she asked, when they had done.

'We shall ride later, if we have time.' Inigo stopped to stare up the track that led back to Córdoba. 'Guillen should be here soon.'

'You want Lord Rodrigo's opinion of what happened at the goldsmith's.'

'Just so. The game can wait. In any case, Guillen will bring us more in the way of supplies.'

The morning slipped by with Inigo teaching Alba to make flatbread. Somehow, her desire to learn to cook overrode his intentions of getting her to clean the storeroom. It didn't really matter. When Guillen arrived, he could do it.

He left her for a moment to go to the door to look up the track when he heard a smothered cry. He turned to see her nursing her right hand.

She'd burned herself. And her skirt was far too near that fire.

His blood went cold as the past rushed back at him, vivid as ever. The stables at Falcon's Castle were alight: Inigo could almost feel the heat; his lungs were choked by smoke; he could hear the shouting. The screams…

Heart thumping, he grabbed the water bucket and was at Alba's side in a trice. He twitched her skirt away from the fire and took her injured arm.

'Here, my lady.' He shoved her sleeve up and

thrust her hand into the cool water. 'Keep your fingers in until the pain eases.'

She did as she was told, her brow furrowed. Thank heaven, she didn't seem badly injured.

'Does it hurt?'

'It throbs a little, it startled me. I was turning the bread to see if it was cooked. I hadn't expected the heat to be so fierce.'

'Next time use the tongs.'

'I will.'

'And be sure to keep your feet well away from the edge of the fire. Many deaths have been caused by skirts catching alight.'

'Many deaths?' She tilted her head, her expression slightly puzzled. 'My lord, you've gone quite white.'

'Have I?' He watched her wriggling her fingers in the water. The burn really wasn't that bad. He willed himself to relax.

'Yes.' She paused, still staring at him. 'My lord, something happened to you. Something to do with fire.'

Her perceptiveness was startling. She drew her hand from the bucket and allowed Inigo to examine it, watching him all the while.

'It looks fine,' he said. 'No lasting damage.'

'Except my pride.' Her hand curled around his. 'My lord, won't you tell me what happened?'

Her jaw had a determined set to it, she wasn't going to let this drop. Releasing her hand, he sat back on his heels with a sigh. 'When I was a youth, there was a fire at Falcon's Castle.' He stopped, he hadn't thought about this in years, it was too painful. He gave her a direct look. 'My lady, I'd rather not go into this, if you don't mind.' He nodded towards the hearth. 'Can't you take it from me that fire is dangerous? Be careful.'

He pushed to his feet. Her eyes followed him and then she too rose. 'Someone died,' she murmured. 'My lord, I am truly sorry.'

And then, Inigo wasn't quite sure how it happened, he found himself talking, the whole appalling incident tumbled out, a grisly shambles of guilt and regret.

'A child died, a little girl and it was my fault.' He shoved his hand through his hair. 'I was a boy, we—the children in the household and I— had been playing hide and seek. A fire started in the stables. Lord knows how it started, but a groom lost his little sister. And my father's favourite mare was killed.'

The dark gaze watched him, unflinching. 'I take it you did not set the fire?'

'Of course not.'

'So how was it your fault?'

'We—the children—were overexcited. I should

have been in the armoury, cleaning weapons, but I wanted to play. So I roped everyone in. My game. My fault. It was fun at first. No one minded our game until a groom noticed his sister was missing. Then the fire started.' Inigo's mouth was dry, merely remembering. 'It was an inferno. Smoke filled the bailey, grooms and squires were falling over each other to save the horses. Alarm bells were ringing. My friends were screaming and crying. She'd been hiding in the hayloft, a tiny scrap of a girl whose only mistake had been to try to join in one of my stupid games.'

'You were a child yourself, my lord. You are too hard on yourself.'

'I was careless.'

'No, my lord. Even the son of a count needs time to play and make friends.' She sighed wistfully. 'I believe I have an inkling of what your childhood must have been like. My sisters and I had each other, we had Inés and our maidservants, but we learned not to make friends with anyone.'

Heavens, Alba's childhood sounded as lonely as his. A tendril of dark hair trembled on her breast. She moved closer, and all he could see was a pair of dark, long-lashed eyes filled with fellow feeling. 'I did have a friend once.'

'You too have known sorrow,' he said, lightly

touching her hand. He ached to draw her closer still, but he resisted. 'What happened?'

Her mouth was sad. 'I was particularly close with one of the maidservants. Her name was Beatriz.'

'Beatriz? Was she Spanish?'

'Aye, like Mamá, Beatriz was a captive. She was more playmate than maidservant. She was very spirited, too much so, as it happened.' Her eyes unfocused as she peered into the past. 'Beatriz was full of joy and energy. Irrepressible. She liked climbing trees and at first no one minded. Then I joined in and someone told my father.'

'You were beaten?'

Her eyes were full of anguish. 'No, my lord, it was worse than that. Beatriz vanished. One day she was there and the next—gone. We never saw her again. I begged and begged for someone to tell me what had happened. I was met with silence.'

Inigo stared. '*Dios mío*, what an appalling tale.'

Her chest heaved. 'It felt like a betrayal.'

'Who told your father? Inés?'

'I don't believe so. I asked her and she denied it. Years later she discovered that Beatriz went to work for a family in Granada. I trust Inés and have no reason to doubt her.' She gave a crooked smile. 'Anyway, after Beatriz vanished, I learned to tiptoe around Father's rules. We all did. My sisters have been my greatest blessing.'

Her expression lightened and she laid her hand on his chest and smiled. There was no trace of the flirt in her demeanour, none.

Reaching out, Inigo cupped her head with his hand and kissed her forehead. It was a gentle kiss, intended to comfort rather than to arouse. None the less, his blood quickened, and he felt the stirring of desire.

Lord, what was wrong with him? Alba was giving him sympathy, sharing past loneliness with him, and he wanted to kiss her? He drew back.

'How's your hand?'

'It's fine, I thank you.'

'You must take care. Fire can be a curse, if not treated with respect.' He forced a smile, slightly baffled at the ease with which they had shared past sorrows.

'I will. I am sorry my clumsiness reminded you of past sadness, my lord.' She gave a gentle smile. 'I thought I was doing so well too—'

The smell of burning had them gazing askance at the fire, but it was only the bread she had made, smoking. It had burned to a cinder.

She sighed. 'So much for bread-making. We can't eat that, it has turned to charcoal.'

Moving away lest he forgot himself and did

something foolish like kissing each of her sore fingers, Inigo reached for the tongs and flipped the bread from the fire.

'We have more flour, my lady, make another,' he said lightly. 'Soon you will be an expert.'

Up went an eyebrow and the edge of her mouth. 'An expert?'

But she set to work again happily, and they sampled the bread later, in the shade of the tall cypress by the stream. The flatbread was only slightly chewy. As they ate, Inigo glanced towards Córdoba.

Where was Guillen? Inigo was becoming increasingly concerned. He wasn't the only one, he caught Alba staring up the track several times. She must be thinking about the assassin. He knew what she looked like and he knew she might be able to identify him.

Thank heaven he had posted those guards along the way.

Chapter Twelve

With every day that passed, Alba's admiration of Lord Inigo grew. Under his tutelage she made more flatbread, and there were no more burned fingers. Another day she made a stew. She did make the odd mistake, but fortunately Lord Inigo was an incredibly patient teacher. Who would have thought that a powerful count would take such pains with her? He understood that learning to manage small basic tasks would give her confidence. He was teaching her to be independent and she relished every moment.

Lord Inigo was an easy companion and his relentless protectiveness was incredibly reassuring. Each night he slept by the door.

'You may rest easy, my lady,' he said. 'I shall guard you against unwelcome visitors.'

'Thank you, my lord,' Alba said.

She found a screen in the storeroom, set it in a corner and made a nest for herself behind it. She slept easily there, happy in the knowledge that he was close.

Each night, as Alba drifted to sleep, she would ponder on how fortunate she had been to fall in with him. If he weren't betrothed to Lady Margarita, and if he weren't so principled, he truly was the perfect man to give her a child. Her breast ached when she looked at him.

She had been so ignorant! It had never crossed her mind that she would meet a man who would turn her ideas on their head. Men could be kind, they could be thoughtful. Physically, Lord Inigo had attracted her from the first. And now?

What she felt went deeper than desire, it would be an honour to give Lord Inigo a child.

It simply wasn't to be. Lord Inigo belonged to Lady Margarita, he'd made that plain and while Alba had yet to fully understand Spanish marriage customs, she must abide by his wishes.

She truly admired him. Once or twice she startled herself by thinking that she wouldn't mind forgoing a child, if it meant she could spend her life with him.

Alba soon forgot the small burn she had received on their first day at the lodge. What she didn't forget was the story Lord Inigo had told her about the fire at his father's stables. He'd been playing with the castle children. Playing.

She frowned up at the rafters. It didn't make sense. In the shepherd's hut, when she'd passed that baby to him, he had been awkward and ill at ease, even muttering about children not taking to him.

Plainly, that hadn't always been the case. In his father's castle he'd been organising children's games. That stable fire had had a profound effect on him, and Alba thought she understood why.

Lord Inigo was dutiful and honourable. It was his nature to be so. And he'd been so distressed by the death of that groom's poor sister, that he had decided to avoid contact with children at all costs.

In fact, Lord Inigo *liked* children.

Alba stared at the screen in the direction of the door.

Lord Inigo might not realise it, but if he could let go of his guilt, he would make a wonderful father. Lady Margarita was the most blessed of women, she had better prove worthy of him. Lord Inigo deserved happiness in his marriage.

After a sennight, Inigo was becoming concerned, there was still no sign of his squire. Had Guillen met with an accident? Or had Rodrigo for some unfathomable reason decided to keep him at Castle Álvarez?

When Guillen finally appeared on the horizon, Inigo hurried to intercept him. They met halfway up the rise.

'You are in good health, lad?' His squire looked well, if a trifle weary. A fine coating of dust lay on his clothes.

'Fine, I thank you.'

Guillen dismounted, and they walked slowly towards the lodge.

'What kept you?'

'Count Rodrigo's absence. My lord, I arrived at the castle to find him away, and you specifically ordered me not to hand your letter to anyone else. I waited for his return.' Guillen reached into his tunic. 'Here's your answer.'

'*Gracias.*' Inigo tore at the seal.

Rodrigo's letter was a revelation. Inigo was reading it a second time when a soft footfall had him glancing up. Alba was standing before him, in a blue linen gown that hugged her neat figure like a glove. What this woman did to him! He wanted to stare. To touch. To taste. To kiss her again. And again...

'I heard your squire arrive,' she murmured. 'Is there news of Leonor?'

Inigo offered her the scroll. 'Here, see for yourself.'

She shook her head. 'I can speak Spanish, my lord, I cannot read it.'

'Very well. In brief, your sister is well.'

'Why was Guillen away so long?'

Inigo grimaced. 'I gave him instructions to give my letter only to Lord Rodrigo, and when he arrived at the castle, Rodrigo wasn't in residence. Nor was your sister. Guillen waited for their return.'

'Where were they?'

Knowing she would hate what he was about to tell her, Inigo braced himself. 'As I understand it, Lady Leonor returned to the Alhambra Palace and Rodrigo, fearing for her safety, took a troop of knights and brought her back.'

Alba's face lost colour and stared blankly at the letter. 'May God preserve her. My lord, Leonor warned me of her plans, but after Father's threats I didn't take her seriously.' Her voice trailed off and those dark eyes met his with a new intensity. 'She went back for Constanza's sake. If you recall, Constanza is—'

'The youngest Princess, I remember.'

She gripped his wrist. 'What happened, my lord? Did Constanza come back with them?'

'I'm afraid not.'

Her face fell. 'Does Count Rodrigo even mention Constanza?'

'Aye, he is determined to get a message to her.'

'That will be impossible. Constanza will be well guarded.'

Inigo agreed, although looking at her woebegone expression, he couldn't bring himself to admit it. 'Lord Rodrigo is nothing if not inventive. He will think of something.'

Alba's eyes took on a faraway look. 'Of the three of us, Constanza was always the timid one. It doesn't surprise me that she wouldn't leave the palace.' Giving a heavy sigh, she smiled faintly. 'You will have gathered that Leonor's character is altogether different. For her to go chasing back into Al-Andalus when Father had banished her was extremely brave. And extremely foolish.'

'Bravery and foolhardiness can be close bedfellows,' Inigo murmured.

'Be that as it may, I thank the stars that Count Rodrigo reached Leonor in time. I shudder to think what would have happened if she'd been captured.' She straightened her shoulders. 'My lord, would you be so good as to escort me back to Córdoba?'

Inigo's eyebrow lifted, she sounded so regal. 'Is that a command?'

She bit her lip. 'It is a request, of course.' Lightly, she squeezed his wrist and his heart gave a tiny jump. 'I know full well that here in Castile I have no influence.'

You have more influence than you know.

Inigo understood what she must be feeling. Save for her sister, Princess Leonor, Alba was alone in Spain. Lord Rodrigo had tracked down her mother's relatives in Baeza, she had somewhere to call home, but those relatives were strangers. Why, she hadn't even met them! She must feel so isolated.

Unfortunately, whoever had murdered the King's man in Córdoba might not have left the district. There was no way that Inigo was going to run the risk of him tracking her down. He kept his expression neutral.

'My lady, it's too soon for you to return to Córdoba.'

'You're thinking about that murder.'

He couldn't deny it. 'Aye.'

'If it's safe for my sister, who looks exactly like me, then surely I too will be safe in Córdoba.'

'Lady Alba, I've warned Rodrigo, he is watching over your sister.'

She frowned and removed her hand from his grasp. Inigo hadn't even noticed he'd taken it.

'Very well, my lord, you may take me to Castle Álvarez. Count Rodrigo can guard both of us.'

Inigo felt his face fall. He hadn't expected that response, though perhaps he should have done. He'd already considered sending her to Castle Álvarez and had decided against it. Should he think again?

If he sent Alba to stay with Princess Leonor in

Rodrigo's castle, he could wash his hands of her. He could return to Seville. It would be the perfect opportunity. It was a sensible solution. Unfortunately, he didn't want to wash his hands of her. Not at all.

What he wanted…

His mind filled with an image of Alba walking with him into his great hall in Seville.

As his wife. Not his mistress. And certainly not as the lover who slipped out of his life once he had given her a child. He wanted her as his wife.

A life with Margarita wasn't for him. He gave a bleak smile.

'My lord?' Alba was studying him. 'What's the matter?'

'How do you do it?' he muttered.

'What? What have I done?'

He felt his face heat. 'You've upset the apple cart, that's what.'

'Oh?'

Inigo shook his head, unwilling to enlarge. He should let her go to Rodrigo and her sister at Castle Álvarez. But knowing her had changed him. If he dismissed her from his life he'd never forgive himself.

Lord, what a mess. He could no longer marry Margarita, yet the entire kingdom knew of their betrothal. The poor woman had wasted the best years of her life waiting for him.

With the whole of Castile expecting their marriage to go ahead, not marrying Margarita could be a diplomatic disaster.

'My lady, you wish to see your sister and so you shall. However, you are not setting foot in Córdoba until I have assured myself you will be safe.'

Her eyes narrowed. 'You intend to find the assassin?'

'I shall scour Córdoba street by street, if necessary. And when, and only when, I am satisfied that all is well, I will come to fetch you.' She opened her mouth, and Inigo forged on. 'Please note that you will be staying with me rather than with Lord Rodrigo.'

Dark eyes watched him. 'My lord, Count Rodrigo's castle is close to Córdoba, yet outside the city. Wouldn't it be better—?'

'*No.* You accept my protection. Do you understand?'

She gave a wary nod. 'If you insist.'

'Guillen will remain at your side here as a guard and companion. He will be instructed to lie low.' Inigo took a step closer, close enough to catch a tantalising hint of jasmine. 'I expect you to do the same. Is that clear?'

That wary look—as though she was braced for

him to lose his temper—was troubling. Yet there was no help for it, she must be kept safe, nothing else mattered.

'Yes, my lord. When do you leave?'

'Dawn tomorrow.'

Conscious that his tone had been a little abrupt, Inigo gave her a brief bow and went to find his squire.

Dawn found Inigo securing his saddlebag to Soldier behind the lodge. He mounted and as he rounded the corner, he saw he wasn't the only one to be up and about. A solitary figure was sitting on the bench beneath the cypress. His breath hitched. *Alba.*

She rose at his approach.

'Godspeed, my lord.'

He drew rein scant inches from her, wondering how it was that he had spent half the night thinking about her when he should have been sleeping. There she stood, a slight young woman with black eyes and black hair. So slender. She looked as though a puff of wind would blow her away. He knew better. Her looks were deceptive, she was far from fragile.

'Come here,' he said. Holding the reins in one hand, he leaned out, half dragging, half lifting her towards him. It was a ridiculous manoeuvre, but he couldn't stop himself.

She let out a startled squeak. Swiftly, he pressed his lips to hers and allowed the kiss to soften. Equally swiftly, he felt light fingers trail a path down his cheek. He smiled, she smiled back, and he set her down. It was over in moments.

'Stay well, my lady.'

Inigo heeled Soldier into a walk and headed up the hill with his lips—and cheek—tingling from her touch.

Alba watched Lord Inigo go with mixed feelings. Yesterday, when she'd enquired about going to see Leonor his abrupt refusal had left her shaken. He'd sounded—almost—like the Sultan. The resemblance was deceptive, at heart Lord Inigo was nothing like the Sultan. Still, he had given her a jolt.

And this morning…she touched her mouth, utterly confused. The way he had swept her up, the strength of his arms, the control, that kiss. He'd had complete mastery, over her and the horse.

Alba gave a wry smile. He'd overwhelmed her, and it had been perfectly delightful.

That night, Alba lay on a bed of straw, listening to the creak of twisting timbers as the air cooled and darkness settled over them. On the other side of the lodge, by the door, Guillen was deep in sleep, his breathing regular and even. Insects were rustling about in the roof, comfortable rustlings Alba had never heard before leaving the palace. She was ruefully aware that these small sounds weren't robbing her of sleep. Friendly and everyday, she'd grown used to them already.

No, the blame for her sleeplessness rested squarely on the wide shoulders of Inigo Sánchez, Count of Seville. Even in his absence, he gave her no peace. She missed him. His absence was an ache that stayed with her. This was loneliness at its worst. She'd felt loneliness before, but never so keenly.

He was away for over a week. At last, when she was making dough, she heard the faint drum of hoof beats. Wiping her hands on a cloth, she went to the door. Guillen was sitting on an upturned barrel, sharpening his dagger.

'Lord Inigo?' Alba murmured.

They stared up the rise.

'I believe so.'

Alba's heart took wing. Lord Inigo was dressed casually in a linen tunic and had discarded his helm. His dark hair was ruffled and his eyes, once they lit on Alba, never left her. She watched him draw near, insides melting. She had more than missed him, she realised, wondering why she had no strength to look away. It was beyond embarrassing. This past week she'd felt as though she'd lost half of herself. Why, she'd missed him more than she missed her sisters. How could that be? She missed her sisters with all that was in her. Yet without him the days had dragged.

Was this love? If so, she was in deep trouble.

Lord Inigo dismounted and came towards her and her whole being warmed. She was vaguely aware of Guillen leading his horse away.

'You are in good health, my lady?' Lord Inigo asked.

'Very well, I thank you.'

Her hand was taken in a firm grasp. He lifted it to his lips and then simply stood there, devouring her with his gaze.

Alba felt herself flush. When he looked at her like that, it was as if she was the only woman in the world. He led her to the bench beneath the cypress.

'You will be glad to hear that Lady Leonor is in the best of health.'

'You spoke to her?'

'I spoke to Rodrigo, who assures me that—save for worrying about Princess Constanza—Lady Leonor is well.'

Alba glanced at her hand. Lord Inigo was rubbing his thumb gently up and down in her palm and disturbing sensations, achingly like those she had experienced when he'd kissed her farewell were sparking into life. It was as though her entire body was waking up after a long sleep.

He was looking questioningly at her, waiting for a response. What had they been talking about? Ah, yes, Constanza. Somehow, she found words.

'Constanza is a worry.'

He smiled, and Alba's unruly heart shifted.

'My lady, it is not all gloom, I have brought more welcome news. Rodrigo informs me that your duenna has reached your mother's relatives in Baeza.'

Alba gripped his hand. 'Inés is unhurt?'

'Save for being worn down by her journey, aye. She wishes to see both you and Lady Leonor. Rodrigo asked me to tell you that he has invited Inés to Castle Álvarez when she has recovered.'

Alba swallowed. 'We must return to Córdoba.'

His mouth went up at the corner. 'Inés is not due for some days, my lady. She will need rest.'

'Of course. My lord, you were concerned the assassin might linger in Córdoba. Has anyone seen him?'

'No, all is quiet. The Guard have searched and

searched. They haven't seen anyone answering to your description.'

'It's possible he's moved on.'

'I pray so.' Strong fingers tightened on hers. 'My lady, to be on the safe side, we will stay at the lodge for another week. If Córdoba remains quiet, then we shall go.'

'Very well, my lord.'

Inigo's brows lifted. 'No arguments? Good Lord, my lady, have you caught a fever?'

She hid a smile. 'Wretch. If Leonor is well and Inés isn't due for a while, there is little to be gained from pressing the point.'

He grinned. 'How reasonable you are today, my lady. I believe I shall take advantage of this rare and wonderful mood by reminding you that you will be my guest, rather than Rodrigo's.'

Alba didn't have to think about it. Last week, when he'd mentioned her staying at his town house rather than Lord Rodrigo's castle, she'd been ready to fight tooth and nail to stay with Leonor. No longer. She was horribly aware she wanted to be with Lord Inigo for as long as possible. Their time together was limited.

'Very good, my lord.'

His jaw sagged and he pressed his palm against her forehead. 'I knew it, you definitely have a fever.'

A pang went through her. Longing. She would ignore it. Kind and amusing as he was, he had refused to give her a child. His marriage was looming, a marriage he desired. Lady Margarita wasn't going to go away.

She kept her voice even and watched for his reaction. 'My lord, did you see Lady Margarita?'

His face became guarded. 'As a matter of fact, I did not.'

'Has she returned to Seville?'

He gave a casual shrug. 'I don't believe so. My steward told me she and her brother are still in their apartment in the Alcázar.'

The casual tone didn't fool her, the moment she'd mentioned his betrothed his expression had hardened.

'Lady Margarita will be sorry to have missed you, I am sure.'

Privately, Alba couldn't help but wonder if that was true. She sighed. If only her knowledge of the world in general and other people wasn't so limited.

Life as a princess had left her woefully ignorant. Alba knew her sisters. She knew Inés and a handful of palace servants. She knew her father, and she had even met one of her uncle's concubines. All in all, it was little experience upon which to form judgements. None the less, Lord

Inigo's betrothal felt completely wrong. It would be hard to imagine two people who were so ill-matched.

Lord Inigo needed a wife who would care for him, a wife who understood that he used humour to keep the world at arm's length, and that he didn't do it because he was cold, far from it. He did it because he cared too much. Lord Inigo *liked* children. That stable fire had given him invisible scars. He would overcome them, she was sure. He'd loved children in the past and deep in his soul, he wanted to love them again.

He pushed to his feet and Alba watched him head towards the horses. Her heart felt as though it was being torn apart. Oh, the irony. She had left her father's kingdom determined to find a man to give her a child. She'd been certain that love between a man and a woman was impossible.

A few short weeks in Lord Inigo's company had shown her how wrong she had been. She still didn't know whether men could love women but this she had learned—women could love men.

I love Lord Inigo.

Resting her head on her hand, she watched him, slowly shaking her head as she imagined Lord Inigo and Lady Margarita as man and wife. The ache inside her intensified. It was unbearable. Was this what it felt to be jealous?

Alba rather thought it was. How very lowering.

Alba was in the storeroom, checking the diminishing supply of flour, when she heard hoof beats. Since no one from the lodge had ridden out that morning, it could only mean one thing—a messenger from Córdoba. She hurried out. The horseman was wearing a green tunic, proclaiming him to be Lord Inigo's man.

Lord Inigo strode up, Guillen at his side.

'All is well, my lord,' the horseman said. 'There's been no trace of the felon and Count Rodrigo has sent word that a woman called Inés will shortly be arriving from Baeza. He said you would know to whom he refers.'

'I do indeed.' Lord Inigo turned to Guillen. 'Pack up our baggage, would you, lad?'

'Immediately, my lord. When do we leave?'

'First light tomorrow.'

Guillen ran off.

Lord Inigo caught Alba's eye and swept her an ironic bow. 'My lady, as you undoubtedly heard, we return to Córdoba on the morrow. There's been no sign of the assassin and I am reasonably sure that you will be safe.'

'Thank you, my lord.'

He stepped closer, took her hand more soberly and dropped a kiss in the palm. The kiss tingled all the way to her toes. 'One further point.'

'My lord?'

'I trust you recall agreeing to stay at my town house rather than at Castle Álvarez?'

'Naturally.' Alba's heart twisted. In truth, as she had already acknowledged to herself, there was nowhere else she would rather stay, though it wouldn't be easy.

At the town house, Alba was given the bedchamber overlooking the central courtyard. As she went to the window and pushed back the shutter to stare at the fountain, she was astonished to feel so at home. She loved this place.

Tears prickled at the back of her eyes. Blinking rapidly, she gazed at the painted screen and the embroidered bedcover and reminded herself that nothing here was hers. The feeling was bittersweet. Her chest ached.

If she kept herself busy, she would doubtless feel better. Washing quickly, she changed her gown, marched back down to the courtyard and hailed a passing maidservant.

'I require an escort to take me to Castle Álvarez,' she said.

The maidservant gave her the strangest of looks. 'You wish to see your sister, my lady?'

'Aye.' Alba found she was clenching her fists. 'Lord Inigo promised I might ride out whenever I wish.'

The servant nodded. 'I know, my lady, but… but I was on my way to tell you. You have visitors, your sister has this moment arrived.'

Alba's mouth fell open. 'Leonor is here? Goodness, how did she know I was back?'

The maidservant smiled. 'I gather Count Inigo told Count Rodrigo you were expected this afternoon.'

Alba blinked. 'That was kind of him.'

'My lady, you might care to know that your sister has another lady with her.' The maidservant curtsied and effaced herself.

The door that led to the stables opened and Leonor and Inés burst into the courtyard.

'Inés!' Alba flung her arms about her duenna and hugged her fiercely, and for a while all was kisses and smiles. 'I was so worried, it is wonderful to see you safe and sound.'

Inés's eyes sparkled. Her round face looked the same as ever, her skin was sunburnt in places and perhaps there were a few new lines, otherwise, she looked remarkably well for an elderly woman who had made her way out of Al-Andalus largely on her own.

'It is good to see you too, my love.' Inés's glance encompassed both Leonor and Alba. 'It has been hard. For a while, I feared you were lost to me.'

Alba led Inés and Leonor to a couch in a shady alcove. 'I am sure you have already told Leonor everything, but I am afraid you will have to tell me too. When I heard that you had taken Constanza's place and that she was still in the palace, I couldn't believe it. What happened?'

'Constanza was too nervous, my lady,' Inés replied, her smile slipping. 'She never left the tower.'

Alba shuddered as she remembered the skin-crawling dash through the underground passageway, the darkness, the feeling of the earth closing in on them. She also remembered the footfall behind her. 'So when I heard someone following me, it was you? It was never Constanza?'

Inés patted her hand. 'It was me, my lady. At first, I thought only to see you and Leonor safely away, I wasn't going to leave.'

'You wanted to look after Constanza?'

'Yes, I thought she'd be lonely on her own.' Inés stared at a floor tile and when she lifted her gaze, her eyes were haunted. She lowered her voice. 'Then I heard Sultan Tariq's hounds and realised how enraged he would be.'

'In helping Leonor and me to freedom, you betrayed him,' Alba murmured. 'So, you tricked Count Rodrigo's cousin into thinking you were Constanza. That must have been hard.'

'Not at all. Sir Enrique assumed I was Constanza.' Inés laughed. 'That man had been drinking so much I suspect he'd have taken up a sack of wheat. All I had to do was keep my face hidden.'

'And when he found out the truth, did he hurt you?

Inés waved a dismissive hand. 'I got the odd bruise when he tossed me off his horse, that's all.'

'*All?* The man's a monster! Leonor told me he deserted you in the middle of nowhere. You must have been terrified.'

Inés gave her a straight look. 'Not as terrified as I would have been if Sultan Tariq's men had caught me.' She sagged a little. 'What truly grieves me is the thought of Constanza being left behind. I should have gone back for her.'

Leonor leaned forward. 'No. Inés, you did the right thing. Father is a vengeful man, it would not have been pretty.'

'Pretty?' Alba grimaced. 'If Father had caught Inés, no question but that he would have had her executed.'

'And Constanza would still be on her own,' Leonor added.

Inés looked dejected, mention of Constanza had lowered her mood. Inés had served the Princesses' mother with great loyalty before going on to serve the three Princesses themselves. Alba had no wish to see her unhappy. She smiled gently at her.

'After parting ways with Sir Enrique, I hear you found your own way to Baeza.'

Inés brightened. 'So I did. My lady, Baeza is more beautiful than I remembered. Naturally, your mother's home isn't as grand as the Alhambra Palace, but Sir Alfredo is most welcoming. All your relatives are anxious to meet you, you will like them, I am sure.'

Alba didn't reply, a lump in her throat was threatening to choke her. Seeing Inés again had made her realise how much had changed since she had left the palace. It had only been a few weeks, yet her former life as the daughter of Sultan Tariq seemed like a dream. Or a nightmare. A nightmare where her every move was dictated by her formidable father.

She was no longer the same person. Back then, reaching her kin at Baeza and having a child had been the sum of her desires.

Today all she could think about was a Spanish

knight with laughing grey eyes and a kiss that melted away all that she had been. If she went to Baeza with Inés…

Her heart cramped. The idea had lost its allure. And as for having a baby which she and Leonor could dote on…that too felt wrong. Alba still longed for a child, having one would certainly give her a role in life, but would it be enough? In Baeza, she'd be a princess in exile for ever.

No, setting up household with Leonor and Inés in Baeza suddenly felt like a backward step. Alba could imagine how it would be. Inés would instruct Leonor and Alba in how to go on in Spain. She'd be the middle sister till the end of her days. There would be new rules. New restrictions.

Well, Alba had had her fill of being instructed. She wanted to find things out for herself. She wanted to be able to make her own mistakes, for she strongly suspected that making mistakes— like burning that flatbread—was the best way to learn.

If meeting Lord Inigo had taught her anything, it was that life was full of surprises. The world might be alarming, but there were wonders in it. Wonders that brought both pleasure and pain, like falling in love with a Castilian knight.

No, Alba wasn't about to return to her old way

of life. Not when the whole of Spain was out there, waiting to be explored.

'There's more to Baeza than you might imagine,' Inés was saying. 'Sir Alfredo keeps hawks and the hunting is excellent. You and Lady Leonor will love it.'

'I will visit soon, Inés,' Alba said. 'I have business to settle in Córdoba first.'

Inés bristled. 'Business to settle, my lady?' She glanced warily about the courtyard and lowered her voice. 'Pray, what do you mean? You cannot be implying that you and Lord Inigo—'

'Inés!' Alba's voice was sharp. Her duenna had taken the place of her mother for so long, that sometimes she overstepped herself. Doubtless, she meant well. Inés would have to learn that her charges were fully grown. *She ought not to be treating us like children.* And she certainly should not be assuming the worst of Lord Inigo. 'Count Inigo is a man of honour. He wouldn't dream of—' Alba broke off, flushing guiltily.

Count Inigo wouldn't dream of seducing me. On the contrary it was I who approached him.

Luckily, Inés subsided. 'I am glad,' she murmured.

Alba felt dreadful. She wasn't lying, though she was uncomfortably aware she wasn't telling the whole truth either. What else could she do?

If Inés got wind of her unseemly proposition—of the way Alba had asked Lord Inigo to give her a child—she would be scandalised. Alba's ignorance of Spanish customs was no excuse, she had been too bold.

Alba glanced at Leonor, willing her to say something. Anything. If Leonor committed to visiting their Spanish kin, it would distract Inés from wondering about Alba's reluctance.

After a long pause, Leonor stirred. 'Constanza will write to us soon, Inés, of that I am sure.'

'If you say so, my lady.' Inés looked sceptical and her tone was doubly so. It was plain that she believed Constanza was lost to them. 'However, I wouldn't pin too many hopes on it. Your father's palace is a fortress, after all.'

Leonor gave a pensive smile. 'That may be so, though I'm pleased to tell you that Lord Rodrigo has contrived to get a message to her. I am confident Constanza will reply, and her reply will go to Castle Álvarez. So, Inés, you will understand why I cannot commit to visiting Baeza quite yet.'

Leonor shot Alba a look, and Alba saw immediately that Constanza wasn't the only reason Leonor wanted to remain in Castle Álvarez. Leonor was as reluctant to bid farewell to Count Rodrigo as Alba was to leave Lord Inigo.

Much to Alba's relief, Inés assumed that Leonor

was speaking for them both and she allowed the conversation to shift. The three of them talked until the shadows lengthened, and then Leonor and Inés took their leave.

'You'll come to Castle Álvarez tomorrow?' Leonor asked, while they waited for their horses to be brought from the stable.

Alba murmured agreement. Tomorrow, she would ensure that she and Leonor had time to themselves. Clearly, Alba wasn't the only one who wanted to explore the boundaries of her new-found freedom.

Chapter Thirteen

Scrolls and parchments were piling up in Inigo's office, yet the next day he found himself at the head of the Princess's escort on the ride to Castle Álvarez. He couldn't seem to help himself. If Alba was surprised to see him, her smile was warm enough for him to understand that she enjoyed his company as much as he did hers. Riding with her had become a delight and a torment. Quite simply, he wanted to prolong their time together. He was neglecting his duties.

As their party clattered out of the city, Inigo recognised the leaden feeling in his stomach for what it was—guilt. Never mind duty, he should have sought Margarita out on his previous visit to Córdoba. He hadn't done so for one simple reason, he had no idea what to say to her.

'Margarita, it is plain you don't wish to marry me.

'Forgive me, Margarita, the feeling is mutual.

'Margarita, a Nasrid princess has turned my head. I can think of nothing but her.'

Inigo had always prided himself on his ability to face realities, but as far as Alba and Margarita were concerned, he had no idea how to proceed. How could he marry Margarita when his mind was filled with Alba?

They reached a crossroad and Inigo found himself studying Alba's profile, the shape of her forehead, her nose. And that wondrous, kissable mouth. He swallowed a groan and forced himself to focus on a distant tree. Looking at Alba's mouth was dangerous. It reminded him of that last kiss, a stolen kiss he would never forget. He could still feel the gentle touch of her fingers as she'd stroked his face. She enchanted him.

In all his life, he had never felt this way. Would it last? Was it just lust? He had no idea. Judging from what had happened to his parents, his feelings for Alba would burn themselves out eventually.

He was tormented by the knowledge that Alba also found him attractive. She had intimated as much more than once. She'd asked him for a child, and he had refused her. If he told her that he'd changed his mind, would she consider taking things further?

A muscle ticked in his cheek. While Inigo was betrothed, his hands were tied. He couldn't go on like this, he had to speak to Margarita. If he prayed hard enough, God would help him find the right words.

The road to the castle cut through lemon and pomegranate groves and the Princess gave every indication of being fascinated by the countryside. She stared at the acres of fruit trees. She ran her gaze along a high stone wall, which was broken by a pair of magnificent wrought-iron gates—the entrance to the Álvarez cemetery. A clever hand had twisted the iron into flowing vines, there were roses and lilies and acanthus leaves.

Through the iron bars the graves were visible, line after line of them. One looked new, it was strewn with fresh greenery and sprays of flowers.

Inigo's guts knotted.

Alba noticed the grave. 'Someone in Castle Álvarez has died recently?' she asked.

'Rodrigo's brother, Diego, lies there.'

'How did he die?'

'He was killed at the border, immediately before my comrades and I were captured.'

She caught her breath. 'The Count's brother died at the hands of my father's troops?'

'Aye.'

'Why didn't you tell me?'

'I'm telling you now. Diego was my friend. He was killed and there he lies.'

Alba stared at the back of her horse's head as though searching for words. Finally, she looked at him.

'I am so sorry, my lord. He was a close friend?'

'Aye.'

'The conflict between our peoples has caused much suffering,' she said sadly. 'I wish it could end.'

'My lady, I too wish it would end.' He heaved a sigh. 'There is blame on both sides. Sadly, matters will probably proceed as they have done for years. Our King will continue to demand tribute from Sultan Tariq, and the Sultan will either refuse to pay or he will take noble Spaniards prisoners in the hope of wringing ransoms out of their relatives.'

'As happened to you and Count Rodrigo.'

'Exactly. However you look at it, it's a mess.'

Alba mumbled agreement and fell silent.

Castle Álvarez lay a little way ahead on their left, rearing up from behind massive stone walls. Rodrigo's red standard was flying from one of the turrets, and sentries guarded the gate, their helmets glinting in the light. On the other side of the road from the castle were more orchards, criss-crossed with water channels.

Inigo glanced at Alba. He had seen similar water channels in Al-Andalus and, hoping to distract her from mournful reflections, he was about to point them out to her, when something else caught his attention. A woman was sitting on a bench beneath an orange tree.

It was Margarita.

Margarita? She was deep in conversation with a man Inigo recognised as Rodrigo's steward, Sir Arnau de Córdoba. The odd thing was that Margarita looked like a different woman. Her face was alight with laughter, and her demeanour was so happy and relaxed that Inigo barely recognised her. He had never seen her look so carefree. Never. What was going on?

Alba's focus was on the castle, she hadn't seen Margarita. Deciding it would be impossibly rude to ignore his betrothed, Inigo was about to mention Margarita's presence when the most extraordinary thing happened.

Margarita glanced up, saw him and her jaw dropped. Quick as lightning, she rose and fled into the depths of the orchard with Sir Arnau striding rapidly after her.

How very peculiar.

For the space of a few heartbeats, Inigo sat as though turned to stone, analysing what he had seen.

Sir Arnau must be the reason for Margarita's lack of enthusiasm to marry Inigo. She had given her heart to Sir Arnau. Inigo felt a smile begin to form. His meeting with Margarita wouldn't be easy, but at least he now had an idea of where to start.

He spurred towards the gatehouse, heart lighter that it had felt for years. A squire he recognised was walking by.

'Miguel, would you please inform Lady Leonor that her sister Lady Alba is here.'

The lad blinked owlishly at Alba and nodded. 'Lady Alba? Heavens, if I may say so, my lady, you truly are the mirror image of your sister.'

Alba smiled, and the young man hurried away.

As they continued into the bailey, a ripple of surprise went around, the young man's astonishment was echoed on every face. Stable boys nudged each other and stared.

'Everyone has noticed the resemblance,' Inigo murmured. 'Don't worry, they will soon become accustomed.'

Alba nodded and Princess Leonor appeared at the doorway to the keep.

'Alba!' With a rustle of silk skirts her sister was upon her, barely waiting for Alba to dismount before giving her a hug. 'Welcome to Castle Álvarez.' She gestured back at the keep. 'I'm in the solar with Inés, would you care to join us?'

Inigo hardly heard a word. His mind was back in that orchard with Margarita and Sir Arnau. A miracle? Lord, let it be so.

* * *

After returning to Córdoba that afternoon, Inigo had left Alba in the care of Lady Raquel and took himself to the garrison. He wanted to know whether there had been any sightings of the cut-throat he and Alba had seen by the market.

After that, he would find his betrothed. Had Margarita returned to her lodgings in the Alcázar? She might still, he supposed, be frolicking in the orchard with Sir Arnau.

Inigo's lips quivered. Margarita? Frolicking? Was his imagination conjuring up things that were not there? Was this wishful thinking?

Captain Gui García was on duty in the chamber over the garrison gate. As they exchanged greetings, it occurred to Inigo that Sir Gui had been present the day he had brought Alba to the garrison.

Inigo's smile faded. He would never forget the way Alba had looked when she'd burst in on him and Margarita in the Alcázar. Her lips had been bruised and her hair awry. Had Sir Gui pressed his attentions on her?

Anger rose like bile in Inigo's throat. He glared at the Captain and Sir Gui's expression became so wary that Inigo knew he had stumbled on the truth. It had been Sir Gui who had upset Alba.

'My lord?'

'You recall Lady Alba, sir?'

Sir Gui flushed. 'Naturally, my lord. Lady Alba came with you to report on that incident in the goldsmiths' quarter.'

Inigo scowled at him. 'Quite so. Should you have the good fortune to meet her again, I will need your assurance that henceforward you will treat her with respect.'

Sir Gui took a wary step back. 'Of course. What happened was a misunderstanding, my lord. I apologise if I caused offence.'

'Don't let it happen again. You have been warned.'

'Very good, my lord.'

Inigo nodded. 'In truth, Captain, I came on another matter.'

'My lord?'

'This touches on that murder near the market—it's been a few weeks now, so are enquiries bearing fruit?'

'Not yet, my lord. A description of the suspect has been circulated around the town and among the troops, but so far—nothing.'

'Very well.' Inigo turned to leave. 'If there are developments. I should like to know immediately.'

After leaving Captain García, Inigo left the garrison and crossed the courtyard to the Alcázar.

Margarita next.

Margarita's maid confirmed her mistress had returned to the Alcázar, so Inigo commandeered the chamber he had used for their last meeting and requested that she meet him there.

He'd not been there long before the door opened, and Margarita stepped in. Her head was high, her cheeks flushed.

'My lady.' Taking her hand, Inigo bowed over it and studied her flushed cheeks. 'That's the second time this afternoon I've seen guilt on someone's face.'

She drew her hand from his. 'My lord, I... I would like to apologise.'

'That isn't necessary.'

'No?'

'No. Come.' A pair of folding chairs stood by the wall. Gesturing for Margarita to take one, Inigo took the other. 'My lady, I believe we owe it to ourselves to be frank with one another. At our last meeting, you affirmed you were still ready to marry me, yet I sensed a deep reluctance. You spoke of your brother's hopes for our wedding, yet never mentioned yours. I should like to know what you think. What are *your* thoughts? Your feelings?'

'Mine? Why, my lord, it is an honour to be—'

He cut her off with a wave. 'No, no, none of that. Not after what I saw this morning.'

'My lord, I believe you misunderstood what you saw. Sir Arnau and I are friends, nothing more.'

He softened his tone. 'Margarita, you don't need to tell me that. You are an honourable woman, that I do know. However, I have come to believe that you want our wedding to take place no more than I do.'

Margarita lowered her gaze. 'My lord, I know how much your father, Count Javier, wanted us to be man and wife. He helped my brother see the many advantages of a union between our families.'

'Yes, yes. Your family's lands and mine share a border. It would be convenient. I understand all that. But what do *you* think? Margarita, I need to hear this from your lips. Do you want to marry me?'

She drew in a deep breath as though bracing herself. 'No, my lord, I do not.'

'Thank you.' Inigo sat back, astonished at the wave of relief that swept through him. 'Thank you.'

She gave him a mournful look. 'Fernando is most insistent, my lord.'

Inigo snorted. 'Hang Fernando.'

'My lord!'

He gave her a narrow look. 'He's not beating you, is he?'

'Heavens, no.' Margarita shrugged. 'Though he mentions our marriage almost every time he sees me. I believe it has become something of an obsession with him. I can't think why.'

Inigo could think of one or two reasons, though he kept his counsel. Baron Fernando was not the best of stewards. He milked his estates for every penny and never put anything back. The Carmona estate was overworked, and its long-suffering tenants lived in broken-down hovels that had needed repair a decade ago.

Inigo had known this for years, yet he'd held to his betrothal because his father had promoted it and he could see the sense in remaining on good terms with his neighbours. That didn't mean he could or should marry a woman who was in love with someone else.

'Margarita, I'll speak plainly. I see no happiness in you and I marrying.' He smiled. 'Judging by what I saw in that orchard, Sir Arnau may be your choice.'

Margarita gave him a troubled look. 'That is as may be, but both you and I know that we can't always follow our hearts. We have our families to consider. Dynasty and duty, as Fernando is constantly reminding me.' She frowned. 'Besides, our marriage has been formally arranged. The King himself has approved it.'

'That is irrelevant. Margarita, with your agreement, I shall write to the King. I shall tell him that we would like to set our betrothal agreement aside. That we prefer to make different arrangements. Do I have your permission to mention Sir Arnau by name?'

She hesitated. 'Is that necessary? I don't want to do anything that might sully Sir Arnau's reputation.'

'Rest assured, I shall stress the need for discretion, at least until the King has made his decision. Do I have your agreement?'

'Very well.' She pulled a face. 'Saints, Fernando will be livid.'

'I shall ask the King to be tactful, Fernando won't know about it until everything's agreed.' Inigo put his hand on hers. 'Margarita, His Grace might not respond immediately, we might have to be patient. If you are uncomfortable living at Carmona, I can arrange for you to stay elsewhere.'

'Thank you, that will not be necessary.'

'Very good. I shall write this eve. My lady, if you find yourself in need of assistance while we wait for the King's reply, please don't hesitate to ask.'

'You are very kind.' Margarita murmured.

'Kind?' He gave a choking laugh. 'Margarita, after all these years, it's the least I can do.'

She met his gaze directly and Inigo had the impression she was at last looking at him. Her lips softened. 'You are a kind man, I know.' She folded her hands together. 'I take it from this change of heart that you too have found love. Is it that girl you brought with you from Al-Andalus? Is it this Lady Alba?'

Inigo looked blankly at his former betrothed. Love? Margarita thought he was in love with Alba?

'Margarita, you understand my views of old. I believe love is an illusion. It never lasts.'

Margarita rose and Inigo did the same. She stepped up to him, eyes serious. 'There we disagree. Love can last. Not everyone is like your parents, Inigo.'

He shrugged.

'You want that girl, at any rate.'

'I won't deny it, she is attractive.'

Margarita's expression softened. 'Inigo, I know you better than you imagine. You want her enough to set our betrothal agreement aside. A betrothal agreement you have held to ever since your father proposed it. If you hadn't met Lady Alba, nothing would have changed. We would have married, and you would have dutifully set aside your mistresses because you saw what happened to your parents' marriage when your mother found out about your father's affair. You didn't want that for our marriage. Inigo, you have good instincts. You love this woman, you want no other.'

'You have been listening to one too many ballads,' Inigo said.

'Delude yourself all you like. You love her.' She dropped into a formal curtsy. 'My lord, I look forward to hearing from you when the King has made his decision.'

Troubled, Alba had taken refuge in her bedchamber. Lord Inigo's manner on the ride back from Castle Álvarez had upset her. He'd responded to all attempts at conversation with brusque monosyllables. He'd not been overtly rude, but his behaviour had so reminded her of the Sultan that all her insecurities had rushed back at her, strong as ever. It had been bad enough when her father kept her and her sisters at arm's length. Lord Inigo's preoccupation made her feel as though she no longer existed.

She'd had the impression that she knew him better than that. They had been getting on so well, or so she had believed. It was extremely disappointing.

Why was he so distant? And why had he

marched off to the Alcázar? What was he doing? If something important had happened, surely he would tell her?

She tried to distract herself by tidying. Not that the bedchamber needed tidying, the maids had done that. She even sorted through her clothes. Not that they needed sorting, everything was so neat, Lady Raquel had obviously beaten her to it.

Keeping busy, however, didn't stop her mind working. Had Count Rodrigo brought troubling news back from Granada? Was the Sultan up to his old tricks? Or had seeing the grave of Diego Álvarez reminded Count Inigo of the bloodshed between their two kingdoms?

While at the hunting lodge, their growing intimacy had led Alba to see Lord Inigo as the closest of friends. Had returning to Córdoba changed all that?

No, that could not be, she wouldn't permit it. The man she'd hoped would father her child had become too dear to lose. If she couldn't have him as her lover, she would have him as her friend.

So, when a sudden burst of activity in the courtyard alerted her to Lord Inigo's return from the Alcázar, Alba rushed to peer through her bedchamber window. She watched him entering his office, smoothed down her skirts and went to greet him.

He was sitting at his desk, staring blankly at a heap of scrolls. Ignoring his startled expression at her sudden appearance, Alba walked boldly in and shut the door.

'My lord, is all well? Was there news of the assassin?'

Rising, he walked around the desk to stand in front of her. 'No news, I'm afraid.'

'Did Count Rodrigo bring ill tidings from Granada?'

'No, no, nothing like that.'

'Then what is it? What is the matter?'

'What do you mean?'

Shamefully, Alba felt her eyes sting. 'Since we left the lodge you have become a…a stranger to me.'

'My lady, I apologise if I am somewhat abstracted.' He gestured irritably at the desk. 'While I was a guest in the Vermillion Towers estate business piled up. Then we went to the lodge and, again, I had no chance of dealing with it. If you would be so good as to allow me to concentrate, I do have much work.'

A tear escaped and rolled down her cheek. Obviously, somewhere along the road, she had become a nuisance. When had it happened? Why hadn't she noticed? Alba was quick to turn for the door, but his expression changed.

'Alba?' Strong fingers caught her arm. 'Crying? You?'

She was pulled against a broad chest.

'I'm a beast, I am sorry. Don't cry.' He urged her to look at him. 'Alba? Tell me you're not crying.'

A gurgle escaped her, and a sniff. 'I'm not crying.'

'Thank heaven for that. Enough tears have been shed in this house, I won't have more.'

His handsome face wavered in front of her, his long-lashed grey eyes were filled with concern. 'It is my wish that this house should be filled with laughter. No more tears. Alba—my lady—I am truly sorry to be so ill-tempered.'

Alba wiped her cheek and stared up at him, alerted by the change in his tone when he'd mentioned tears being shed here. What did he mean?

She gave him a wobbly smile. 'Tears are not allowed?'

'Not one. Crying is forbidden. Especially for you.'

There it was again, that slight catch in his voice. Something about crying. This house held sad memories for him. Suddenly, she had it—his mother! This touched on Inigo's parents, Countess Elena and Count Javier. At the Córdoba Alcázar, after Alba had interrupted Lord Inigo's reunion with Lady Margarita, Lord Inigo had mentioned his mother's distress. His father had suddenly brought home an illegitimate daughter, Pepita. It had been easy to work out that Pepita was the reason Inigo was so determined to remain faithful once he had married. He didn't want that kind of misery infecting his marriage. This was why fidelity meant so much to him.

Alba pushed her distress to the back of her mind. 'What happened here? Inigo?'

He would have turned away, but Alba kept him in place with a light touch to his cheek, and her gaze clung to his. 'Inigo, please. Tell me.'

He shrugged, affecting a carelessness that was not mirrored in his eyes. 'This house belonged to my mother.'

'I knew it,' Alba murmured.

He took a deep breath. 'I believe I mentioned that my parents' marriage was troubled. My mother acquired this house when relations with my father were at their worst.' His mouth twisted. 'I came to think of it as the house of tears. My mother had adored my father and when she learned about Pepita—my half-sister—her love soured.'

Alba glanced about her. 'Countess Elena left Falcon's Castle and came to live here.'

Inigo nodded. 'She used the bedchamber next to yours. Father couldn't bear to be away from her, he was truly repentant. His one thought was for reconciliation. He sent me to convince her to see him again. It wasn't easy. Alba, you may have noticed how sound carries in these houses. Even though I slept on the lower floor, I would lie awake night after night, listening to my mother weeping.'

'You succeeded in the end though, your mother agreed to meet your father.'

'Yes.'

His voice was curt. Full of pain and hurt and, most bitter of all, guilt. Alba laid her hand over his heart, she knew it was aching.

'You did your best, Inigo. You were not responsible for the storm that took their ship. That was fate.'

His chest rose and fell under her hand. His expression was inscrutable. Wishing she could free him of the guilt, Alba pressed on.

'My lord, you were not responsible for your mother's grief, any more that you were for that storm. You wanted your parents to reconcile and the Countess will have taken comfort from that. She must have been proud of you, in so many ways.' She cleared her throat. 'I am sure she loved you.'

Grey eyes narrowed. 'Are you?'

'How could she not?' Alba asked lightly. She rather imagined his face softened, though she couldn't swear to it. At least he hadn't pushed her away.

Chapter Fourteen

A few mornings later, Inigo had set down his quill and was headed for the stables with Guillen when Sir Nicolás drew him aside.

'My lord, if I may have a word?'

Beginning to feel as though duty had him under siege, Inigo managed not to grimace.

'Can it keep until later? I've promised to escort Lady Alba to Castle Álvarez again.'

It was Inés's last day in Córdoba. On the morrow, she was to join Sir Alfredo in Baeza.

Inigo knew Alba wanted to bid her duenna farewell and he was extremely relieved that Alba had shown no sign of wanting to meet her Spanish relatives for herself. Inigo was set on escorting her again today because he suspected Inés might beg Alba to go with her.

That couldn't be allowed to happen. He had changed, for which the Princess was responsible. She was like the sun. For years, Inigo had hidden his feelings behind walls of ice. A short time with Alba and the ice had melted.

This could be the last time I act as Alba's escort.

Guilt had become a familiar companion. Inigo

was honour bound to keep to his betrothal vows until the King confirmed that Inigo and Margarita might marry elsewhere. If the King refused his request, the Princess and he would have no future. And, even if the King agreed, Inigo was grimly aware that what he felt for Alba might not last.

The feelings he had for her—the obsessive desire for her company, being unable to tear his gaze from her face whenever she was near, and, yes, lust—were damned uncomfortable. And so incredibly powerful, it was inconceivable that they should last. Even though he knew this, the idea that Alba might choose to go off and live with her mother's family filled him with dread. And not just because he wanted her.

If Alba departed for Baeza, he might never see her again.

Daily, Inigo reminded himself that passion, in whatever form, usually burnt itself out.

It didn't help. Whenever he was with Alba, the knife twisted. How long would he have before the passion faded? And, if they were separated, what would happen? Would Alba ask someone else to give her a child? Would she marry? Would her husband care for her?

'My lord?' Sir Nicolás was watching him quizzically. 'You need to hear this.'

Duty calls. With a sigh, Inigo caught his squire's eye. 'Guillen, you are to join Lady Alba's escort today. Bring her safely home.' *Please God.*

'Yes, my lord.'

Back in his office, Inigo ushered Sir Nicolás to a chair. 'Well?'

'I was in The Mill last eve, my lord.'

Inigo nodded. The Mill was one of the busiest taverns in town. It stood on the riverbank, close to the old Roman bridge.

'My lord, the silk merchants are in town and there'd been some deep drinking. Tongues were loose and there was troubling news concerning King Henry's treasury in Seville.'

Inigo tensed. 'Someone's broken into the Seville Alcázar?'

The Alcázar in Córdoba was but one of King Henry's palaces, there was another in Seville. Holding title to much of the land surrounding the Seville Alcázar, Inigo felt a certain responsibility for its governance.

Sir Nicolás hesitated. 'The merchant talked a lot of nonsense, my lord, it wasn't easy to sift the wheat from the chaff. He was hazy as to whether there had been an actual robbery. However, I did gather that while you have been away, there have been unsettling murmurings about the treasury accounts.'

'Go on.'

'The merchant says the accounts don't tally and that there is less in the treasury than there ought to be. I couldn't work out whether he was talking about embezzlement or outright theft.'

Someone had been tampering with the accounts? Inigo swore softly. 'This must be investigated, and the King's treasury secured.'

'Quite so. There's more, I'm afraid, and it concerns Lady Margarita's brother, Baron Fernando.' Sir Nicolás cleared his throat. 'My lord, were you aware that a few days since, the Baron left Córdoba?'

'Drunk or no, that silk merchant was a mine of information,' Inigo said drily.

'No, my lord, this titbit came from the local garrison. Captain García sent word that the stolen Book of Hours has been recovered in Seville.'

Mind grappling with the realisation that his idyll with the Princess could be at an end, Inigo was finding it hard to focus on what his steward was saying.

'My apologies, Nicolás, my mind was elsewhere. What was that?'

'The Book of Hours, the one that was stolen the day the King's envoy was killed—it's turned up in Seville.'

Inigo stared. 'What?'

'Baron Fernando found it. The King is delighted and is making much of it, the Baron is to receive a reward.'

Inigo rubbed his temple. 'Nicolás, does it strike you as strange that the Book of Hours should go missing in Córdoba while the Baron is in residence and then, when he returns to Seville, it reappears?'

'It is rather a coincidence.'

'Where is Margarita, do you know?'

'She went with her brother to Carmona.'

Inigo gave a pained sigh. Any relief he might have felt that there was no longer any chance of Margarita and Alba running into each other in Córdoba was swiftly tempered by the realisation that he would have to follow Baron Fernando to Seville. The Baron needed watching. He was known to be a spendthrift, had his coffers run dry? Was he raiding the King's treasury and tampering with records to cover his tracks?

His steward looked at him. 'When do you leave, my lord?'

'At once.' Recalling he'd charged Guillen with taking Alba to Castle Álvarez, Inigo added, 'Nicolás, find Luis, would you?'

'The groom, my lord?'

'Aye, he's a bright lad, I've a mind to try him out as a squire.'

With luck, teaching Luis the responsibilities of a squire would take his mind off other matters. Like the pain in his heart at the thought of a lifetime in a cold world with duty as his bedfellow.

'Very good, my lord.'

Inigo trudged back to his office with a heart like lead. There was no way he could take Alba with him to Seville. To do so, before the King had responded to his letter, would be to insult Margarita in the worst way possible.

He told himself all was not gloom, here was his chance to take command of his feelings. What he felt for Alba wasn't likely to last. Hard though he might find it right now, a period of separation would be telling.

He would simply have to pray that Alba didn't take it into her head to go and meet those relatives in Baeza. In the short time Inigo had known her, she had helped him so much. For years he'd felt despair over the breakdown of his parents' marriage. Alba's sympathetic and no-nonsense reaction to what he'd told her had made him realise that his mother's sorrow wasn't his responsibility. He'd done his best to heal his parents' wounds, the rest had been down to them.

Further, Alba's certainty that his mother had taken solace in her relationship with him was warming. His mother had loved him. He smiled. Most mothers loved their children, it wasn't re-markable, but it was warming.

Alba was a clever woman, despite her shel-tered upbringing. That tale about her luckless maidservant had gone some way to explaining her need for a child. She wanted someone to love, someone who couldn't be taken from her like an old toy.

Well, if Inigo's plans came to fruition, he might be fortunate enough to give her the child she so desired. A legitimate one.

Dusk had stolen most of the light. On her re-turn from Castle Álvarez, Alba handed her horse to Guillen with a smile and found herself blink-ing through the gloom at Sir Nicolás. He had just told her that Lord Inigo had gone away. She must have misheard.

'Lord Inigo is no longer here?'

Sir Nicolás bowed. 'Just so, my lady. The Count has urgent business in Seville.'

Sir Nicolás offered Alba his arm and they pro-ceeded towards the courtyard.

Lord Inigo—gone? Her stomach felt hollow.

Having bade farewell to Inés, Alba had already been feeling low, but this—her heart cramped. Coming to a standstill at the fountain, she turned to Sir Nicolás.

'Did Lord Inigo say when he would be back, sir?'

'At present, the Count has no plans to return. He sends you his compliments. He wishes you well, and he has asked me to ensure that you give me your direction were you to leave.'

Alba looked blankly at the steward. 'I'm to give you my direction? That is all? He said nothing more?'

'I'm afraid not.'

A slight frown creased Sir Nicolás's brow. Clumsily, he patted her hand. Alba realised this interview troubled him, he understood how upset she was.

'My lady, this house is to remain at your disposal for as long as you require.'

'I see.' Except Alba didn't see, not really. 'The Count has lands in Seville,' she said. 'And Lady Margarita lives nearby. Do you know if she went ahead of him?'

Sir Nicolás looked thoughtfully at her. His eyes were kind. 'Lady Margarita accompanied her brother to Carmona some days since.'

Throat tight, Alba nodded. This wasn't entirely

unexpected; Lady Margarita was obviously still preparing for her marriage. None the less, it hurt. She felt devastated. 'I see. Thank you for telling me, sir.'

'My lady, whatever you decide to do, you must know that Lord Inigo holds you in great esteem.'

Esteem. Alba's eyelids prickled. Fearing sympathy would be her undoing, she lifted her hand from his arm. 'Thank you, sir.'

'It has been a pleasure knowing you, my lady. You will forgive me if I speak out of turn, but Lord Inigo is the better man for meeting you.'

'Thank you. Sir, when you next communicate with him would you please convey my thanks for his assistance?'

'Naturally.'

The fountain tinkled. Lamps were being lit in the alcoves around the fountain, and the pain in Alba's heart was agonising. *I can't stay here.* She straightened her back. 'I believe I shall be joining my sister at Castle Álvarez tomorrow, Sir Nicolás.'

'If you think that would be for the best, my lady.'

Alba cleared her throat. 'Is your lady wife about? I would like to thank her for her help. If she is free, would you ask her to join me in my bedchamber?'

* * *

Several gowns were spread over the embroidered bedcover and Alba's eyes stung as she looked at them. A couple had never been worn, they'd been made on Lord Inigo's orders and had only arrived today.

The latch clicked and Lady Raquel put her head round the door.

'My husband tells me you're leaving?'

'Aye, Count Inigo is called to Seville.' Alba spoke brightly, hoping to hide the hurt in her breast. 'It isn't appropriate for me to stay. Before I go, I wanted to thank you for being such a help. Your advice has been invaluable.'

'You are most welcome, my lady.'

Alba stared bleakly at a gorgeous green damask draped over the bed.

How could he leave in such a manner?

Sir Nicolás had been polite, but Lord Inigo's message had been insultingly brief. And cold. After what they had shared—how could he? It was galling to discover that the man who had taught her that men and women could treat each other with affection could dismiss her so easily.

I thought I loved him. I imagined that he was beginning to reciprocate.

Lady Raquel leaned forward to smooth the skirt of the green gown. 'Is this fabric from France?'

'I believe so. Lord Inigo found it.'

'It's very pretty.' Lady Raquel lifted her gaze. 'My lady, Guillen told me that you witnessed the murder of one of the King's men. I know about the missing Book of Hours. I also know that Lord Inigo took you to the hunting lodge to keep you safe. Did my husband tell you that the King's book has been found in Seville? A few gems have been levered from the cover, otherwise it is, apparently, still glittering with jewels.'

'Sir Nicolás made no mention of that,' Alba said slowly. 'I assumed Lord Inigo was returning to see to his estates.'

'Well, that is certainly true. He will also be seeing Lady Margarita.'

Alba watched Lady Raquel run her frowning gaze over the other gowns on the bed, and every fibre of her being felt as though it was in revolt. This was intolerable. How could she go to Leonor when every instinct was urging her to follow Lord Inigo? Their relationship couldn't be at an end. It couldn't. What she had with Lord Inigo had come to mean the world. Heavens, she wanted him even more than she wanted a child. She wanted him on any terms. Could she have misunderstood him? If he'd left in such a hurry, maybe there'd not been time for him to compose a more measured message.

If I want him, I must fight for him. If I fail, I may still lose him, but I must try.

'What will happen to these gowns, my lady?' Lady Raquel asked.

Alba replied absently, 'I thought perhaps you might like them.'

Lady Raquel frowned. 'But Lord Inigo wants you to have them.'

'Does he?'

'Most certainly.'

Alba focused on the green damask, she longed to keep it. In truth, she wanted all the gowns. Whatever happened, they would be a memento of her extraordinary time as Lord Inigo's guest.

A thrill ran through her. She would keep them. She was going after Lord Inigo, and she would need decent clothes.

'Lady Raquel, I must warn you, I am about to be extremely rash.'

Lady Raquel's face lit up. 'I knew it, you're going to Seville!'

'I am indeed.'

'My lady, I believe you have captured his heart.'

'I hope so.' Alba paused, thinking. For her part, the bond between her and Lord Inigo felt strong enough to last an eternity. Might he feel the same? She wasn't blind to his doubts, but instinct was telling her that what she felt couldn't possibly be one-sided. She must go after him, she had to find out what was in his heart. He had one, she knew.

The decision made, her despair evaporated. Alba felt energised, and a little nervous. 'My lady, I cannot travel alone.'

'Certainly not, there are outlaws everywhere, which means you will need a travelling companion. And an armed escort. And—'

'Sir Nicolás might object.'

'Not he, he likes you.' Lady Raquel looked thoughtful. 'And if he does object, we shall ignore him. Although for the sake of propriety, he is bound to say that you will need a female companion. Lady Alba, I would be honoured to come with you. May I?'

Alba took Lady Raquel's hand. 'I would love you to be my companion. Thank you.' She nodded in the direction of the clothes on the bed. 'I will need these in Seville. The only problem is that I don't have a proper travelling chest.'

'That's easily remedied, you may have one of mine.' Lady Raquel grabbed the hand bell and rang it energetically. 'I can't wait to see Count Inigo's face when he sees you. And please, my lady, since we have become friends, you must call me Raquel.'

'And you must call me Alba.'

'Thank you.' Raquel hesitated. 'Would it be impertinent to ask, well, who are you?'

Alba blinked, startled to discover that the idea of telling Raquel who she was didn't fill her with alarm. She trusted this woman, she wanted to tell her. 'Raquel, you must keep what I am about to tell you to yourself. Here in Castile, I am merely a lady. But, in Granada, I was the Princess Zoraida, Sultan Tariq's second daughter.'

Raquel gasped. 'A princess! I see.'

Seville. When they reached the city, astonished by the bustle, Alba reined in.

On one side lay a busy river port, crammed with wharves and quays. Seagulls mewed, swooping low over a forest of masts. Rope hoists creaked, chests and barrels swayed precariously in mid-air as they were lifted out of ships and barges and on to carts and waggons. On the other side, streets ran off into the heart of the town. Most of the houses and workshops were wooden, they leaned together like old friends. Here and there a scattering of stone buildings rose tall above the rest.

'That is the Golden Tower,' Raquel told her, pointing with her riding crop at a crenellated building sitting on the edge of the river. A similar tower was positioned on the opposite bank, its jagged merlons looked like great teeth, snapping at the cloudless sky.

'Watchtowers,' Alba murmured.

'They guard the river,' Raquel added. 'Seville is well protected. A great chain runs across the riverbed. When it's raised, it blocks the waterway, stopping enemy ships from coming upstream.'

Alba nodded absently and shifted in the saddle. She was hot and tired, and longing for a bath. Doubtless her escort, which included Guillen and some men-at-arms pressed upon them by Sir Nicolás, felt the same.

'Not far now.'

Raquel spurred forward, and Alba cast a final look at the port.

Anxious cloth merchants were shouting warnings as bolts of fabric, wrapped in oilskin to protect them from the elements, were lifted clear of the decks. Alba's attention was caught by a hooded man hurrying along a gangplank and her breath stopped. The man was carrying a small chest and something about his gait disturbed her. The way he walked, his bow legs—she would know that gait anywhere.

It was the man who had killed the King's envoy in Córdoba. Then, as though sensing he was being watched, the man twisted and looked back. His gaze found Alba and her blood froze.

He let out a hoarse cry, tossed the chest into the barge and jumped on to the quay, eyes blazing murder. Alba clapped her heels to her horse's side and was off, galloping blindly into a side street.

Raquel's cry of alarm came after her. 'Alba! My lady!'

Alba bent over her horse's neck, instinct was telling her she must race for her life. More cries followed.

'Stop, my lady, stop!'

A woman stepped into her path, saw Alba's frenzied approach and leaped out of the way. A flock of chickens scattered, squawking. Feathers flew.

Alba thundered down one street and into another. She had no idea where she was, all she could think was that she must get away. She charged past house after house, then, reining back to a trot, she listened.

No one was shouting, there were no footsteps, she could hear nothing save her frantic breathing and pounding heart.

Ahead stood a handsome gateway, flanked by half a dozen guards. *Half a dozen* guards? Was this the Royal Palace? Dear God, let it be so, a murderer would surely avoid the Alcázar like the plague. Glancing over her shoulder, she headed for the gateway.

'Excuse me, sir?' she said, addressing the nearest guard.

'My lady?'

The guard eyed her uncertainly, as well he might. With the dust of the road on her and panting as though she had run all the way from Córdoba, she must look a fright. No matter, she had to get into the palace. Back straight, ignoring the way the other guards shifted to bar her passage, she pressed on.

'I have missed my way and require your assistance.'

Another guard let out a hoot of laughter. 'And lost your escort too, I'll be bound.'

She quelled him with a lofty look. 'Quite so. As you can plainly see, I am exhausted and in need of refreshment.'

'And your name is...?'

Alba shot a swift look behind her. Mercifully, there was no sign of the assassin. 'My name will mean nothing to you. I am an acquaintance of Count Inigo Sánchez.'

The guards exchanged glances. 'Count Inigo?'

'I believe he is well known in the district.'

She held her breath as more glances were exchanged. There was a little muttering and the guards' faces relaxed. God be praised, they stood aside to let her pass. Alba breathed again.

'You're in luck, my lady, Count Inigo is here. You'll find the stables on your left. Leave your mount with a groom and someone will direct you.'

'Thank you.' Alba smiled. 'Thank you so much.'

Leaving her horse to be cared for in the stables, Alba made further enquiries and was directed along a path in the shade of a high wall. The shade was welcome, her clothes were sticking to her skin and she felt horribly dishevelled. It wasn't important. With the assassin in Seville, all she could think of was that she must reach Lord Inigo.

She passed an orchard and a small tree-filled square with a fountain in the centre. The idea of splashing water on her face was beyond tempting, she resisted and hurried on. She'd reached a stone-flagged terrace that was screened with vines, when she became aware of someone behind her.

'Pretty lady, why the haste?'

The voice was wheedling and not one she knew. Her skin crawled even before she turned.

The assassin stood three paces away, an ugly smile lighting his dour features, his hand resting on the distinctive black and gold hilt of his Toledan sword.

'Well met, pretty lady.' His eyes were dead, this was a man who had no soul.

Alba's legs stopped working. He'd been on foot, how had he got here so quickly? And how had he got in? Her heart was in her mouth and it was a struggle to speak.

'Wh…what do you want?'

Steel hissed as he drew his fine sword. The glittering point came to rest on her breast.

'Your silence.'

Held by fear, everything around Alba was suddenly vibrant with life. The fragrance of lavender was sharp and sweet; the hum of bees and the cooing of doves was a song of peace; the splash of a distant fountain was the best of blessings. The gardens were filled with light and shade and life, so beautiful they brought tears to her eyes.

I will never explore this place, I am going to die.

The assassin's hand shifted and his blade, sharp as only Toledan steel could be, sliced through the bodice of her gown.

She took a step backwards and a vine-covered trellis pressed into her back.

'No escape that way, pretty lady.'

His hand shifted again, a silver line cut through the air and a section of her veil drifted away. He was playing with her.

Lifting her chin, Alba scowled. 'I warn you, I am about to scream.'

His laugh was as ugly as the rest of him. 'Scream away. I shall say I caught you in the treasury and you threatened me with violence.'

She managed a scornful laugh. 'I am unarmed, and you are a coward.'

His sword glinted, razor sharp.

Footsteps. God be praised, someone was tearing down the path, she wasn't alone.

'My lady!'

Guillen. Alba was scarcely able to breathe for fear of goading the assassin further. There were more frantic footsteps and Raquel hurtled into view, her face as white as whey.

Guillen snatched out his sword.

'Be careful, Guillen,' Alba got out. 'Raquel, please find Lord Inigo.'

'Where—?'

Alba pointed at a flight of steps. 'That way, I think. For pity's sake, hurry!'

Raquel fled.

The next few minutes were a waking nightmare. Guillen danced about the assassin, sword drawn, driving him away from Alba. The gardens were uncannily quiet. Alba prayed that Lord Inigo would arrive before his squire was butchered.

The Toledan sword flickered, a bright white line. Guillen skipped nimbly out of the way.

The assassin closed in, stabbing and slashing like a madman. Again, Guillen leaped aside.

Another stab. A slash. Saints preserve them, the Toledan steel hit its mark, ripping through Guillen's tunic at the shoulder. A faint streak of red appeared.

The assassin grinned and beckoned Guillen forward. 'Come on, boy, can't you do better than that?'

'Stand down, Guillen, I have him.' Lord Inigo strolled coolly on to the terrace. His eyebrows lifted. 'Martin Díez, who would have thought it? Care to cross swords with me?'

Alba gasped. Lord Inigo knew this man?

The deadly dance began again, and confusion was forgotten as one thought dominated the rest. What if Lord Inigo was hurt? Alba couldn't bear to watch, yet she couldn't not watch. Her mouth dried. Watch she must. She had never seen a sword fight, and each time this Díez slashed and lunged, her stomach cramped. Steel rang out as Lord Inigo parried every thrust, and the cramps worsened. He mustn't be hurt! He mustn't! He hadn't even looked Alba's way and that, she told herself, was a blessing. It was focus or die.

She was vaguely aware of Guillen nursing his shoulder. His eyes never left his lord.

Raquel's face was the colour of snow and at every feint and pass, she gasped. When Lord Inigo drew blood and a small red line appeared on the back of Díez's hand, she moaned and swayed. Fearing the steward's wife was about to faint, and that her lord would be distracted, possibly fatally, Alba slipped to her side.

'Hold firm,' Alba murmured, and they clung to each other. 'My lord is in command here.'

Raquel nodded. 'I know. It's hard though.'

Alba couldn't argue with that. When she tasted blood, she realised she had bitten her tongue to stop herself from crying out. She willed Lord Inigo to take care. *Stay safe, my lord.*

The assassin was puffing and blowing like a bellows, winded, but not yet fully spent. He made a clumsy lunge, a feint. Steel clashed, and his blade rasped up Lord Inigo's all the way to the cross guard.

A line of silver flashed as Lord Inigo parried, the Toledan sword almost shaved his cheek. Alba held her breath. Was Lord Inigo toying with the man? He was a formidable swordsman, when he followed through with a couple of swift, deadly passes, red bloomed on the assassin's arm and again on his chest. He staggered back and leaned against a pillar, panting.

To Alba's dismay, Lord Inigo didn't press home his advantage.

'Tell me, Díez,' he spoke almost conversationally, 'whose banner do you march under these days?'

'Go to hell!'

'Last I knew, you were employed here in Seville.'

The assassin's face twisted. 'Not any more.'

Lord Inigo flexed his sword arm, a negligent movement that was oddly threatening. 'Oh, and why is that?'

'None of your damn business.'

Lord Inigo's eyes were hard as slate. 'Díez, there are two ways this can go. You can offer your testimony about the events leading up to the death of the King's envoy in Córdoba, and I give you my word I'll speak up on your behalf. Fail to do that and I promise you nothing save a bleak and bloody end.'

'Liar.' The assassin's face twisted into a sneer. He pushed away from the pillar, pointing his sword at Lord Inigo's chest. 'No lord ever spoke up for a mercenary.'

'This one will, if you make a full confession. Think about it.'

'When hell freezes over.' Martin Díez spat at the ground and lunged.

The clash of steel sent doves hurtling from their perches. Save for the whirr of birds' wings and the harsh breathing of the duellists, it was ominously quiet.

Lord Inigo made a careful pass. Alba knew she was watching a master, his slightest movement was considered—from his stance, strong and certain, to the calm way his eyes never left his opponent.

Díez was all anger, he had no finesse. Another measured pass was parried so clumsily a bunch of grapes was sliced from the trellis and fell to the ground. The mercenary flinched, his eyes were bulging like those of a frightened horse. His chest heaved, he was almost blown.

'Sweet Mother, Díez, see sense. You're no duellist. You have a fine sword, the pity is your skill doesn't match it.'

Díez replied with another wild swipe, slipped on the grapes and almost lost his footing. A couple of deadly passes followed and the Toledan sword clattered to the ground.

'I yield, damn you.' Díez lifted his hands in surrender.

Guillen moved in and kicked the sword out of reach.

'Are you all right, lad?'

'Yes, my lord, just a scratch.'

'Then bind him.'

'Aye, my lord.'

Lord Inigo rounded on Alba, eyes blazing. 'My lady, what in the name of all that's holy are you doing here?'

Chapter Fifteen

Alba released her death grip on Raquel and stumbled towards Inigo. All she wanted was to fling her arms about him and reassure herself that he was whole, but he was glaring at her as though she was the last person he wanted to see.

'It's good to see you too, my lord.' Alba looked meaningfully at the assassin. 'This Díez is definitely the man I saw outside the goldsmith's house.'

Inigo took a deep breath and those penetrating grey eyes searched hers. 'You'd swear to that?'

'There's no doubt. I know you didn't see his face, but I saw it clear as day. He is the murderer.'

'Thank you, my lady. Having you as a witness will help in the interrogation.' Lord Inigo bent to pick up the discarded sword. 'Toledan steel, just as you told me,' he murmured. 'Luis?'

'My lord?'

Alba blinked, she'd been so taken up with the sword fight, she hadn't noticed that several other people had appeared, among them a boy she had seen working in the stables at Lord Inigo's Córdoban town house. Furthermore, beyond the vine-covered trellis, a cluster of courtiers was watching, wide-eyed.

Alba was bursting to ask what else Lord Inigo knew about the assassin, but with half the Seville court present, it wasn't the right moment.

'Assist Guillen in taking Díez to the lock-up, Luis,' Lord Inigo was saying. 'I shall question him shortly. And, Guillen?'

'My lord?'

'Borrow some of the palace guards, Díez mustn't escape.' Inigo sheathed his sword and crooked his arm at Alba. 'Come, my lady, permit me to show you to a guest chamber. Lady Raquel, you too.'

Alba took Lord Inigo's arm. She was so thankful he wasn't hurt, she couldn't help hugging it. His manner was carefully formal, but he covered her hand with his and she felt the faintest of caresses as his thumb swept over the back of her hand. She hid a smile, she loved it when he did that. In his heart, he was pleased to see her, though he would never make a grand display, particularly since they had an audience.

The courtiers parted to allow them through, and they ascended the steps and entered the Alcázar. The antechamber was breathtaking, Alba was taken aback by the resemblance to her father's palace in Granada.

Plasterwork was painted and gilded in gorgeous colours and tiled floors gleamed. Horseshoe arches gave tantalising glimpses into magnificent state chambers and pillared courtyards. Ladies in silks and satins promenaded slowly along the colonnades. There was even a peacock, its long tail trailing across a marble floor as it made its stately way past a fountain.

As they went deeper into the palace, Alba caught Raquel giving her and Lord Inigo more than one sideways glance. Her new friend had noticed Lord Inigo's fingers were entwined with Alba's.

Blushing, Alba made to pull free. Lord Inigo wouldn't permit it. He strode purposefully on, through glittering rooms where light from multi-coloured windows tinted delicate plasterwork with reds and greens and blues. He came to a halt outside a polished wood door.

'You will find refreshment inside, my lady,' he said, running his gaze over Alba in a way that made her all too conscious of how travel-stained she was.

'Thank you, I am sure I look quite dreadful.'

'You are as enchanting as ever,' he murmured. With a bow, he released her. 'Lady Raquel, is your husband aware you are here?'

Raquel bristled. 'Naturally, my lord.'

'That is a relief.' Lord Inigo's voice was dry. 'If you came without his blessing, I would assuredly never have heard the end of it. Lady Raquel, would you be so good as to attend Lady Alba?'

'My lord, you have no need to ask.'

Alba caught his gaze. 'Shall we see you later, my lord?'

'After I've interviewed Baron Fernando's mercenary.'

Alba's breath caught. 'Baron Fernando's?'

'Aye, I know Martin Díez of old, the last I heard he was in the employ of Baron Fernando.'

Turning on his heel, Lord Inigo walked back the way they had come, leaving Alba and Raquel staring after him with their mouths agape.

'Baron Fernando is Lady Margarita's brother,' Alba said wonderingly.

'So he is.' Raquel pushed at the door. 'Come, my lady, I'm sure you are as eager for refreshment as I.'

The sky over the palace gardens was bright, although beyond the western wall several rosy, gold-tinted clouds warned that sunset wasn't far away.

Inigo and Guillen had been searching high and low for Lady Alba for what seemed like an age.

Guillen spotted her first. 'There she is, my lord.'

She was with his steward's wife, walking along a path by two palms.

'Guillen, be so good as to ask Lady Raquel if she and Lady Alba have everything they require,' Inigo said quietly. 'I'd like to speak to Lady Alba alone.'

'Yes, my lord.'

Inigo took Alba's hand and lifted it to his lips. Her eyes were sombre, though she smiled at his touch. It was heartening to see that gentle smile again, he'd been all too aware that his earlier greeting had been less than welcoming. When Lady Raquel had run to him saying that Alba and Guillen were being attacked in the gardens, his heart had missed several beats. And by the time he'd noticed that part of Alba's veil had been cut away, a red mist had blocked his vision. There'd been no room for niceties.

Alba had changed into a fresh gown which was very becoming, apricot in colour, it was edged with cream. Her veil was also cream and, thankfully, whole. She looked more herself. Inigo felt his tension drain away.

'You look rested, my lady. I hope they took care of you.'

'Thank you, everyone has been most kind. Lady

Raquel arranged for my clothes to be fetched. My old veil—'

Inigo's jaw tightened. 'I noticed that Díez had cut it about. I trust you yourself are unharmed?'

'I am fine, my lord.' She peeped up at him through her eyelashes, eyes anxious. 'You mentioned knowing this man of old?'

'He's a mercenary. Hires himself to the highest bidder. I ran across him when he was working for Baron Fernando.'

'You have finished questioning him?'

'For the moment.' Inigo kissed her hand again. He was going to win this woman, even though winning her was like working his way through a maze. He'd wanted her from the first, despite the many obstacles. She'd asked him to give her a child and he hoped and prayed that she would only have done so because she was attracted to him. Perhaps more than attracted. For so long he hadn't believed in love. Nor, as he recalled it, had she. With her arrival in Seville, was it possible that she had changed her mind?

Was he deluding himself? Alba had come after him…

The maze twisted this way and that. Until he heard back from the King, Margarita remained an obstacle, though it seemed wrong to peg his betrothed as an obstacle. None the less, he would win Alba, her hand *and* her love, for he had come to understand that he couldn't have one without the other. Until today, despite his desire to win her, he'd not been confident of success. Her presence here had changed all that. She had come after him. She wasn't ready to bid him farewell.

I will win her.

Heavens, what he felt for her was so all-consuming, it even seemed possible it would last.

'My lord, I've been thinking about Díez.' Puzzled dark eyes held his. 'When I saw him by the quayside, before he gave chase, he was on foot. I was on horseback. How on earth did he get to the palace so quickly?'

'There's not an alley and side street he doesn't know, I expect he took a shortcut.'

'And how did he slip past the guards?'

'Rank bribery.'

'What?'

'Aye. He slipped some coin to a dolt of a guard, told him he was on an urgent mission and the other fools were persuaded to let him in. They are being disciplined.'

With a swift glance about her, Alba leaned in and whispered, 'Did he kill the King's man on the Baron's order?'

He pressed his finger gently to her mouth.

'Hush, my lady, until my investigation is concluded, we must be wary of what we say.'

She looked solemnly at him. 'I understand.'

Inigo spoke softly. 'I suspect there's more to this than the theft of a jewelled book by a disgruntled mercenary. Baron Fernando is known to be a poor steward, he has run his estate into the ground. I'd assumed he had reserves to draw upon, but perhaps his coffers are empty. My lady, I received word that, while I was subject to your father's hospitality, Crown revenues were going missing here in Seville.'

Mention of her father brought colour to her cheeks and she looked swiftly away. 'I don't know how you can look at me, never mind speak to me, my lord,' she whispered.

Gently, he turned her face back to his. 'My lady, I hope you know that I am not so unreasonable as to hold you responsible for the Sultan's sins.'

She stared at him for a long moment before nodding. 'You have always shown me kindness. My lord, you must know I hold you in the highest esteem.'

He felt himself smile. 'That is good to hear.'

'Lord Inigo.' Her voice sank to little more than a whisper. 'About the Crown revenues, what else did Díez say?'

'Thus far, very little. Never fear, if he's left to cool his heels long enough, I am confident he will say more.'

A bench stood beneath a tumble of pink roses and Inigo guided her towards it. It was late in the season for roses and the air was heady with their scent. Alba sat neatly next to him, her thigh lightly brushing his. She was looking through an arch towards Lady Raquel and Guillen, giving Inigo the perfect opportunity to study her profile.

Lord, she was pretty. The deepening twilight did nothing to hide the curve of her brow, the length of her eyelashes and the fullness of her lips. Inigo's heart thumped, and his thumb went on caressing her hand. He couldn't stop if he tried. On the contrary, the impulse to tug her towards him was irresistible. He ached to turn her face to his and look deeply into those black eyes. In this light, would he see those golden flecks?

He followed the direction of her gaze. Lady Raquel and Guillen were partially hidden by another screen of roses.

The dusk thickened. The warmth in Alba's smile drove away reason and sense, all Inigo wanted was to pull her into to his arms. No one would see. Apart from Lady Raquel and Guillen, no one else was about…

Cupping her face with his palm, he leaned in. 'My lady, I—'

Then his lips were on hers and he forgot what he had been about to say. The garden fell away, and both Margarita and Díez were blinked out of existence. Nothing was real save the warmth of Alba's mouth and the way her body leaned into his. The elusive scent of jasmine mingled with that of the roses. Alba gave an inarticulate murmur and he drew back.

'My lady?'

Above them, the sunset flared gold and crimson. She shook her head, lifted her lips to his and kissed him back. With passion. With sweetness and promise.

Inigo's pulse thudded, and he felt a strong echo in his loins. He knew he should stop, none the less, the kiss deepened. Her tongue was touching his and he was unable to help himself. Kissing Alba was all that there was. It was both right and necessary and he was caught in a curious enchantment in which longing, desire and need merged into one.

Lady Raquel's voice broke the spell. In a trice Inigo was back in the garden, sitting under a shower of pink roses with a Nasrid princess in his arms.

A princess who was trembling and who carefully extricated herself from his grasp.

'My lord, anyone might see us.'

She sounded breathless and was flushing as brightly as the roses. She looked adorable.

He reached for her hand. 'I apologise, but I needed that. I wanted to kiss you earlier, only not with half the court looking on.'

With a sigh, he leaned back. He wanted to do more than kiss Alba, but he wouldn't be so crude as to admit it. It was beyond frustrating. At that moment, he would have given his entire estate to be able to tell her what had passed between him and Margarita. He wanted Alba to know that Margarita hoped to marry Sir Arnau, and that if the King agreed, he would be a free man. As matters stood, his hands were tied.

'I feared you might be angry,' she murmured.

'With you? No. Afraid you'd been hurt? Yes.' He nudged her shoulder with his. 'As for kissing you just now, I couldn't help myself.'

'I understand, my lord, I feel the same.'

She had Inigo utterly bemused. Nothing had prepared him for Alba. In his experience, women rarely spoke with such straightforward honesty. He leaned in and pressed a swift kiss to her cheek. More at ease than he'd felt in an age, he pushed to his feet. 'I am honoured. Come, my lady, allow me to direct you to your quarters.'

'Thank you.' Alba stood and shook rose petals from her skirts. In the dusk her eyes gleamed like jet. 'Will we be staying in the Alcázar until your business with Díez is concluded?'

'I think that's best, I need to be on hand. Owing to the shortfall in revenues, I've put the treasury under surveillance.'

'You suspect Baron Fernando has turned to thievery?'

'Time will tell. If the Baron is as desperate as the rumours have it, he will eventually show his hand. So, for the moment, we remain here.'

In truth, Inigo wanted to carry Alba to Castle Sánchez, but that wasn't possible. A princess deserved some respect. Not to mention that until he had resolved matters with Margarita, there was no way he was going to shame his betrothed by installing another woman in territory she had long viewed as hers.

The following morning, Alba ventured alone into the palace gardens. Raquel had vanished, and Alba assumed that the Spanish King's affairs were demanding Lord Inigo's full attention.

Finding a large pond filled with water lilies,

Alba perched on the rim. Fish were gliding beneath the lilies, bright splotches of gold, white and black. As she dipped her fingers into the water, several swam to the surface. Perhaps they were hoping for bread.

She was conscious of a strange melancholy, and knew it was in some way connected to Lady Margarita. Alba needed to know Lady Margarita's true mind. Did Lady Margarita wish to marry Lord Inigo? Alba instinctively felt she did not. The only time Alba had met her, in the Córdoba Alcázar, Lady Margarita had reacted with cold anger. If Lady Margarita believed Alba was Lord Inigo's mistress, the anger was understandable. Her pride had been hurt. But why the coldness? Alba could understand it if Lady Margarita didn't wish to marry Lord Inigo.

She sucked in a breath. Lady Margarita didn't want to marry him, she was marrying him on sufferance.

Was she being coerced?

Alba's stomach turned over. She was reminded of her meeting with Gui García. The Captain was personable and certainly handsome enough to give her the child she'd longed for, yet his touch had repelled her. Put bluntly, Sir Gui wasn't Lord Inigo. Having a child with Sir Gui—impossible.

What did Margarita think about her betrothal? What did she want?

The Spanish nobility set much store by duty, and Alba understood the necessity for dynastic marriages. She knew that Count Javier had proposed the alliance between his family and Lady Margarita's. None the less, she couldn't believe that Lord Inigo, the kind and thoughtful man she'd come to admire, would wilfully ignore Lady Margarita's distress. He was an honourable man, not a cruel one.

A shadow fell over her. Raquel was hurrying along the path, her face bright with happiness. She looked so pleased, Alba thrust her misgivings aside.

'Raquel, what's happened?'

'I'm sorry I kept you waiting.' Raquel sank down next to her and leaned in conspiratorially. 'My lady, I have the best of news. I… I was unwell this morning. I believe I am carrying a child.'

Confused, Alba gripped Raquel's arm. 'You were ill? Please tell me the baby wasn't harmed by the journey from Córdoba.'

'No, no, not at all.' Raquel put a hand to her belly, still smiling. 'Women often suffer in the mornings when they conceive a child.'

'Do they?' Alba let out a relieved laugh. 'You

will have to excuse me, I am woefully ignorant. Please accept my congratulations.'

'Thank you. Sir Nicolás and I have been trying for an age. I was beginning to fear it would never happen.'

'It is wonderful news. Children are such a blessing,' Alba said. As the words left her mouth, she stilled. How she had changed! Much as she wished for a child herself, having a child was no longer her main concern. She wanted Lord Inigo far more than she wanted a child. She wanted a soulmate to stand beside her, someone with whom she could share her hopes and fears.

Eyes glittering, Raquel danced to her feet. 'And now you must excuse me again, I need to write to my husband.'

She was gone before Alba had a chance to ask whether she knew if Lord Inigo's interrogation of the assassin had been concluded and whether anyone knew how Lady Margarita was faring.

Alba gazed pensively into the pond. Lady Margarita had been miserable when Alba had seen her in Córdoba. Baron Fernando had to be insisting she married Lord Inigo. Poor woman, no one should be forced into marriage.

Alba clenched her fists. Something must be done.

Lost in thought, she glanced down the path on

her right. It was the path that led to the terrace where Lord Inigo and Díez had fought their duel. It was beyond strange that the assassin should turn out to have been in the Baron's pay. Alba had been listening to the court ladies, and while everyone had been discussing the shocking sword fight in the palace gardens, a place where no one was meant to bear arms apparently, none of them had mentioned Baron Fernando. Lord Inigo's determination to keep the Baron's name out of it was proving a success.

What was happening? She burned to know.

Most importantly, why wasn't Lord Inigo doing more to assist Lady Margarita? He, of all men, was well placed to do so. Why was he dragging his feet? Did he intend to pursue the marriage, despite her apparent reluctance?

Alba stared into the pond, praying that she hadn't misjudged him. She was sure she loved him, the feeling felt true. *I love him.*

When she'd first come to Castile, all she'd wanted was a child. Lord Inigo had made it easy to choose him for the father. That longing hadn't faded, but it paled in comparison to her longing for Lord Inigo himself.

What would happen if Alba marched into the palace offices and demanded to speak to him? As far as the Spanish court was concerned, she would have no right to know—about anything. She was a foreigner and a woman. And the Count was betrothed to Lady Margarita.

Alba was on the point of rising to go and find him, when brisk footsteps pulled her from her reverie.

Lord Inigo's broad shoulders blocked out the light. He reached for her hand. 'Good day, my lady. Heavens, what a dour expression, what have the poor fish done to you?'

'Nothing, my lord.' Alba waved in the direction of the palace. 'I was wondering how to find you in that great labyrinth.'

'Ask for Guillen or Luis, they usually know where I am.'

'Thank you.'

He settled beside her on the edge of the pond. 'How are you?'

'You want the truth?'

'Always.'

'I am anxious. And angry.'

His expression sobered. 'How so?'

'Lady Margarita.'

'Ah.'

'My lord, it has occurred to me that her brother might be coercing her into marrying you.'

'You are as perceptive as ever,' he murmured.

She gave him a confused look. 'What are you doing to help her?'

He held her gaze, grey eyes steady. 'My lady, I'm pressed for time, so I must be brief. I came to tell you that last evening, I used the King's seal to summon Margarita to the Alcázar.'

Alba's eyes widened. 'Lady Margarita is coming here?'

'She arrives today. My lady, I believe this is the moment to tell you what I saw when you first visited Castle Álvarez. You will recall the orchard by the gates?' At Alba's nod, Inigo continued. 'Lady Margarita was sitting on a bench in that orchard, engrossed in conversation with Lord Rodrigo's steward, Sir Arnau. I barely recognised her, she looked so changed.'

'I don't understand.'

'The Margarita on that bench was the old Margarita, the one I hadn't seen in years. She was happy and carefree. Full of life.'

Alba watched him, unmoving. 'She was?'

'Alba—my lady—what I saw prompted me to speak to Margarita. She has admitted that she no longer wishes for our marriage to go ahead.' He smiled. 'She is in love with Sir Arnau.'

'Lord Rodrigo's steward.'

'Aye. That is why I have arranged for her to come here. She'll be free of coercion in the palace.'

Alba bit her lip as a surge of happiness swept through her. He was setting aside his betrothal! She forced herself to remain calm and to concentrate on what he was saying. 'And if her brother the Baron accompanies her?'

'So much the better, he will walk straight into custody.'

'I don't understand.'

Triumph gleamed in Lord Inigo's eyes. 'In the small hours, Díez confessed to stealing the King's book on the Baron's orders, he was told to get hold of it, whatever the cost. That poor wretch whose death you witnessed in Córdoba merely had the misfortune to get in his way.'

Alba ran a fingertip along the rim of the pond. 'Lady Raquel mentioned that the Book of Hours had been returned. I hadn't realised that Baron Fernando claimed credit for finding it. It seems incredible that he would order it stolen only to hand it back. Why do such a thing?'

'The Baron is desperate to win the King's favour and in "finding" that Book of Hours he has done exactly that. My lady, you may not know, but illuminated books of such quality are priceless in Castile. Monks take years to decorate the pages, and the jewels on the cover are as valuable as the contents.' Lord Inigo's mouth thinned. 'Baron Fernando is a wastrel and a spendthrift, he could have been angling for a monetary reward. Díez became extremely talkative when I offered to plead for his life and his testimony has confirmed my suspicions. The Baron rarely settles his debts. Díez didn't expect to be paid for his services. He has confessed to prising a few gems from the cover before passing the book to the Baron.'

Alba shuddered. 'Poor Lady Margarita, I feel for her. Her brother sounds vile.'

'I agree, I don't think she knew where to turn. I'm partly to blame. If I'd made more of an effort to understand her, she might have trusted me with the truth.'

'My lord, you can't shoulder the blame for everything. As I understand it, you were young when the responsibilities of your estate were thrust upon you.'

'It's true my parents' deaths set me back. However, that is no excuse. I neglected Margarita and she has suffered as a result.' He sighed. 'My interview with Díez has cast light on another matter. You may remember my mentioning that Crown revenues in Seville were running low.'

Alba went still. 'Baron Fernando is responsible for that too?'

Lord Inigo nodded. 'Díez overheard him conspiring to withhold Crown revenues and tamper with the accounts. Furthermore, Díez has confirmed it before witnesses.'

'It seems incredible that the Baron never paid him,' Alba said. 'If Díez knew his murky secrets, it would have made sense for the Baron to keep him sweet.'

'I dare say he planned to pay Díez, eventually.' Lord Inigo laughed. 'What a pair they make— Díez too impatient to wait for his pay, and the Baron delaying payment until the last possible moment.'

She grimaced. 'Not an ideal partnership.'

'I'd say it was doomed from the beginning.' Lord Inigo caught her hand, kissed it and rose. 'If you will excuse me, there's much to do before Margarita arrives. Be assured, you are ever in my thoughts.'

Alba caught his arm. 'My lord?'

'My lady, I really must go, the King needs to know his revenues are secure.'

'This won't take long.' Lord Inigo was still looking down at her, so Alba rushed on. 'It concerns Sir Arnau.'

'What of him?'

'It's occurred to me, do you think…would it be possible to send for him too? I assume that since he is a vassal of Count Rodrigo he will be reliable.'

Lord Inigo's face softened into a smile. 'He is, very much so. Sir Arnau has no lands of his own, but he is the rarest of men, honest and genuinely noble. I'd trust him with my life.' Drawing her to his feet, he briefly caressed her cheek. 'As always, your thoughts align with mine. I sent for Sir Arnau late last eve.'

'Bless you.'

Impulsively, Alba took his hand, pressed her forehead against it and kissed it. Lord Inigo's face was a picture, he looked absolutely bemused. Pleased, but bemused. And not a little embarrassed.

'Saints, my lady, there's no need for that.'

'There is every need.'

Smiling, he shook his head. 'You do realise that Margarita will be here before Sir Arnau, her brother's lands are close to the city. You might also care to know that I shall keep the King fully informed. About everything.' He took a step back and bowed. 'I beg your leave, my lady.'

Turning, he stepped into a patch of sunlight and strode towards the palace.

Alba watched him go, her heart aching with an agonising combination of hope and fear.

You are ever in my thoughts.

Count Inigo had summoned Lady Margarita to the Alcázar to keep her safe, and her brother seemed to be on the point of being arrested. He'd summoned Sir Arnau too, who would doubtless lend aid if trouble flared between the Baron's supporters and those of Count Inigo. But what kind of aid? As a landless knight, Sir Arnau would have no troops at his command. The only reason that Alba could think of for summoning Sir Arnau was as a companion for Lady Margarita. And finally, the King was being kept fully informed about everything, whatever that might mean.

Lord Inigo must be hoping that Lady Margarita would make a match of it with Sir Arnau.

If so…

A rush of longing swept through her and she moaned aloud.

'My lady?' Raquel was back, her face creased with concern. 'Are you well?'

Alba wrapped her arms about herself and gave a wry smile. 'I have no idea.'

Chapter Sixteen

The following day, the atmosphere in the women's quarters was close and stuffy. The women were busy with needlework, and Alba found the chatter oppressive. She felt stifled and shut in.

She truly needed to know Lord Inigo's mind. Was he hoping that Lady Margarita would marry Sir Arnau? Doubtless, there would be obstacles. Lord Inigo was a great lord, and his betrothal was long-standing. The King would surely be involved in releasing him from his betrothal.

'I need a walk,' she murmured to Raquel. 'Can I lure you outside?'

'With the sun at its height? It will be very warm.'

'I need exercise and would enjoy your company.'

Raquel rose with a smile. 'In that case, a walk would be pleasant.'

Alba had already done some exploring and it hadn't taken long for her to see the similarities between the Seville Alcázar and her father's Alhambra Palace. Both were fortress palaces.

Like the Alhambra, this one was protected by

a high curtain wall, on top of which were regularly patrolled walkways. Inside, everything was far less military. The top of the garden wall, for instance, was an elegant covered terrace that was usually crowded with courtiers. Alba had seen them promenading along the terrace with their entourages, partly to be seen, partly for exercise and, above all, to observe.

From the terrace, a series of arches overlooked shimmering fountains, dark fish ponds and trellised courtyards. Using the walkway, the lords and ladies of Seville could keep an eye on those in the gardens below. People rarely looked up, and an unguarded word from someone wandering in the gardens was easily overheard. Promenading with apparent languor along the high terrace was the perfect way to gather information about what was happening elsewhere in the palace. Discreetly. And without the use of spies or a large network.

It was stifling outside; the air was still and heavy. Hoping the heat had driven everyone inside, Alba gestured at the stairs to the garden terrace.

'There'll be a breeze higher up. Let's find a cool spot.'

They found a couch in the shade and Alba's luck was in. No one else was about. She heaved a relieved sigh. 'My apologies for dragging you out, I couldn't stand it in there a moment longer.'

The abrupt tolling of a bell fractured the peace of the tranquil gardens. Gathering up her skirts, Alba hurried to a nearby arch and peered through.

'It's coming from the gatehouse.'

Raquel's shoulder brushed hers, she too was staring through the arch.

'That's an alarm bell,' Raquel said. 'My guess is that Lady Margarita has arrived. Her brother must be with her.'

Angry voices reached them. Men were shouting and swearing. Then came a slight pause, like the eye of a storm, and a lone male voice was raised in outrage. Steel clashed, a chilling, brittle noise, peculiarly incongruous in the sultry air. A harsh cry went up and the alarm stopped ringing.

Silence.

Gradually, the voices began again. One of them, a man's, was achingly familiar.

'That's Lord Inigo,' Raquel said.

Alba hurried to the next archway, desperate to know what was happening. Frustratingly, her line of sight was blocked by the fronds of a palm tree.

Raquel let out a huff of impatience. 'How irritating, we can't see a thing from this standpoint.'

Alba lifted an eyebrow. 'What say you to a walk past the gatehouse?'

'Lead on.'

They picked up their skirts and flew down the steps and into the garden.

It was maddening. By the time they reached the entrance to the gardens, the outcry had died down and there was no sign that anything untoward had happened. Bunches of grapes sagged heavily on the vines, a dove cooed from a nearby trellis.

Raquel gave her a sympathetic look. 'If we can find Lord Inigo, he will tell us what's happening.'

Alba hesitated. 'If that was Lady Margarita and Baron Fernando, Lord Inigo will be fully occupied. There's nothing for it, we shall have to return to the women's quarters, one of the ladies is bound to know something.'

They went back inside. The ladies were still at their embroidery. Needles flashed silver in the sun. Tiny scissors snipped at silken threads, gold, crimson, green. The talk was desultory, the atmosphere dozily carping, it was as though everyone was half asleep.

'Did you see Lady Sofia's new gown? Silk from Cathay, could it be?'

'I don't care where it's from, in my view it's criminal to wear it with quite so many yellow ribbons. The woman looks like a—'

The door flung open and a stately woman sailed in, puffed up with self-importance. Her name,

Alba recalled, was Lady Jimena. Lady Jimena's broad forehead was dotted with perspiration, she had clearly hurried from some dark recess of the palace and was agog with scandal.

'Just listen to this,' Lady Jimena said, breathlessly addressing the room at large.

All eyes turned her way, needles paused mid-stitch as Lady Jimena launched into an account of what had happened at the gatehouse.

'Baron Fernando Marchena has been arrested.'

Several ladies gasped.

'Aye, is it not strange?' Lady Jimena continued. 'Lady Margarita was summoned by her betrothed and the Baron headed her escort. However, no sooner had the Baron ridden into the stables than Count Inigo had him in irons.'

The ladies stared, open-mouthed.

A woman in her middle years leaned in. 'On what grounds? Why was he arrested?'

This was Lady Valeria. Her cheeks were wrinkled like old apples. Alba had already learned that Lady Valeria knew everyone and that many of the ladies deferred to her wisdom.

'He's to answer charges of embezzling the King's revenues.'

'Lady Jimena, that's impossible.'

'Not so, Lady Valeria, I assure you.'

A subdued muttering began.

Lady Valeria held up her hand. 'Quiet, for pity's sake. What of Lady Margarita?'

'Count Inigo has taken her under his protection. She has been given an apartment close to his.'

Ice ran down Alba's spine. A couple of noble-women looked down their noses at her and she found herself struggling to maintain her calm. Lady Margarita had chambers close to Lord Inigo's, while she'd been housed in more general quarters with the other ladies. Hurt twisted inside.

The ladies muttered to one another behind their hands. Doubtless, they knew of Alba's connection with Lord Inigo and were wondering what to make of it.

Alba's cheeks were hot. Did these women, like Captain García, assume that Alba was Lord Inigo's mistress? The disdain in their expressions was yet more proof that a mistress in Spain was not viewed with the same tolerance as a concubine in her father's harem.

She sat stiff-backed and told herself that the opinion of these women was irrelevant. What mattered was that only yesterday Lord Inigo had treated her as a trusted friend, even going so far as to say their minds were aligned.

We are friends. Close friends.

Lord Inigo had taken her to task about her ill-advised plans to get with child. He'd mentioned disparagement, he would never demean her. Just as he would never demean Lady Margarita, who remained his betrothed.

She would have to trust him.

Alba's faith in Lord Inigo was sorely tested, the sun rose and set several times before she saw him again. What was he doing? It was a question she asked Lady Raquel daily, and daily the answer changed. Count Inigo was in a council meeting. He was talking with the King's Treasurer. He was meeting with the Captain of the Palace Guard.

Essentially, Lord Inigo was too busy to see her.

It didn't help that there had been no sign of Lady Margarita either. What was going on?

Patience at an end, she finally went in search of Guillen. With luck, he would know more. She found him in the stables, grooming his horse.

'Guillen, Lord Inigo said that if ever I wanted to speak to him, you would be able to help. I'd like to see him.'

Guillen leaned against his horse's rump. 'I regret, my lady, that may not be possible. Lord Inigo is closeted with the King's advisors.'

'Again? Will he be busy all day?'

'I believe so. It's a council meeting,' Guillen said. 'They always drag.'

'Drag? It seems they are interminable. Are they held every day?'

'My lady, there is much for Lord Inigo to do, while he was away, the County's finances—'

'Yes, yes, I know about the embezzlement.'

Guillen eyed her sympathetically. 'My lady, you might like to know that my lord has written to the King to advise him that the Baron of Carmona has been dipping his fingers into Crown Revenues. His Grace also knows that Lady Margarita was being forced into marriage. Lord Inigo had made several suggestions, he awaits the King's response.'

'My lord has told the King that Lady Margarita was being coerced?' she asked.

Lord Inigo had mentioned that he was keeping the King fully informed, this must be what he meant.

Guillen hesitated, seeming to pick his words with care. 'Lord Inigo has been entirely frank with the King. But until we hear from His Grace, my lord's hands are tied. My lady, the entire court is on tenterhooks.'

'Thank you, Guillen. When you next see Lord Inigo, please be sure to give him my best wishes.'

A shadow shifted in the doorway, Lord Inigo was leaning his shoulder against a wooden beam, watching her.

His lips curved. 'At last, I find you.'

Alba's face flamed. She was embarrassed at being caught asking questions and angry that she had had to resort to hunting poor Guillen down in the stables.

'You were looking for me, my lord?' Her voice was dry. 'I am sorry to have inconvenienced you, I am sure.'

She strode to the door. Lord Inigo caught her arm as she squeezed past and threaded it through his.

'At odds with me?' His eyebrow quirked upwards. 'You feel neglected.'

'Neglected?' Alba stopped dead in the middle of the stable yard. 'Why should I feel neglected? I am not your betrothed. You owe me nothing.'

'True.' He patted her hand which, strangely, fired her rage. 'As you say, my lady, you are not my betrothed. May I suggest a walk through the gardens?'

Alba narrowed her eyes at him. It was on the tip of her tongue to insist he return her to the women's quarters, but that would achieve little. Besides, she had been looking for him.

'There's something I wish you to see,' he added.

'Very well.'

They passed under the arch and into the gardens and they'd scarcely gone three paces when

Alba was brought up short before an arbour framed by falls of luxuriant purple flowers.

Lady Margarita sat on a low wall, half hidden by foliage. Her hands were folded primly in her lap and her face was lit with happiness. Next to her sat a man in a dusky blue tunic. They weren't touching, yet their delight in each other was plain to see.

'That can only be Sir Arnau.'

'Aye.' Lord Inigo cleared his throat. 'I take it Guillen explained that I'd written to the King suggesting Margarita should marry Sir Arnau rather than me.'

Her eyes widened. 'No, he didn't give me any details.'

Strong fingers covered her arm. 'So, now we wait. His Grace is almost certain to allow the marriage. Sir Arnau knows much about managing an estate and he has built up a reputation for diligence and good stewardship. Let us leave them in peace.'

They brushed past a flowerbed edged with lavender, and a cloud of white butterflies rose into the air. Alba barely noticed. Longing was an ache in every fibre of her body. Lord Inigo had asked the King if Lady Margarita could marry elsewhere. Agonising though it was, she must react calmly.

'My lord, by all accounts you yourself are a good steward. What if the King continues to promote your marriage with Lady Margarita?'

'I doubt he'll do that.'

Alba thought of her father and felt unbearably sad. Sad and hideously conflicted. 'Can you ever be certain what a king will do?'

Lord Inigo smiled. 'I cannot, however, I know King Henry pretty well, he usually takes my advice. Rest assured, the instant we have his reply, you will be informed.'

Another question hovered on the tip of Alba's tongue. If the King agreed to Lady Margarita marrying Sir Arnau, Lord Inigo would, for the first time since she had met him, be truly free. Free to choose his bride. She stole a sideways glance at him.

Would he choose her? Doubts engulfed her. She had grown to be fond of this man, no, she must be honest with herself, she loved him with all her heart. That didn't mean that she was blind to Lord Inigo's many responsibilities. How could he marry her, when he had the County of Seville to think of and his King to answer to?

The time for dreaming was over. She must be realistic. Why would the Count of Seville choose a Nasrid princess? She had nothing to offer, save a handful of jewels. Her father the Sultan was the worst of neighbours. He broke peace treaties and refused to pay the tribute he owed to the Spanish Crown. Countless Spanish lives had been wasted in petty border disputes, including the life of Lord Inigo's comrade and friend, Diego Álvarez. And if that wasn't bad enough, Alba had been banished from her father's kingdom. A banished princess was surely worthless.

I have been banished, and if I became Lord Inigo's wife his position in Castile would be weakened. He is far too dutiful and honourable to choose me. And even if he did, for his sake I ought to refuse him.

She had been living in a dream world. Hollow-hearted, Alba walked along the paths with her hand on his arm, seeing nothing. Feeling numb.

'My lady, Sir Arnau brought a report from Castle Álvarez that will interest you. Lord Rodrigo has succeeded in getting a message from your sister, Lady Constanza.'

Alba pushed her sadness behind her. 'Constanza wants to escape my father's palace?' She even found a smile.

Lord Inigo grimaced. 'No, my lady, nothing has changed in that regard. Lady Constanza wrote to Lady Leonor making it plain she will be staying with Sultan Tariq. Arnau said something about Lady Constanza insisting her name was not and never would be Constanza. She calls herself Zorahaida. I dare say you will understand it, for I'm blessed if I do.'

'My father calls her Zorahaida. It is her Moorish name.'

'Her Moorish name,' Lord Inigo murmured. 'Yes, I remember, you are Zoraida.'

Alba gave him a steady look. 'I wonder sometimes what I am.'

Dark eyebrows twitched into a frown. 'You are upset about Lady Constanza.'

She lifted her shoulders. 'More disappointed than upset. Truth to tell, I didn't really expect she would try to escape, not on her own.'

'Sir Arnau asked me to add that Lady Leonor will shortly be writing to you herself.'

They strolled down another path and sadness filled her. Much as Alba enjoyed Lord Inigo's company, their friendship was likely to become ever more awkward. She was a diplomatic embarrassment. This might be the last time they walked together.

Lord Inigo paused before a wooden pavilion set in the dappled shade of a ring of olive trees.

Alba lifted an eyebrow. 'I've not seen this before. It reminds me of Count Rodrigo's hunting lodge.'

Grey eyes smiled back at her. 'It's a mite smaller

than Rodrigo's hunting lodge. Come, the interior might surprise you.'

Hand clasped in his, Alba stepped into the shade and was confronted by a long divan which was almost lost beneath a tumble of cushions. It was the only piece of furniture. The rest of the pavilion was extraordinary, it was like walking into a tent. Almost every inch of the walls was draped with golden silk, artfully gathered together to form a peak above their heads. The golden silk was enhanced by delicate embroidery. Red, white and blue butterflies hovered above sprays of flowers. There were bees, doves, rabbits…

'The work in this!' She made her voice bright. 'It almost seems alive.'

Lord Inigo murmured agreement, although Alba couldn't help but be aware that he wasn't looking at the silk, he was watching her, eyes intent. He tugged gently on her hand and turned her to face him.

'My lady, I understand you are upset about Lady Constanza.'

'As I said, disappointed rather than upset, truly, my lord.'

He studied her. 'Something else troubles you?'

Alba shook her head. 'A little melancholy, that's all.' And she mustn't allow it to spoil their remaining time together. If this was all they had, she would make the most of it.

'I hoped you'd feel comfortable in Seville, my lady. The last thing I want is for you to live to regret fleeing Al-Andalus.'

Her fingers tightened on his. 'I don't regret a thing, my lord.' Caught between an irresistible urge to tell him she loved him and the knowledge that they were unlikely to have a future together, she bit her lip.

With a half-smile, he reached up to touch her mouth. 'Don't do that.'

'Why not?' She moistened her lips and the atmosphere in the pavilion grew warm.

Inigo leaned in. 'Because it invariably makes me want to do this.' He hesitated, long enough for her to understand what he was about to do, and his lips met hers.

Paradise. The moment their lips touched, it was as though Alba had walked into Paradise. Her doubts, her fear that the gulf between them would never be bridged, all of that faded. Lord Inigo was everything. As his mouth moved softly over hers she gave a breathy moan. Her body leaned against his and her breasts pressed firmly against him. She felt no embarrassment and no shame. Each kiss, each sigh, was drawing her into a sensual web from which there could be no escape.

This was what she wanted. This, with this man. The chance might never come again, and her body knew it. Realising his hand was on her breast and that far from objecting, she had pressed herself more closely against him, she managed to pull back. There was something she must say first.

'My lord, I need, I need...'

'Mmm?' He trailed a row of meltingly gentle kisses along her neck and when he looked at her, his grey eyes were dark with what she recognised was desire. 'Tell me what you need.'

His voice was husky. She was surrounded by his scent—spicy, male and achingly familiar. Her legs felt weak. Shooting a glance at the cushion-covered divan, she gripped his tunic. She must tell him she loved him before what was left of her common sense deserted her.

'My lord, I love you.'

A crooked smile appeared. 'You do?'

'Very much.' Alba looked intently at him.

He kissed her neck again, slowly working his way to her mouth. 'That's good.'

'Is it?'

'Mmm.' His gaze softened and she saw a new vulnerability in his expression. That crooked smile reappeared. 'Alba, I shouldn't be saying this so soon, but I have never felt this way before, with any woman. I adore you. I'd hoped to wait till the time was right, but you overwhelm me. I adore your eyes.' He kissed her eyelids. 'Your face.' He kissed her cheek. 'Every inch of your body.' A strong warrior's hand shaped her breast and his voice cracked. 'Alba, I can wait no longer. I will make things right between us.'

Alba's heart took flight. All she'd really heard was that he adored her. For some reason, hearing him say the words made her unbearably shy. Fighting the urge to bury her face in his chest, she forced herself to watch his expression. 'You adore me.'

Warm lips nuzzled her cheeks. 'You know it, my love. One moment, if you please.'

The golden drapery at the entrance of the pavilion was held back by silken cords looped around brass hooks. Inigo released her long enough to unhook the cords and a swathe of gold swished neatly across the doorway. They were left in half-light, a discreet and shady bower.

He gestured at the couch.

'Your thoughts align with mine, my lady?'

Alba swallowed hard, she had to clear her throat before she could speak. 'Yes.'

Her thoughts lost all coherence as he led her to the couch. She was nervous and excited and blissfully happy. *He adores me.*

Gently, he sat her down and knelt on the floor

at her feet. 'My lord, please,' she said, tugging at his hand, conscious only that she wanted him on the couch next to her.

'There's no need to be nervous, my sweet.' He caught her hand, dropped a kiss on her knuckles and tenderly, and far too respectfully, set about removing her veil. 'We can take our time. I respect your innocence.'

A frustrated laugh escaped her. 'You think I'm nervous.'

A dark eyebrow lifted. 'Aren't you?'

He reached for her foot and deftly removed a shoe. Then the next. It was all very decorous. He was being so careful she had to smile.

'Impatient, perhaps, not nervous. Not with you.'

His eyes darkened. He made a sound that she had never heard before, it was part groan, part growl. Pure want. A heartbeat later, he was beside her on the couch.

His hands were everywhere. Unlacing her gown, slipping it from her shoulders, and gently, so gently, stroking her skin. Everywhere his hands went, his lips followed. Warm, sensuous, tantalising. When she felt his mouth on her breast, Alba arched towards him and heard a new sound, one of her own making. She was pure want herself. It felt wonderful. He felt wonderful.

'That's...'

He lifted his head. 'Good, I hope.'

'Do it again.'

'As you command. Lord, Alba, you are lovely.'

'So are you.' Alba wove her fingers into his hair and brought his mouth back to hers. She was rewarded with a feral groan that told her that he didn't hold all the power here. They were equals. She pushed at his chest and curled her fingers into his tunic.

'This must come off.' Alba had never seen a man's body and she had to see his.

He adores me. Briefly, a dark recollection broke through the haze of desire. He'd not mentioned love. Indeed, he'd told her that love never lasted. He might desire her today, but tomorrow? So much stood between them. This might never happen again.

A crooked smile pushed away her doubt, and his belt and tunic went the way of her shoes and veil. Alba's dress, she realised, was bunched about her waist. She didn't care, she was too busy staring at his chest. He was strongly, beautifully formed, with muscles that cried out to be caressed. When she touched him, his sensuous groan reached deep inside.

For today, it was enough. He moved over her, and words lost their value. Thoughts tangled and, as he rocked into her, Alba gasped.

'All is well, my love?' His voice was thick, as though he too was having difficulty thinking.

She managed a nod and stroked her hand down his back. Gripping his hips, she went with him to a place where guilt no longer existed. All doubts were swept aside. All that remained was a world without barriers, a world where two people became one in a dazzling flash of delight.

For two days, Alba trod the thyme-scented pathways of the Alcázar gardens in a bliss-filled daze. She thought about Lord Inigo from dawn to dusk. All she wanted to do was to sit on the lichen-encrusted rim of the fish pond, crushing lavender between her fingers, remembering. Making love had been a revelation. Lord Inigo had been so gentle, effortlessly sweeping her away on a tide of passion, teaching her that her expectations of what it meant to join with a man had been based on prejudice and fear. Men could be trusted. They could be loved and making love wasn't something to be endured for the sake of begetting a child. It was meant to be beautiful.

I love him. She gave a heavy sigh. Did he love her in the same way? Love, she was learning, did exist between men and women. Look at Lady Raquel and Sir Nicolás, at Lady Margarita and her Sir Arnau. Love achieved miracles. It could bridge great divides.

Could it bridge them all?

Overhead, swifts screeched as they wheeled through the sky. The year was turning and the swifts would soon be gone. Alba's chest ached. As far as she and Lord Inigo were concerned, she had a terrible suspicion that time was running out like sand in an hourglass.

The King's reply was due any day. In the meantime, Lord Inigo continued to be elusive and Alba had little choice but to leave him alone. Council meeting followed council meeting. There was nothing to be gained by harrying the man.

Lord Inigo and I made love and it was exquisite.

As one day slid into the next, Alba kept returning to the pond. Her faith wavered. She might have to live on her memories, they were certainly bright and beautiful enough to last several lifetimes.

Had Lord Inigo given her a child to remember him by? He had never explained how to avoid getting with child and, given his concerns about illegitimacy, it seemed likely he would have been careful. Pain sliced through her. A child would be wonderful, though she would far rather have the man himself.

'My lady? *Lady Alba!*' Guillen was sprinting down the path. 'The King's courier has come.'

Alba braced herself. This was it, the King's decision would surely put an end to their liaison.

'Noblemen are gathering in the council chamber.' Guillen paused briefly to catch his breath. 'It's filling fast, everyone wants to hear the King's decision. Lord Inigo regrets that you cannot attend.'

She smiled sadly. 'I never expected to attend.'

'No, my lady. However, my lord wanted you to know about the alcove adjacent to the meeting room. It's discreet and you will be able to hear everything.'

Alba stared at Guillen and came slowly to her feet.

The alcove walls were tiled and blue and white. A sturdy, high-backed armchair, carved from walnut in the Spanish style, stood firmly in the centre. Alba gathered up her skirts and sat down.

'My lord will speak to you later,' Guillen said. 'Would you care for refreshment?'

'Thank you, Guillen, some fruit juice would be welcome.'

Guillen nodded and drew a curtain across the opening, leaving Alba in isolated glory on the armchair. When the curtain rings stopped rattling, she became conscious of other sounds: the murmur of voices in the council chamber, sandaled feet scurrying along marble corridors, a sudden crack of laughter.

The curtain shifted and drew back to reveal a girl bearing a cup.

'My lady, this is orange and pomegranate, will that be to your liking?'

Alba took the cup. 'Thank you.'

The girl curtsied and the curtain closed. Alba sipped the juice, unable to pinpoint exactly why she felt so ill at ease. She could hear voices from inside the council chamber. Lord Inigo had suggested that she should listen, yet she felt incredibly guilty, half hidden as she was. She felt like an eavesdropper. It wasn't pleasant.

Beyond the silken curtain, a herald bellowed for order and started running through an impressive roll call of names. Alba recognised a few of them.

'Lord Inigo Sánchez, Count of Seville, who is presiding. Count Inigo is acting as the King's judge in this court. His decision is final and irrevocable.

Lord Ramíro Herrera...

Baron Fernando Marchena de Carmona...

Baron Fernando's sister, the Lady Margarita Marchena de Carmona...

Sir Arnau de Córdoba, Steward to Rodrigo Álvarez, Count of Córdoba...'

The list continued with names Alba didn't know. It was as interminable as the council meetings and her mind wandered. She finished the juice and set the cup on the floor with a gentle clack.

Despite the warmth, she shivered. Her sense of disquiet was hard to shake. She frowned at the blue and white wall tiles, at the painted ceiling, at the curtain hiding her from the rest of the court. She was staring uneasily at the floor when it came to her.

There were alcoves exactly like this in the Alhambra Palace. Adjacent to the audience chambers, they were designed with one purpose in mind. Her father's favourite concubine would recline on a couch in case the Sultan—when he had finished his business with his knights or advisors—should have need of her.

Alba's eyes filled, and the pretty blue and white wall tiles merged together in a rush of tears. This was Lord Inigo's way of telling her what her role in his life would be. She was to be his lover, she would never be his wife. Her throat ached. She told herself she had no right to be hurt, he'd never deceived her. She'd known all along what to expect, and she'd chosen to make love with him anyway. She should have remembered that in Spain, the only way a man and woman could remain together with honour was in marriage.

Voices from the council chamber faded in and out as Alba gripped the arms of the chair and struggled to accept what waiting in this alcove truly signified. Lord Inigo was kind and straightforward, he was not a man of evil. There were worse fates than being the lover of a kind and straightforward man.

She had been foolish to hope for more. That sense of connection between them had led her astray. It had made her believe that anything might be possible.

Mouth twisting, Alba stared blindly at the curtain. When she'd set out from Granada, the idea of having a child had been her only goal. After that tryst in the curtained pavilion, Alba ached for more. She wanted what Raquel had with Sir Nicolás—the chance to build a life with the man she loved. She wanted to prove that love could last.

Baron Fernando's name jolted Alba back to the present. Lady Margarita's brother was being stripped of his lands and titles. She heard shouting, the rattle of chains and more shouting. A door slammed.

Lord Inigo wants me as his mistress.

Her mouth tasted bitter.

In the council chamber, the herald launched back into speech.

'His Grace, Henry of Trastámara, King of Castile and León, hereby approves the marriage of Lady Margarita Marchena de Carmona to Sir Arnau de Córdoba on the understanding that Sir Arnau will steward Lady Margarita's family lands. Lady Margarita is a virtuous lady who deserves a man of honour and Sir Arnau's reputation is spotless.'

Alba was pleased for Lady Margarita and Sir Arnau, but she felt utterly worn. Prey to doubt, she leaned her head on the chair back. What would happen to her? There was no place here for a Nasrid princess. She would never achieve her heart's desire—Lord Inigo as her husband. The King was bound to disapprove. She was an enemy princess and as such, she would surely never be permitted to marry one of Spain's most prominent lords.

Perhaps, when our days together have run their course, I shall set up house with Inés in Baeza.

That had been her original plan, she might have to go back to it. The thought was dark and cheerless. In Lord Inigo's company she had stepped into a bright new world. Lord Inigo had shown her the true meaning of freedom. And, improbable though it had seemed back in her father's palace, she had fallen in love. If she joined her mother's relatives in Baeza, she would feel as though she was in a prison.

'And now, my lords,' Lord Inigo's voice caught her attention. 'You need to know that His Grace has sent me a private document concerning my own marriage.'

Alba's breath caught and she leaned forward, straining to hear over the thumping in her ears.

'I asked His Grace to consider a new, possibly less orthodox alliance. In brief, the King has agreed. This letter grants me permission to solicit the hand in marriage of Lady Alba, formerly known as Princess Zoraida of Al-Andalus.'

The council chamber fell pin-drop quiet. A few shocked laughs were followed by a handful of barbed remarks.

'Princess Zoraida? A Nasrid princess?'

'My lord, have you run mad?'

'A concubine? That one will bring you nothing but trouble.'

Other voices were more supportive.

'Bravo, my lord. Bravo!'

'Congratulations, my lord.'

Someone cheered, a desultory clapping began and gradually the noise increased.

In a heartbeat the mood in the chamber had

turned from incredulity to rejoicing. Alba stared at the curtain, startled by the speed the mood had changed. Her heart pounded.

A door hinge creaked. Footsteps sped past the alcove, a babble of chattering rose and faded. Abruptly, the curtain was whisked back. Lord Inigo was smiling down at her, offering his hand to help her rise.

Alba seemed to have lost the power of movement. Had she heard aright? Lord Inigo had asked his King for permission to marry her? Not to make her his concubine, as she had assumed when he had had her seated in this alcove. He wanted to marry her.

Was it possible that he loved her as much as she loved him? That he believed love might last?

Head high, heart twisting in an agony of hope, she accepted his hand to rise.

He bent to kiss each of her hands in turn. 'You heard His Grace's decision regarding our marriage?'

Alba stood very still. It was true, he wanted to marry her. 'Our marriage?'

'I told the King I wished to marry you, my lady.'

Her stomach turned into a cloud of butterflies. 'Lord Inigo,' she said, keeping her voice cool only with great effort. 'Why would King Henry permit one of his right-hand men to marry Sultan Tariq's daughter?'

The grey eyes softened, Lord Inigo was still smiling.

'Because like me, the King hopes to build peace between our people. Besides, I told His Grace that I would have no other woman to wife.'

'I cannot believe you would dictate to your King in such a manner.'

He looked down at her, eyes slightly perplexed. 'My lady, if the King had refused me, I was ready to be stripped of my titles, though I didn't believe it would come to that.'

'You would have done that for me?'

'Of course.' He shrugged, as though giving up his titles and status for her was a small thing. 'My lady, will you do me the honour of giving me your hand in marriage?'

'You truly wish to marry me.' Her voice sounded strange. Inside, she was dancing.

'With all my heart. My lady, you know I love you.'

'Love,' she said, watching him carefully. 'You don't believe love can last.'

His mouth went up in that dear, crooked smile. 'I hope you are not going to hold my ignorance against me, I said that before I knew you. With you, my love, anything is possible.' A brief frown flickered across his handsome face. He leaned in, breath tickling her ear as he whispered, 'You are a tease, my lady. You know how I feel, particularly after our tryst in the garden.'

Her cheeks scorched. 'I didn't realise you were thinking of marriage.'

He studied her expression and caught his breath as though stunned. 'You doubt me? Even after what happened in the pavilion? My love, I thought you understood. You have taught me to feel. Until you, I imagined the best marriage was based on logic and planning. Feelings were irrelevant. You have shown me the error of my ways. Forgive me for not declaring myself sooner. I was unable to do so because—'

'You were not officially free.'

His gaze held hers, steady and sure. 'In part, though in the pavilion I must confess that passion ran away with me. I could barely think for wanting you.' His hands came to rest on her shoulders, warm and strong. 'Do you think, my sweet, you might give me an answer? Will you marry me?'

Spirits soaring, Alba darted a glance in the direction of the audience chamber. 'We will be the talk of the court.'

Cupping her cheek with his hand, he turned her

face back to his and leaned in. 'I care not. The King approves, people will fall in line, eventually.'

'Truly?'

'Truly.'

Alba allowed the joy to well up inside her and flung her arms about his neck. 'Oh, yes. Yes, please, my lord, I would like to marry you above all things. I love you.'

Strong arms enclosed her, and warm lips covered hers in the gentlest of kisses. When he pulled back she was looking at that wry smile she loved so much.

'One thing further, Alba, my love. My name is Inigo, could you bring yourself to use it occasionally?'

'Inigo,' she murmured, reaching up to press a kiss to the pulse on his neck.

His eyes gleamed. 'Again.'

'Inigo,' she said, kissing his cheek. 'My love.'

Inigo caught her into his arms and whirled her about. 'Alba, I love you.'

He glanced back over his shoulder and grimaced. Two maidservants and Guillen were watching them. Guillen's face wore a knowing grin.

'Saints, is there no privacy?' Lifting a dark eyebrow, Lord Inigo—no, *Inigo*—frowned at the carved oak chair and then at the curtain. 'Not here, I think.'

She stifled a laugh. 'Anywhere but here.'

'As you wish.'

Inigo took Alba's hand and ushered her through the audience chamber, down several twisting corridors, past a sunlit courtyard and up a short flight of stairs.

A door closed with a click. They were in a large bedchamber, light tumbled through cracks in the shutters and dust motes shone like tiny stars.

Inigo, soon to be Alba's husband and, God willing, the father of her many children, glanced at the bed and set his hands on her shoulders.

'Well, my love?'

Alba moved towards him. 'You remember I would like children, Inigo? Lots of them.'

His eyes gleamed. 'How could I forget it?

She stood before him and, fingers trembling only a little, set to work undoing his belt buckle. 'So we will have to do this a lot, Inigo. It will be very tiring for you.'

His lips curved. 'I am entirely at your mercy, my love.'

* * * * *